T0243225

# AFTER HE'S GONE

# AFTER HE'S GONE

## Katherine Bolger Hyde

SEVERN
HOUSE

First world edition published in Great Britain and the USA in 2023
by Severn House, an imprint of Canongate Books Ltd,
14 High Street, Edinburgh EH1 1TE.

Trade paperback edition first published in Great Britain and the USA in 2023
by Severn House, an imprint of Canongate Books Ltd.

severnhouse.com

*British Library Cataloguing-in-Publication Data*
A CIP catalogue record for this title is available from the British Library.

ISBN-13: 978-1-4483-1033-3 (cased)
ISBN-13: 978-1-4483-1052-4 (trade paper)
ISBN-13: 978-1-4483-1034-0 (e-book)

*All Severn House titles are printed on acid-free paper.*

Typeset by Palimpsest Book Production Ltd.,
Falkirk, Stirlingshire, Scotland.
Printed and bound in Great Britain by
TJ Books, Padstow, Cornwall.

*To all the survivors*

# ONE

It's Charles. I know it's Charles even though he's lying on his face with blood all over his head. I know that stubborn little curl of hair on the back of his neck, the arrogant set of his shoulders, his elegant, tapering fingers, even though they're covered, drenched, drowning in crimson, coagulating blood.

I know it's my husband. I know he's dead. What I don't know is whether I killed him.

*September 2015*

I can almost remember what it was like when I first met Charles. Almost recapture how handsome I thought him, how dashing and debonair – back then I actually used words like 'dashing' and 'debonair.' How I thought the steely glint in his eye denoted strength, or daring, or determination. Before I realized it was just a reflection – of other people's hopes, dreams, needs, lives. His eyes reflected them back because he could never take them in.

We were students at the same law school, at Santa Clara University, but the one year he was ahead of me might have been a century. The gap between his father, who not only approved his choice of career but insisted on it and could pay for every penny of his education, and mine, who grudgingly allowed me to attend law school on scholarship only because there was nothing he could do to stop me, stretched as wide and deep as the Grand Canyon. When Charles stooped to my level, it was like God bending down to pick up a flea.

I remember our first conversation as if it were yesterday. It's the me in that conversation that's cloudy, out of focus, like a bad print of an old black-and-white film that crackles and spits its way through the projector. How could I not have seen where things were heading? How could I not have understood that in choosing to climb the cliff that was Charles, I was dooming myself to fall?

It started innocently enough, I suppose. I was sitting in the courtyard of the law school with my laptop and a cup of coffee, trying to wrap my head around California's arcane and bewildering child custody laws, when I heard a voice from on high, like the voice of God talking to Charlton Heston in *The Ten Commandments*: 'May I sit here?'

It startled me, not only because I was immersed in another world but because God doesn't usually ask permission when he wants to invade my life. At least not in so many words. I looked up, and there he was – Charles Crenshaw, smiling on me with his teeth gleaming like the beam of a lighthouse beckoning me to shore. I'd seen that beacon trained on others but never dreamed it might one day turn toward me. Nor did I remember in that moment that lighthouses do not beckon but warn.

I plunged ahead. 'Of course.' I scooted my laptop and coffee over to give him room, then made to return to my work, assuming he had only asked to sit with me because there was no other place free. But a glance to my left showed several open tables. I felt myself begin to blush and willed the blood away from my face, back into my brain, where I was clearly going to need it. But my blood did not obey.

He set his coffee on the table and his backpack on the ground, not moving to take anything from it. I felt his eyes on me, pulling mine like a magnet until I could no longer resist. I glanced at him, and he smiled again. I was hooked now, like Ulysses with the Sirens, only I hadn't had a chance to chain myself to the mast.

'You're in my family law class,' he stated. From his mouth the words sounded profound, like some great insight into the workings of the universe. I could only nod.

'I've noticed you. You have some good things to say, *Miss Taylor*.' One eyebrow went up, along with the opposite corner of his mouth, and I knew that was my cue to supply my first name. First names were never used in class. I knew his because it was carried on the air throughout the law school – *Look, that's Charles Crenshaw*, as if he were Barack Obama or Benedict Cumberbatch.

'Abby.' I could feel the blush rising again and cursed my transparent skin.

'Charles.' He put out his hand, and I stared at it for a moment, noting the strength and size of it, along with the smooth, uncallused skin, the long fingers, the square, perfectly manicured nails. But one thing was odd – his ring finger was as long as the middle one. I'd never seen a hand like that before.

I shook myself a little, sure I'd been staring at his hand for at least five minutes, though his smile hadn't faded. I slipped my hand into his and watched my fingers disappear in his firm, dry grip. But he didn't shake my hand; he held it for a fraction too long, and then slowly released it. I snatched it back and stuck it under the table, resisting the urge to stare at my own hand as if it had touched a holy relic.

He talked some more, and I answered, the speech center of my brain working on autopilot while the rest was a seething jumble of thoughts and emotions, a little-gray-cell soup. I can't remember what we said because I was hardly aware of it at the time – all I could think about was his eyes, his smile, both trained on me as if I were the center of the universe, when all the time that position really belonged to him. All I do remember is that at the end of our conversation – if you could call it that – he said, 'I know a place that does great Afghan food. Want to try it sometime?'

I found the presence of mind to laugh. 'Afghan food? Is that even a thing?'

'It is now.' As if his acknowledgment had made it real. 'Saturday?'

'Sure.'

He rose, swung his backpack up to his shoulder, picked up his empty cup in his left hand, and put his right out toward me again. 'Till Saturday.'

I touched my fingertips to his, not wanting to get swallowed up again. 'Till Saturday.'

He turned to go, and in the vacuum left by his going, I saw my friend David staring at me from the next table, his eyes full of reproach. He hadn't been there when Charles arrived. Had he been listening to our conversation? Why hadn't he come over to say hello, since he could have no other business at the law school except to see me? Well, that was obvious – Charles's magnetism had created an invisible force field around our table. David would have felt it, seen the shimmer of its edges. He'd gotten as close as he could.

Only then did I remember I had plans for Saturday – I'd promised to go to the expo David's computer science class was putting on at the student center. I beamed across at him and gave him a little wave. He wouldn't mind if I didn't show. He'd been downplaying the thing as pointless, laughable even, ever since he first told me about it. It wouldn't make me a terrible friend to not show up. Maybe I could even tell Charles I wanted to stop by after dinner – it was a stop-by-any-time kind of thing.

I made a show of glancing at my watch. It was time for me to go to my next class, so I hurriedly gathered my things. At David's table I paused and said, 'Hey there. I didn't see you. Why didn't you join us?'

His look withered me, almost literally, like the fig tree Jesus cursed. 'You didn't look like you wanted company.'

'We were only talking about law. I barely know Charles. Met him properly for the first time just now.'

'But not the last.'

I smiled brightly. 'No, probably not the last.' I glanced at my watch again. 'Listen, I have to get to class, but let's do lunch later, OK?'

His eyes dropped away, fastened on his laptop. 'Maybe. I might have a thing.'

'Sure. Text me.'

He nodded. I squeezed his shoulder, which shrank away from my hand, and moved on – my feet heading to the classroom, my soul trudging off on the first leg of what promised to be the mother of all guilt trips.

David had that effect on me. His devotion was a crushing weight I could never shrug off. We'd been friends since high school, and he was practically the only real confidant I had, so I couldn't tell him to take a hike. But neither could I ever muster up in myself a feeling to match what I knew he felt for me. My heart never lifted in David's presence; it only sagged. Sometimes, like now, it threatened to sag right out the soles of my shoes.

David's huff gave way before lunchtime, of course; he texted me at eleven thirty to meet him at Benson, the student center-cum-food court. That was our usual venue, not only because David hated to take the time to walk anywhere off campus but because we could never find a restaurant that suited both our tastes. He was a burgers-and-pizza kind of guy, while I thrived on salads with a little grilled chicken or fish. It wasn't a weight-watching thing; it was simply that I found heavy foods clouded my brain, and I needed it sharp to stay afloat in the shark-infested waters of law school.

'I can't stay long,' I said as we reconvened at a table after getting our food from separate booths. 'Exam tomorrow. This prof has a rep for gruesome exams.'

'Tell me again why you want to be a lawyer?' David said for the gazillionth time. Not one to stop beating a horse just because it's dead, was David. 'You're really not the lawyer type.'

'I keep trying to tell you, there is no "lawyer type." People go into law for a lot of different reasons. I want to help people who might not be able to get justice on their own. Women and children, specifically.'

'And what makes you think you'll be able to succeed in that where thousands before you have failed? Aren't the halls of justice littered with the shed skins of idealistic young things like you? They all turn into sharks in the end.'

'You may be right, but I have to try. If you see me turning into a shark, you have my permission to pull me out of the water so I have to become human again or die.'

He humphed and tucked into his burger, a double stacked so high with trimmings I had to stare in wonder as his jaw opened wide enough to fit it in. He'd just bitten through when I heard the voice of God at my shoulder.

'Well, hello again,' Charles said. 'Long time no see.'

So original, but his voice – deep and smooth as the finest chocolate, every nuance controlled – made the commonplace sound like the apex of wit. Juries would melt before that voice. I hoped he was going into criminal law – he'd be wasted otherwise.

I managed to smile brightly up at him. Mustn't blush in front of David. 'Oh, hi, Charles. This is my friend, David Dunstable.' Maybe a little too much emphasis on *friend*. 'David, Charles Crenshaw.'

Mouth bursting with burger, fingers smeared with drippings from same, David nodded at Charles and glared at me. I gave him a tiny shrug. It wasn't my fault he'd been caught at a disadvantage.

Charles raised one eyebrow. 'Pleasure.' I could see him sizing David up – from his untamable mousy hair to his indoor-pale, slightly pockmarked skin to his geeky-humor T-shirt stretched over a pudgy belly – and filing him in the box labeled *Unthreatening*

*Nerdy Guy Friend*. Which, to be fair, is what he was, but I couldn't help feeling sorry for David being dismissed so summarily.

I'd been about to invite Charles to join us, but at this I thought better of it. He saved me by saying, 'Gotta run. See you Saturday.'

'See you.' I gave him my best smile, willing David not to have picked up on the *Saturday*.

My mind-control skills needed work. 'Saturday?' he said accusingly, glaring at me through his horn-rims. Even though the cool kids, the hipsters, were wearing horn-rims in those days, David still managed to look nerdy in his. And not in a good way. 'What about my show?'

I tried a smile, but it didn't quite work. 'You said the show was stupid, remember?'

'That doesn't mean I don't want you there. You know I can't handle stupid without you.'

True. He could never hide his boredom and frustration at having to explain to the computer-semiliterate things that were laughably basic to him but arcane mysteries to the rest of us. He needed me to run interference, supply the social skills he lacked.

'It's just dinner, with Charles. I'll come by after.'

'I'll hold you to that.' But his look showed he didn't really believe he could. All he'd be able to do was guilt me afterward for not showing up.

I dreaded that guilt enough to make an effort. But even I knew the chances of my getting away from Charles that quickly were slim.


# TWO


*Monday evening, February 26, 2018*

*Peter*

I get the call at five thirty p.m., half an hour before my shift is supposed to end. A body on Highview Drive on the West Side, one of the richest neighborhoods in town, near the university. Not the kind of neighborhood that runs to murder.

Probably accident or suicide, I speculate as I drive up there from downtown through the pouring winter rain. I know from experience – not my own, but what I've witnessed – that the kind of money these people have doesn't necessarily buy happiness. More often it buys divorce, alcoholism, estrangement from children. Depression, despair, sometimes suicide. But hardly ever murder. The people who live on the West Side are much too civilized for that.

So I get a surprise when I see the body. Suicides don't bash themselves on the head, as a rule.

I take in the scene. Living room nicely furnished in a modern style – black leather upholstery, white carpet, glass tables, stock photos in black frames on the gray walls. Not much personality in the room. Other than a small heap of ashes in the fireplace, everything is super clean, even sterile.

Except for the body. There's a heck of a lot of blood around it, suggesting he didn't die quickly. But there's no sign he put up a struggle or made any effort to get help, so chances are the blow rendered him unconscious at least. The wound is too much of a mess for me to make any guess as to what caused it. The forensics guys will find the weapon if it's still here.

The pathologist is bending over the body, performing his mysteries. 'Any idea as to time of death?' I ask.

He raises an eyebrow at me. 'Can't be accurate at this point, but it looks pretty recent. He's barely cold. For now, I'd say within the hour. Could be less.'

'Thanks.' I straighten and look around for the responding officer. His nametag says *Spinelli*. He stands feet apart, hands together, head a little bowed.

'Who found the body?' I ask him.

'His wife.' He nods toward the far corner of the room, voice low and respectful. 'Abigail Crenshaw. Victim is Charles Crenshaw, Junior.'

I peer into the relative darkness beyond the circle of the floodlights over the body. Huddled in the corner between the end of a loveseat and the wall is a young woman, so slight as to seem almost a child, holding a sleeping baby against her shoulder and rocking to and fro. Her eyes are dark abysses of horror.

I go over and kneel in front of her, not too close. Those eyes go straight through me. Does she even know I'm here?

'Mrs Crenshaw?'

She nods, her teeth chattering.

'I'm Detective Peter Rocher. Why don't you sit on the couch here, and we'll get you a blanket? I think you're in shock.'

Numbly she allows me to take her hand and help her on to the sofa with her feet up. I call to a paramedic, who brings her a blanket and a cup of cocoa. She waves the drink away, gesturing toward the baby. I guess she's worried about spilling the hot drink on the child.

I scan the room for a female officer, figuring Mrs Crenshaw might be more comfortable handing her baby over to a woman. I see a vaguely familiar-looking face among the forensics crew and beckon her over. 'Mrs Crenshaw, this is Officer—' I stop. I don't know the woman's name.

'Inez Montoya,' she supplies.

'Would you let Officer Montoya hold your baby for a minute while you drink your cocoa? You need to get something warm into you or you're going to be ill.'

The officer leans over Mrs Crenshaw and gives her a reassuring smile, and she reluctantly hands over the child. The baby – a girl, judging by its pink outfit and hair bow – nestles into Montoya's neck without awakening. She's a cute little thing with a headful of golden curls. Mrs Crenshaw draws the blanket close about her shoulders and sips the cocoa, never taking her eyes off her daughter.

'Now, Mrs Crenshaw, I need to ask you a few things if you're ready. Do you think you can answer some questions?'

Her eyes swivel toward me for the space of a nod, then snap back to her baby. 'Call me Abby. Not Mrs Crenshaw anymore.'

That's awfully fast to repudiate a husband's name, with him not even cold on the floor. But maybe they were separated? Or divorced?

'OK, Abby. Can you tell me what happened here?'

'I–I don't know. I don't know what happened.'

'OK, let's back up. Were you out this afternoon?'

She nods.

'When did you get home?'

'I'm not sure. After five, I think.'

'Where had you been?'

'At my sister's. In San Jose.'

'And you had the baby with you?'

'Emma. Yes.' She rubs her brow as if to coax her thoughts into order. 'I remember coming home, putting the car in the garage. Taking Emma out of her car seat. And then . . . I was in here, without Emma, and he was there. On the floor. Covered in blood.' She shivers. 'Then I called the police.' Her eyes cut toward me again. 'You.'

'You don't remember what happened in between? When you first came into the house?'

She shakes her head slowly.

'Was the door locked? Was anyone else here?'

She gives a helpless shrug.

I noticed on the way in there was no sign of forced entry. 'You don't know for sure whether he was dead when you got here?'

She shakes her head again. I didn't think her eyes could get any wider or deeper, but now they do.

I've seen this kind of thing before – shock and trauma can make a person black out, lose their short-term memory. But was it the shock of finding him . . . or the trauma of killing him?

'So you had a blackout, apparently. That's not uncommon in this kind of situation. Your memory will probably come back in a few days.'

She shakes her head.

'No? You don't think so? Why not?'

Her teeth start chattering again. 'Not the first time.'

'Not the first time what?' Not the first time she's come home to a murdered husband? Not the first time she's killed? Occam's razor: stick with the obvious. 'You mean you've had blackouts before?'

She nods. 'It's been happening . . . kind of a lot . . . lately.'

'Lately, as in days? Weeks? Months?'

She screws her eyes shut, then opens them. 'A few months.'

'Has anything . . . bad ever happened during one of your blackouts before?'

She stares at me, the word *duh* written plainly on her face. 'How would I know?'

'I mean, you didn't find out about anything after you came out of it?'

'Not . . . bad, exactly. Just strange. Things missing, stuck where they don't belong. Lots of gas gone from the car. Emma—' She shudders. 'One time I woke up and I was changing Emma at ten in the morning, and she was crying. God knows how long she'd been awake, and I had no idea. Her diaper was soaked through to the blankets. If I hadn't come to when I did . . .'

Her face drains of color, and I call the paramedic back. He gives her another blanket and a fresh cup of cocoa. 'I think we better take her to the hospital,' he says to me.

I stand to speak to him, my legs protesting at having been in a crouch for so long. 'Yeah. We need to get the shock treated, sure. Then we need to find out what's been making her black out.'

I shake out my legs and squat in front of Abby again. 'A couple more questions, Abby, then I'll leave you alone. Would your husband have left the house unlocked while he was here?'

She shakes her head. 'He's paranoid. Always locks it whether we're here or not.'

'Does anyone else have keys to the house?'

'Our cleaner. But she only comes on Fridays.' This is Monday. 'And Charles's parents.'

'Where do they live?'

'Los Altos Hills.'

I make a mental note to get their full contact info so I can notify them. 'Abby, we need to take you to the hospital now. Something's wrong that's making you black out, and we need to find out what it is. Is there someone who can take care of your baby for a few days?'

Her mouth quivers, and she reaches for the baby. 'No, not Emma! You can't take Emma away from me!'

I lay a hand on her arm, gentle as I can make it. 'Nobody's taking anybody away, Abby. We just need to make sure Emma is safe. You wouldn't want to have another blackout and risk her getting hurt, would you?'

She shakes her head so rapidly it looks like another shudder. 'My sister. Ellen. Ellen will take her.'

'That's good, Abby. That's very good. This is the sister who lives in San Jose?'

She nods.

Great. An hour away. 'Is her number in your phone?'

She nods again.

'Where is your phone?'

She blinks, then feels in her pocket and pulls out an iPhone, the latest model.

'Unlock it for me?'

I watch her put in her code, memorizing it for later. She taps to her favorites list, hands me the phone. Ellen Stepanovich is at the top of the list.

'Great. I'll call and have her meet us at the hospital. Officer Montoya can take care of Emma till then.'

Abby turns worried eyes to Montoya. 'She'll need a clean diaper as soon as she wakes up. And a bottle. There's some expressed breast milk in the fridge. And her car seat's in my BMW. In the garage. The diaper bag might still be in there, too.'

Officer Montoya smiles and pats Abby's arm with her free hand. 'Don't worry. I've got five nieces and nephews, and I babysit them all the time. We'll do fine.'

I call the sister, who agrees to meet us at Dominican Hospital as soon as she can get there – which, at rush hour, is not going to be as soon as we all would like. I need her not only as a babysitter but hopefully as a source of an outside perspective on the Crenshaws' recent situation. When I finish the call, I pocket Abby's phone.

Abby lets the paramedics lead her away to the ambulance, her eyes never leaving her baby until she's out of sight. I have a word with one of them to be sure the hospital keeps her clothes intact and examines her for blood spatter. I didn't notice any on her face or hands.

I get up, shake out my cramped legs again, and go over to Spinelli. 'Do a house-to-house. Ask if anyone else was seen entering the house this afternoon. And see if you can find out exactly when Mrs Crenshaw got home. How long before she called us.'

'Right. I'm on it.'

That piece of information is going to be critical, and I pray we can get it. A thirty-second interval and Abby Crenshaw will be in the clear. Ten or fifteen minutes, and we may have a problem.

# THREE

I spent most of Saturday afternoon agonizing over what to wear for my date with Charles. My wardrobe consisted mostly of jeans and casual tops, plus one gray suit for official law-school occasions and a couple of all-purpose dresses. All purposes, that is, except dinner at an unknown restaurant with a nearly unknown but ultracool, difficult-to-impress kind of guy.

In desperation I called on my roomie, Morgan. We were room-mates for convenience, not because we were BFFs; I guess I could imagine someone more different from me, but it would take some doing. An ancient crone in a loincloth in the African bush might have been more different, for example. But possibly more like me in the limitations of her wardrobe.

Morgan's clothing collection bulged out of her closet on to hooks and dressers and shelves that filled the walls of her room. We were about the same size. She was bound to have something perfect.

I told her my dilemma and she stared at me, mouth open. '*You* have a date with Charles Crenshaw.' I could see her eyes turning green. Clear subtext: *I've been angling for a date with him for months. How could a little mouse like you succeed where gorgeous me has failed?*

I didn't understand it myself, unless Charles was the kind of guy who only wanted what didn't throw itself abjectly at his feet.

'Just dinner. No big deal. I think he wants to pick my brain about our family law class. He's probably hoping to get enough from me so he doesn't have to do the reading.'

She gave me a *yeah, right* look and a heavy sigh. 'All right, I'll help you look good. I don't want to be humiliated if he finds out we're roommates.' So generous.

We went into her room, and she pulled down a series of dresses that looked to me like tube tops for a Barbie doll. 'I can't wear these,' I told her. 'I'd feel like I was out in public in my underwear.'

Another heavy sigh. She went into the closet and pushed all the way to the back. 'Here. This is what I wear for a formal dinner at my parents' house. Is that boring enough for you?'

Black, knee-length, a bit of sleeve, rounded V-neck. The fabric didn't stretch, so it couldn't fit like shrink-wrap. I tried it on and looked in the mirror. It skimmed my curves without hugging them, and the neckline showed a tantalizing shadow of cleavage. Not bad.

'You'll do,' Morgan said, and started hanging stuff back up. I noticed she was holding those tube tops up to herself in front of the mirror in the process. Probably planning what she'd wear that night to upstage me in case I brought Charles home. Which I would not. For all kinds of reasons.

I reached the dorm lobby, where Charles and I had agreed to meet, promptly at six, and he was waiting. But instead of the suit and tie I'd expected, he was wearing chinos and a polo shirt. In my Little Black Dress and heels, with my long hair in the sleekest updo I could manage, I felt as out of place as a penguin at a hyena convention.

I thought about disappearing before he saw me, but it was too late. He smiled, waved, and headed in my direction.

'Maybe I'd better change,' I said.

'Why? You look great,' he replied. 'Besides, I don't want to miss our reservation.'

He held out his arm, elbow crooked for me to put my hand there, as if he were wearing a tux. But with his short sleeves, that meant I was touching his bare skin. Why does touching the inside of an elbow feel so much more intimate than a handshake? I was sure he must have been aware of the tiny thrill that went through me as I rested my fingers lightly on his arm. In fact, I was pretty sure he'd counted on it.

We drove to Fremont, into a neighborhood where the signs shifted from English to Arabic script. 'This area is called Little Kabul,' Charles told me. 'The restaurants here are mostly frequented by Afghans. Not fancy, but authentic and quite good.'

'Oh dear,' I said, suddenly conscious of my bare knees and slight shadow of cleavage. 'Should I have worn my burqa?'

He smiled. 'They're used to Western women,' he said. 'The men may avoid looking at you, but they won't kick you out. Best to let me do the talking, though.'

'Right. Women are supposed to be silent. Preferably invisible. No minds or souls, just a body draped in black.'

'Guys' paradise.' He laughed.

The restaurant was unexpectedly lovely, with the geometric designs I think of as Moorish, but which are apparently common to many Islamic cultures. Deep-red walls surrounded pointed arches that framed mini murals of what I assumed were scenes of Afghan life. There were plenty of tables at regular height with ordinary chairs, but around the perimeter I saw low tables surrounded by cushions as well. I was relieved when the host escorted us to a table with chairs. My narrow skirt would have made cushion-sitting extremely tricky.

I was also relieved to see that none of the women present wore the full-length burqa, though I did see many wearing a hijab, the scarf that covers the head and neck. But there was also a smattering of women in ordinary Western clothes, so I only had to be self-conscious because I was wearing a nice dress while all the others were in jeans.

And, of course, because the only thing on the menu I could recognize or pronounce was *kabob*. Fortunately, Charles had it all down pat and was able to explain to me what dishes like *bodinjon borani* and *sabzi challow* were. The latter was nothing more exotic than a spinach dish with lamb shank, which turned out to be the tenderest, most flavorful lamb I'd ever eaten.

The meal came in several courses, and no one seemed to be in any hurry. By the time we'd finished eating and were sipping a thick, sweet Arabic coffee, it was seven thirty, and David's show ended at eight.

'Charles, would you mind awfully if we dropped in somewhere for a few minutes? David's department is having a presentation, and I sort of promised I'd show up. Before we made this date, that is.'

His eyebrows rose slowly over a look in his eyes that I couldn't quite pin down. If he'd been in court, I'd have thought he was about to pose a question in cross-examination that would make the witness squirm. I was squirming a bit myself by the time he answered.

'Of course,' he said, beckoning to the waiter for the check. 'If that's what you want. I did get tickets for *Hamilton*, though. It starts at eight.'

My stomach dropped. Tickets to *Hamilton* were nearly impossible to get, and I'd been longing to see it. No way would I ever have another chance. And despite his apparent flexibility, I knew if I insisted on going to David's show, I'd never have another chance with Charles.

'Oh,' I said in a small voice. 'You didn't say.'

'I wanted to surprise you.' Accompanied by the full-on dazzling smile.

'I'm dying to see *Hamilton*.' I swallowed my guilt and smiled back. 'David will understand.'

He wouldn't, really. But he would put up with it. David would put up with anything from me. I tried not to take advantage of that fact, but tonight was going to have to be an exception.

The show was fantastic, and I left with a song in my throat, as I always do after a good musical. I wouldn't have minded a career in theater, but I never had the confidence I could be good enough to make it in that tough, competitive world. So I opted for the tough, competitive world of law instead.

Charles laughed as I skipped down the steps of the theater, tra-la-ing my way through King George's number, 'You'll Be Back,' one of the more melodic songs of the show. Charles followed at a normal pace, and at the bottom he caught me with his hands around my waist. 'My, my, Miss Taylor. We don't see this side of you in family law class.'

'I have a lot of sides you haven't seen,' I said lightly, though the look in his eyes put a catch in my throat. 'I'm a multifaceted personality.'

'And I want to uncover each one,' he purred. Then he leaned in for a kiss.

I considered ducking out of his embrace. Honestly, I did. For a nanosecond. But that was long enough for me to lose the chance to get away.

I'd never experienced a kiss like his before. It blocked out all my other senses, focusing my entire being in my lips – and his. By the time he released me, I belonged to him. And the tiny smirk in his hooded eyes said he knew that very well.

I tried to avoid David the next day, but he tracked me down at lunch. 'Missed you last night,' he said, attempting to sound casual. But I knew him too well.

'I'm sorry, David. I thought it was just going to be dinner and then I'd have time to come by after. But Charles had tickets to *Hamilton*. I couldn't not go.'

David's eyes drilled into me. I concentrated on my salad.

'You couldn't not go to some stupid show. But you could break your promise to your oldest friend.' He let that sink in while I sank into the floor. 'I don't think I know who you are anymore, Abby. I never thought you were one to let a pretty face turn your head.'

'He's not just a pretty face. And he hasn't turned my head. It was a one-time thing.'

'Bullshit. Your head's turned so far around you're looking up your own—' He stopped. He wasn't quite angry enough to say *that* to me. Yet.

'Look, David, I'm really, really sorry. But obviously you survived. How did it go?'

He snorted. 'It went. The time passed and it ended. That's the best I can say.'

'But there wasn't anything riding on your show, was there? I mean not a grade or anything?'

'No.' He made the admission grudgingly. 'It's the work that counts, not showing it off. The show's for the department's PR.' He pointed his fork at me. 'But that doesn't let you off the hook. I needed you there, and you knew it.'

I sighed. 'Let me make it up to you. We'll go to that pizza place you love downtown. Maybe a movie. My treat.'

His gloom lifted slightly. 'Tonight?'

I had a ton of work to get through to make up for losing study time the night before. But I'd already made a date with Charles for the following weekend. 'Tonight.'

# FOUR

*Abby*

My God, my God, all that blood. How could one man have so much blood in him? That's almost Shakespeare, isn't it? *Macbeth*. The Scottish play. Unlucky to say the name. Unlucky to be in that house tonight. Unlucky to be me.

If only I'd stayed away. I thought about it. Then someone else would have found him, and I would have known it wasn't me. But who? Who else would find him? Will or Colin, maybe, if he didn't show up for work Tuesday morning. Or Consuelo, our cleaner, on Friday. He would have lain there for days in that case. No, I'm glad it wasn't Consuelo. She doesn't deserve that.

I'm babbling. The mental equivalent. Have to concentrate, think. What happened between the time I walked in with Emma and the time I saw Charles lying on the floor? Was it two seconds or two hours?

*Think*, Abby. I left Ellen's at four. Then the drive home: traffic heavy but not too slow – say an hour, maybe a little more. So I probably got there a bit after five. And what time did I call the police? What time is it now? Wish I'd never stopped wearing a watch. It's dark outside. But it's February – could be any time after, say, five thirty.

I would have had time to kill him. I could have put Emma down, gone into the living room, picked up – what? Who knows? – something and bashed him in the head. God knows I've been driven to the brink often enough. It wouldn't take much to push me over.

But that would mean I really am crazy, like he's been telling me all along. Forget the hospital. They should take me straight to the funny farm. If such things exist anymore. Straitjackets and shock therapy – do they still do that stuff? Or is it only in old movies? Whatever, if I did that, I deserve it. Need it, even. I'm not safe out.

But then what would happen to Emma?

Ellen would take her, raise her as one of her own. Good old Ellen. They don't make them saner than her. Emma would be safer with her aunt than with her crazy mother.

And without Emma, I would have nothing left to live for. Nothing at all.

*Peter*

I have roughly half an hour before I need to leave for the hospital to meet Ellen Stepanovich. May as well use it to examine the scene a little more. Can't let the forensics guys do all the work.

I start with the body itself. It's lying on the carpet between a black leather sofa and a glass-topped coffee table. No obvious blood on either. The table seems farther out from the couch than it should be, too far to reach a drink easily. I take a closer look at the carpet. At the far end, where there's no blood, I see dents in the pile a good foot closer to the sofa than the table is now.

'Anybody move this table?' I ask the room. Negative responses all around.

Did Crenshaw move it himself before the attack? If so, why? Did the killer move it, before or after? Again, why? To check if Crenshaw was dead? Did Abby move it, to try to help him? No marks in the blood on or around the body to show anyone got close.

If the table was closer to the couch when he was hit, surely there would be obvious blood spatter on both. Should be some on the couch regardless. Unless the killer cleaned it up for some unknown reason. Clean up the area but leave the bloody corpse in plain sight? What kind of sense does that make? Am I dealing with the Mad OCD Killer who can't stand to leave a mess behind? That would kind of go with this whole sterile room.

And that would make Abby the most likely killer. My gut goes tight at the thought.

Well, forensics will find out if any cleaning happened – there will be traces left behind no matter how zealous the cleaner was.

Could Crenshaw have been attacked elsewhere in the room and then moved? The off-white carpet shows no drag marks, no blood spatter beyond the immediate vicinity of the body. Crenshaw bled too much for him to have been knocked out and then moved before death without leaving any trace, and the way the blood lies on the body and the carpet around it shows he was definitely still bleeding when he got to that position.

This is beginning to look like that detective's nightmare: the murder that could not have been committed. Not because there's no person who could have done it, but because the situation doesn't add up. Oh, well. I have a whole investigation ahead of me to make sense of it.

There's no more I can do here for now. I leave forensics to their work and head to Dominican Hospital.

# FIVE

*Fall 2015*

Over the next few weeks, we tried Ethiopian food, Australian food, Vietnamese food, Russian food. I barely tasted any of it. My senses were entirely filled by Charles. As were my waking thoughts and my nightly dreams. It's a miracle I didn't flunk out that semester, because law was a very distant second priority at that point. And other people, like David and my sister, Ellen, had practically fallen off the bottom of the scale. Ordinarily I told both of them pretty much everything, but, for different reasons, I knew neither of them would want to hear about Charles.

At the Russian restaurant, Charles ordered beef Stroganov. After resigning myself to the fact that there was apparently no such thing as light food in Russia – no doubt they needed all those carbs and fat to keep warm – I settled for chicken Kiev. I handed my menu to the server, smiling my thanks because I figure wait staff need all the encouragement they can get. He moved off, and behind him I glimpsed the last two people I wanted to see at that moment: Ellen and her husband, Pavel, coming in the door.

I whipped my face away, but Ellen's sisterly radar had already detected me. She pulled Pavel toward our table.

'Abby! What are you doing here?'

'Having dinner,' I said in a voice as dry as the Pinot Grigio I was drinking. Seeing Ellen's frown, I caved and answered the question she wanted to ask but didn't. 'Ellen, Pavel, this is Charles Crenshaw. Charles, my sister and her husband.'

Charles stood and shook both their hands. 'Won't you join us?' he said. I tried to telegraph to him my profound objection to this invitation, but once again my mind-control skills fell short. 'I've been wanting to meet Abby's family. She's hardly told me anything about you.'

Ellen raised an eyebrow as she pulled out a chair and lowered her eight-months-pregnant body into it, leaning heavily on her husband's arm. Pavel caught my eye with a glance that said, *Do you want this?* He's always been the more sensitive partner in that marriage. I gave him a tiny shrug and eye roll. Once Ellen makes up her mind, it's pointless to stand in her way. Pavel took the remaining chair with a half smile that told me he'd do his best to rein her in.

'So, Charles, what do you do?' Ellen asked. Straight to the third degree, no preliminaries. Ellen should have been the lawyer instead of me.

'I'm a law student, like Abby. Only I'm in my final year.'

Ellen's gaze took in Charles's perfectly tailored gray suit and subtly patterned tie – he'd come straight to dinner from a job interview – then flicked to Pavel's black turtleneck, leather jacket, and pressed jeans. This time both eyebrows went up as she looked at me, then returned to normal as she turned back to Charles. 'What's your specialty?'

'Family law.'

'Oh, like Abby. But I wonder if you're doing it for the same reasons.'

I telegraphed, *Whoa, slow down!* but Ellen only smiled and plunged ahead. 'I suppose you know her motivation?'

'No, actually, we've never discussed it.' Charles turned to me with an inquiring smile. 'I'm just following in my father's footsteps, frankly. What made you choose this branch of the law?'

My insides turned to jelly, and not in a good way. The skeleton in our family closet wasn't one of those plastic Halloween jobs that flies out with a wail when you open the door. It was a rotting corpse with strips of putrid flesh still hanging from its twisted bones.

Pavel, of course, already knew everything. Unlike me, Ellen had reacted against the secrecy in our family by keeping nothing private from anyone she cared about. She'd probably told Pavel our history on their first date, and he'd absorbed it all with his usual empathy and tact. But Charles was so perfect – I was sure his family must be perfect as well. Although, come to think of it, he'd said as little about them as I had about mine.

'It's because of . . . something that happened when we were kids.' My eyes begged Ellen to get me out of this mess of her making.

She came to my rescue, if you can call it that; some might call it dropping me in the soup. 'Our parents were divorced. We were pretty young, young enough our mother should have gotten custody. But our father fought her, citing her chronic depression, and won.' She stared at me with a little gesture that handed the ball back to me.

I wanted to throw that ball all the way out of the restaurant, but it probably would have hit the nice waiter on the way, or knocked over the huge silver samovar that sat on a lacquered table near the door. I closed my eyes for a second, trying to center. I told myself that since I was falling in love with Charles, it was a bad idea to have secrets from him. Or, to put it another way, if he was going to run a mile after hearing about my background, I'd as soon he did it now, before I got in too deep.

'Mother's depression had never been that serious before – nothing that prevented her being a good parent. But after the divorce, she got much worse. About a year later, she . . . committed suicide.'

Even that was the expurgated version. The rest would have to wait for a more intimate setting, preferably involving darkness and a far deeper level of trust than Charles and I had yet established.

Charles gave a low whistle. 'So you want to prevent that kind of injustice from happening to other families.'

'Exactly.'

He reached over and squeezed my hand. 'I should have known it was something noble. You never did strike me as the typical predatory lawyer type.'

'Like you?' Ellen said it with a disarming smile.

Charles laughed. 'Like me.' He beckoned the waiter over with a practiced, imperious flick of his wrist. 'What will you two have? It's on me.'

'Oh, no, I can't let you do that,' Pavel put in – his first speech of the evening.

Ellen explained what her husband preferred not to mention. 'Pavel's a VP at Apple,' she told Charles. 'I hate to cook, so we used to eat out every night. Now we have a toddler at home, so it's mostly takeout – going to an actual restaurant is only an occasional treat.' She caressed the top of her bulging belly. 'And this may be the last for quite some time.'

'All the more reason for me to congratulate you ahead of time. Besides, I owe you a debt of gratitude for getting your sister to open up to me. And I always pay my debts.'

Pavel graciously backed down. He and Ellen ordered, and we talked of less personal topics for the rest of the meal. Over dessert, Ellen asked, 'So, Charles, how many generations of lawyers have there been in your family?'

'Four or five. My three-times-great-grandfather moved to San Francisco from the Midwest and made his pile catering to the Gold Rush crowd. He was a tiny bit shady, to tell the absolute truth. His son wanted to get more respectable, so he became a lawyer and eventually a state congressman. My grandfather was a judge – he died of a heart attack last year. My father's only a founding partner of a successful firm at this point, but he's hoping to make judge one day.'

Ellen whistled. 'Quite a history.' She shot a smile at Pavel. 'We're just the new money at the table, aren't we, love?'

Pavel returned her smile with no shadow of self-consciousness. He'd chosen his field because he loved it and had risen to the top because he was good at it – the money was an unsought bonus.

'And I'm the no money,' I quipped. I didn't mind being poor; I only minded being made to feel it.

'Not for long,' Charles said. On the surface, I assumed he simply meant I'd be making my own money as a lawyer soon. But the look in his eyes as he said it raised the first fluttering hope that he might mean something more.

The next day, Ellen summoned me to her house for brunch after she and Pavel got home from church. I considered begging off, but

I knew the pending conversation was inevitable. May as well get it over with. Besides, I had a little matter to discuss with dear big sister myself after the previous night.

Ellen dragged me into the kitchen to help cook, and the bombardment began. 'Abby, are you sure you know what you're doing?'

'At the moment, I'm chopping vegetables for an omelet.' I glared at her across their immense kitchen island – an island in the same sense Australia is an island – knife in hand. 'Did you know what you were doing last night? Exposing me in front of Charles?'

Ellen started, her eyes widening momentarily. She wasn't used to me challenging her. She's five years older than I am, and she'd been acting like my mother since before we lost our real mom. Most of the time I just took it – she was pretty good at being supportive as well as bossy, so it wasn't a bad deal overall. But last night she'd gone too far.

She recovered quickly and scrabbled on to the high ground again. 'I did it for your own good. If you're going to date a guy like that, you have to go into it knowing where you stand.'

'What do you mean, a guy like that? Because he's handsome, rich, and charming, you think he's out of my league?'

She tied on an apron, then hefted a large frying pan off the copper rack above the island and set it on the range across from me. 'It isn't that, exactly. I mean, I'm hardly one to talk about getting involved with someone from a very different background. Pavel was born in Russia, for pity's sake, not to mention being Orthodox. But Charles isn't merely from a different background.' She hesitated, making a business of laying bacon strips in the pan.

'Come on, out with it. It must be something pretty bad for *you* to hold back. Do you know something about Charles that I don't?'

'Not about Charles himself. About his father.' She put a spatter screen over the bacon and looked up at me. 'One of Pavel's coworkers, Joanne, got divorced a few months ago. Her husband hired Charles Crenshaw, Senior.' She swallowed, fiddling with her apron strings. 'They took her for everything she had – and custody of the kids into the bargain. And there was no justification for it – none whatsoever. Except that Joanne works long hours, but her ex does, too. He leaves the kids with a nanny.'

I opened my mouth to say something: that my Charles was not his father, that we didn't know the whole story; probably Joanne's husband was to blame and his lawyer was only following instructions. But Ellen went on.

'I talked to Joanne about it at a staff picnic. She said before he hired Crenshaw, her ex was perfectly happy with asking for joint custody and an equitable distribution of property. Crenshaw egged him on and made him go for blood.' She turned her attention to the bacon, which was protesting loudly that it wanted to be turned. 'And that's not all. She heard rumors that Crenshaw and the judge were cronies. There was nothing fair about that judge's decision.'

I opened my mouth again, but nothing came out. The situation was too much like what we had gone through as children – except, in our case, our father himself was out for blood from the word go.

I focused on the vegetables, slamming the knife into a tomato and squirting juice and seeds on my top. I, of course, had neglected to put on an apron. *Charles is not his father*, I told myself. *He would never do a thing like that.* I wanted to say those things to Ellen, but the words wouldn't form on my tongue.

'So it's not that I think he's too good for you, sweetie.' Ellen came around beside me and put her arm across my shoulders. 'I think chances are you're way too good for him.'

I shrugged her arm off. 'Don't be ridiculous. How could I be too good for Charles Crenshaw?'

'You're brilliant and beautiful and sweet.' Ellen always said those things, but she had to; she was my sister. Her saying them didn't make them true. 'But that only puts you at his same level. More importantly, you have integrity and compassion and a true sense of justice. Can you be sure the same is true of Charles?'

I finished chopping the tomato and plunged my knife into an onion. 'To be perfectly honest, I can't be sure of much of anything where Charles is concerned. But we're not that serious. We've only been dating a few weeks.' I used the knife edge to scrape the chopped vegetables into a bowl. It was only the onions that were making my eyes sting. Really. 'Nine chances out of ten, he'll have a little fun with me, and then he'll drop me. Like he's probably done with dozens of girls before.'

'And you're OK with that?' Ellen's eyes bored into me.

I shrugged. 'What Charles wants, Charles gets. Who am I to say no?'

Ellen took me by the shoulders and gazed into my eyes. 'It looked more serious than that to me. On his side, as far as I could gauge without knowing him, and definitely on yours. Please, Abby, don't let yourself get sucked into something that will break your heart in the long run. Promise me that.'

I managed a pale smile, but I couldn't make the promise. I was already in. If a broken heart was in my future, there was no way I could avoid it now.

# SIX

*Monday evening, February 26, 2018*

*Abby*

Where am I? What is this place with the white walls and strange beds and beeping instruments all around? And where is Emma?

'Emma!' I cry, sitting up on this funny, hard bed.

Some woman in navy scrubs says, 'Don't worry, Emma's fine. She's being well looked after. Your sister will be here in a few minutes to take her home.'

Ellen. Of course. Always count on Ellen. I lie back down. My head hurts. I'm cold and I'm oh, so very tired. The bed is still hard. The instruments keep on beeping.

Scrubs. Instruments. This must be a hospital.

Why am I in a hospital?

I was in an ambulance. I remember that. Must have passed out. Or had another blackout. But why?

My vision goes red. Something wrong with my eyes. No, no, it's not my eyes; it's the blood. Charles's blood. All over him. All over his precious white carpet. Nothing's going to get that clean.

Oh Lord, the blood.

'Abby?'

It's a voice I've heard before, but only lately. I look around. Oh, it's that policeman who was at the house. What was his name?

Detective Somebody. He was kind to me. He'll be disappointed when he finds out I killed Charles.

If I killed Charles.

I remember the blood. I remember calling 911, going to Emma to make sure she was all right, still sleeping. But what happened before the blood? What happened in that black time, the nothing time, the sucking emptiness that's been eating up more and more of my life?

I have to find out. Because I know I wanted Charles dead. God help me, I did. I have to know whether I actually killed him.

'Abby?'

That nice policeman wants to talk to me. 'I'm here.' Now. In the present. Good place to stay.

'Have you remembered anything more?'

'No. Nothing more. Just the blood.'

'The blood?'

'All over Charles's head. All over his precious white carpet.'

'What about the couch and the coffee table? Did you see any blood there?'

Starts to fade in, then fades out again. 'Don't remember. Sorry.'

'That's all right. Take your time. The important thing right now is for you to get well, stop having these blackouts.'

Nod. 'Get better. Better for Emma.'

Nurse says something, detective turns around, then back to me. 'Your sister's here. Do you want to talk to her?'

'Ellen. Yes. Ellen.'

He moves aside, and Ellen is there. Grab her hand and hold on for dear life.

'I'm here, sweetie.' Strokes my hair, like Mama used to do. 'Everything's going to be all right.'

'Emma?'

'Emma's fine. I met that nice policewoman who's taking care of her. Emma's awake and happy. She's had her bottle and her diaper, and they're playing peek-a-boo.'

'And you'll take her home with you?'

'Of course. She'll be fine for as long as you need to stay.'

'Worried, El. Something's wrong with me.'

'It's the stress. Your life has been pretty miserable lately. You need a good rest, and then you'll be fine.'

She doesn't say it, but we both know. I'll be fine now that Charles is gone.

*Peter*

After the sister gets through talking to Abby, I pull her aside into a waiting room. 'Mrs Stepanovich, I need to ask you a few questions, if I may.'

She glances about as if looking for an escape route, but there is none. 'All right.'

I sit us down in catty-cornered chairs. 'Are you older than Abby or younger?'

'Tactful, Detective. I'm five years older.'

'And your parents?'

'Our mother died when Abby was six. Our father is alive, but we don't have much of a relationship.'

'Does he live around here?'

'No. His fourth wife took him to Washington.'

'I see.' You get someone with more than three spouses, the picture is usually pretty clear. 'Any other family? Siblings, cousins?'

'No. Just Abby and me.'

'You knew your sister's husband fairly well, I imagine?'

'Better than I wanted to.' She shifts in her chair, looks away from me. 'He was a first-class jerk.'

Not quite what I expected, given Abby's reaction to his death. But it does fit with her saying she isn't Mrs Crenshaw anymore. 'There are jerks and jerks. Can you be a little more specific?'

'I'm not a psychologist, but I'd say he was an emotionally and sexually abusive narcissist. Possibly a psychopath.'

I whistle. 'Can you give me an example?'

'You've seen Emma, right?'

'Yeah. Cute kid.'

'Very. But Charles would have nothing to do with her because she isn't the perfect boy he was hoping for. And, of course, it was all Abby's fault she came out wrong. Everything was always Abby's fault.'

I stare. 'That's a first-class jerk, all right.'

'Indeed. I've been trying to get Abby to leave him since before they were married.'

'And how long ago is that?'

'They were married – it'll be two years in June. Dated for maybe eight or nine months before that.'

'Did you see from the beginning what he was like?'

'Not precisely. I didn't even meet him until they'd been dating a while. But I knew his family by reputation. It didn't seem like a good fit. They're at the top of the social scale, and we were only ever middle-middle.'

'How did they meet?'

'In law school. Santa Clara. Abby was there on scholarship.'

'Does she practice law now?'

'No. She managed to get her degree, barely, before Emma was born, but then she decided to be a full-time mom. At least for a while. She never took the bar exam.' A slight headshake. Disapproving of little sister wasting her talents?

'How about her husband? Where did he practice?'

'A branch of his daddy's firm in Santa Cruz. Crenshaw, Hopkins, and Melrose.'

'What kind of law?'

'Family, mostly. Expensive divorces, property settlements, estates. That sort of thing.'

'So not likely he'd have criminals out for his blood.'

'No. Maybe a disgruntled divorcé who didn't get the settlement they wanted. But I'd hardly think that would be a sufficient motive for murder.' She shrugs. 'You'd know better than I.'

Have to agree with her there. But I need a lead – any lead. 'Do you have any idea who might have wanted to harm Charles?'

She stares at me as though I have a dunce cap on. 'You mean besides Abby? No, I don't. But I promise you . . . wait. Did you tell me *how* Charles was killed?'

'No. We haven't officially determined cause or manner of death.'

'But was it violent? Was there blood?'

I don't think it can hurt to tell her that much; Abby's sure to say something eventually. 'Yes. A lot of blood.'

'Then I can promise you, Abby didn't do it. She's incapable of violence.'

'Very few people are genuinely incapable, Mrs Stepanovich. It just takes the right provocation.'

'No, you don't get it. I didn't say she's incapable of *killing*.

Poison or something, maybe, if her life or Emma's life depended on it. But she has an unusually strong aversion to violence. Blood in particular. She absolutely can't stand it.'

The light goes on. That would explain her extreme reaction to the death of a man she must have hated. And it also explains why she can't remember anything except the mere sight of his smashed skull and all that blood.

'Abby can't remember exactly what happened tonight. She says she's been having blackouts for several months. Were you aware of that?'

She nods. 'She didn't tell me when they first started, but it came out eventually. I put it down to the stress of living with that man.'

'Has she consulted a doctor?'

She huffs and shoves back her short brown hair with both hands. 'No. She was afraid it would get back to Charles. I was going to take her to my own doctor as soon as I could get her in.'

Afraid to go to a doctor? What kind of marriage was this? 'Sounds like Abby was pretty unhappy in this marriage. Why did she stay?'

'As a matter of fact, I think she was ready to leave him for good. She stayed as long as she did mainly because of Emma. Abby was afraid Charles would try for custody – and given his daddy's reputation, he'd probably have gotten it.'

'Why would he want custody if he didn't care about the child?'

'Just to spite Abby, I suppose. Plus, she's maybe a little paranoid on that point because of our own family history. Our father got custody of us when we really should have gone with our mom.'

Mrs Stepanovich probably doesn't realize she's just handed me a powerful motive for Abby to kill her husband instead of simply leaving him. Dead men can't get custody.

'OK, one last thing. Where were you this evening between five and five thirty?'

'Me?' She looks startled for a second, then laughs. 'Oh, I see. You think I might have killed him to protect my sister. I won't deny I'm glad he's dead. But I didn't kill him. I was home all afternoon until you called me, whenever that was. My husband can vouch for me from five o'clock on.'

'All right. I'll give him a call. Thank you, Mrs Stepanovich. You can take your niece home now.'

# SEVEN

*October 2015*

For the first couple of months we dated, Charles and I were always alone, except for the one accidental meeting with Ellen and Pavel. In my darker moments, I suspected he was embarrassed to introduce me to his friends, as if I were some guilty pleasure he indulged in only in secret. So I was surprised – one might say relieved – when, one balmy Saturday in late October, Charles invited me to join a group of his friends surfing in Santa Cruz.

I'd surfed a little in high school but had never been serious about it. 'Isn't it kind of late in the year for that?' I asked. 'The water will be freezing.'

'We'll find you a wetsuit. You're not afraid of a little cold water, are you? I thought you were tough.'

When he put it that way, I could hardly refuse. Though what I had done to give him the impression I was physically tough, I couldn't imagine.

Charles had borrowed his mother's Mercedes SUV so we could all ride together. We picked up the other two couples, Colin and Jennifer and Will and Melissa. Melissa, who was about my size, had scrounged an extra wetsuit and board for me; my own board was long gone.

The three guys sat in front, and during the hour-long drive to Santa Cruz, they teased and baited each other in loud voices nonstop. Melissa gave me a wry smile now and then to let me know she would have talked to me if she could have been heard, while Jennifer just stared out the window.

When we'd parked at the beach and struggled into our wetsuits, the three guys ran into the turbulent waves immediately, with Jennifer hard on their heels. Melissa hung back with me. 'Does anyone else think surfing in late October is a little bit mad?' she murmured.

I gave her a grateful smile. 'Absolutely. But I guess we have to at least make it look like we're trying.'

She grinned. 'I'm getting to be an expert at that. Follow me.'

Melissa and I paddled out a few feet and caught a couple of the smallest waves, spending most of our time in the shallows. Jennifer struck out on her own, surfing real swells but not huge ones. Meanwhile, the guys were going for the biggest and longest waves they could find, some of which struck me as rather alarming. One in particular proved too much for Colin and Will; they both dropped out, shaking their heads. But Charles mounted his board and rode the huge wave all the way to shore.

He grabbed his board in one arm and flung the other fist into the air. 'Ha! I beat you suckers! I beat you all!'

Melissa and I exchanged a baffled look. 'I didn't realize this was a competition, did you?' I asked.

'Honey, I've known Charles for years. And let me tell you: with him, everything is a competition.'

I shook my head, but part of me couldn't help admiring his triumphant muscular form encased in skin-tight black rubber, goggles raised to the sky. He could almost be some sort of superhero. The Unstoppable Surferman. Though how one could defeat the bad guys by surfing, I couldn't quite imagine. Maybe if the bad guys were alien supersharks.

We adjourned to a nearby hotel, where Charles had rented two rooms so we could all take hot showers and change in comfort. As we girls dressed, Jennifer said lightly to me, 'So, how goes it with Mister Wonderful?'

Something in her tone put me on alert. 'Fine, I think.'

'That's what they all think at this stage.' The words were muffled as Jennifer's head disappeared inside the turtleneck she was pulling on. I wasn't sure I'd heard her correctly.

'Wh–what do you mean?'

'Don't pay any attention to her,' Melissa put in. 'She's pulling your chain.'

'Me? I'm not the chain-puller. You'll find out for yourself eventually,' Jennifer said. 'Don't say I didn't warn you.' She grabbed her things and strode out of the room.

I turned to Melissa. 'What did she mean? I have a feeling I need to know.'

Melissa hemmed and hawed, then finally admitted, 'Charles has a bit of a reputation. As a ladies' man. Jennifer dated him for a while when we were undergrads. Before she started dating Colin.'

My voice went small. 'I see.'

'But honestly, I've never known him stay with anyone as long as he's stayed with you. Usually it's a couple of weeks, a month tops, and then he moves on.'

'We're at six weeks now. That doesn't exactly feel like safe ground.'

Melissa put a hand on my arm. 'Well, maybe the time isn't that significant, but I've never seen him look at anyone the way he looks at you. It's different with you. And you're a different kind of girl. Most of the ones he's dated weren't worth staying with. Well, Jen would have been, but they weren't a good match. She challenged him too much. I can see you two staying together for the long haul. Honestly, I can. And I'm sure Charles can, too.'

I appreciated Melissa's attempt at reassurance – and her friendliness, even more – but I was only partly reassured. The two women's words stayed with me all through dinner, which we ate at a casual seafood restaurant on the wharf. I picked at my popcorn shrimp, feeling like an invisible observer as Charles joked and bantered with his old buddies. This was a side of him I'd never seen in our private times together, and I wasn't sure I liked it. With me alone, he seemed confident, but with the guys, he displayed a need to show off that revealed a deep insecurity. But I felt pretty insecure with this bunch myself. I'd never had a group of friends like this, who had known each other from grade school. Despite Melissa's kind attempts to include me in the conversation, I didn't know if I could ever fit in.

But once in a while, Charles would turn from the general chatter and enfold me in a smile that shut out everyone else, and I knew it didn't matter whether or not I fit in with his friends. Melissa was right. I had Charles, and that was enough.

By the time Christmas break was upon us, Charles and I were nearly inseparable. Despite Jennifer's dark hints, Charles showed no sign of leaving me, and I couldn't imagine how he would have time to be with anyone else in addition. I barely had time for my studies.

But I made it through my semester finals and was packing to spend the break with Ellen, looking forward to cocoa-pajama-and-movie parties with my sister and playing with two-year-old Nicky and newborn Katya to my heart's content, when my father called. I stared at the phone as if the numbers it displayed were some indecipherable alien code. My father? Calling me? I must be in the Twilight Zone.

'Hello?'

'Hey, Abigirlie.' The hated nickname. It really was him. 'It's Dad.'

'I . . . sort of gathered that. Has something happened?'

'What do you mean? Does something have to "happen" for me to call my best girl?'

Uh, no. Ellen had always been his best girl, and even that position was not one most daughters would envy.

'It's just . . . you haven't called for a while.' About two years, as a matter of fact. Since I decided to go to law school instead of following him into teaching. And two years, it turned out, was not long enough.

'Well, I'm calling now. Vicki and I want you to come up for Christmas.' Vicki was his fourth wife. And 'up' was Bellingham, Washington. About as 'up' as you could get without a passport.

'Gosh, Dad, that's pretty last-minute. And I'm not sure my car would make it.' My 2005 Mazda coupe was running decently, but I certainly wouldn't trust it in the snow I'd no doubt have to drive through along the way.

'I'll pay for you to fly. Already got the ticket, in fact, so this is an offer you can't refuse.' That *I'm only joking around* tone couldn't fool me. My father had laid out money – nonrefundable money – and that meant if I didn't board that plane, he'd find a way to teleport down here and drag me on to it.

Thank God my plans had only been with Ellen and not with Charles. He was going skiing with his parents over the break. Ellen would understand the Dad factor, but I still feared the Charles ice was too thin under my feet to withstand it. 'When do I leave?'

'Tomorrow. Returning December twenty-eighth.'

Tomorrow was the sixteenth. That meant almost two weeks with Dad and Vicki. All the Dickens Christmas ghosts rolled into one might not suffice to get me through.

I unloaded my suitcase and started over, cramming in all my heaviest sweaters. I'd have to wear the fur-lined boots, which meant hot feet until I got there; no way would they fit in the suitcase. Then I drove to Ellen's house to drop off my gifts for her family and break the news.

'You know he's got to have some hidden agenda,' Ellen said.

'I know. But I have no idea what. And it doesn't look like I can get out of it. I'm sorry to ruin all our plans.'

'Chalk it up to Dad the Destroyer. I'd say have a great Christmas, but that might be too much to expect.'

'Well, merry Christmas to you guys, anyway. You know I'd rather be here watching Nicky rip off all the ribbons and try to feed them to Katya.'

After that I had to brave the pre-Christmas mobs to buy gifts for Dad and Vicki. Regardless of the short notice, I'd never get away with arriving empty-handed. Dad wasn't too difficult to shop for; he loved techie toys, and the stores in Silicon Valley were full of them. But I was clueless about Vicki. We'd only met at their wedding a little over two years ago. She seemed nice enough, but I'd had no chance to get to know her. What colors had she chosen for the ceremony? My memory was blank. I guess I'd been too focused on surviving the day to notice. I wandered the mall aimlessly, picking things up and putting them down again. Right before closing time, I grabbed a big box of locally made high-end chocolates. Surely every woman liked chocolate. I just hoped she wasn't on a diet.

I arrived in Bellingham the next day to a frigid wind that bit through my thickest California coat. Dad met me with a frown. 'Unprepared as always, Abigirlie. You should have checked the weather reports.'

'This is the heaviest jacket I own. We don't need parkas in Santa Clara. Raincoats, yeah, but not parkas.'

He humphed. 'Vicki can lend you something while you're here.' Vicki was about five-two and at least a size sixteen, to my five-five and size six. But whatever. It would be better than freezing.

Vicki smiled her acquiescence. 'Of course. Meanwhile, let's get you out of this wind.'

We drove from the airport to their home on the outskirts of Bellingham – not my childhood home, which had been in San Jose, but a nice Cape Cod cottage nestled under a thin coverlet of snow. I was allowed half an hour to settle into the guest room. It was a good thing I hadn't tried to guess at Vicki's taste – apparently it ran to pastels, frills, and Precious Moments figurines. Polar opposite of my own preference for earth tones and a warm but uncluttered ambience. Still, it was only for thirteen days. I was counting them.

A handbell sounded – the signal for dinner since time immemorial in the households of Jeremy Taylor. I put down my hairbrush and ran down the stairs. Lateness was an unpardonable sin.

Dinner was dry meatloaf with runny mashed potatoes and canned green beans. I choked it down and told Vicki how much I'd missed good home cooking.

'We have a guest coming for dinner tomorrow,' Vicki said with a sidelong glance at Dad.

'Oh? Anybody I know?'

'One of my old students,' Dad said. 'Mark Fleming. He's doing his student teaching at Bellingham High.'

My stomach plummeted. A young man my own age – and a teacher to boot. This could only mean one thing. The chosen suitor for my hand – my own personal Prince Charming, who probably had no idea of the high honor he was destined for.

But then, Dad had no idea about Charles. I kept my response noncommittal for now. Any protest would only make things worse.

The next day, Vicki insisted I accompany her to the beauty parlor. Since Vicki herself had never yet insisted on anything, I assumed this directive issued from Dad. He'd always been as dissatisfied with my appearance as with everything else about me.

I'd never set foot in such a place in my life – a hair salon once or twice, but this was a real old-fashioned beauty parlor, complete with dome dryers, magazines, and gossip. I would have thought you'd need a senior-citizen card to get in. Vicki was in her early fifties, I guessed, but not among the blue-haired yet.

As soon as we walked through the door, the proprietress pounced on my thick, untrimmed, waist-length chestnut mop.

'Look at all this gorgeous hair! The color! And the wave! Oh, I could do wonders with this!'

I drew back, horrified, visions of beehives dancing in my head. Vicki said diplomatically, 'Don't you think just a little trim, dear? And maybe a little shaping around the face? Your hair is lovely, but it could flatter you so much more.'

I thought of Jennifer and Melissa, who had the kind of haircuts that are meant to look natural but actually cost the earth. 'Well, maybe a little trim. But it has to stay long.' My hair hadn't been short since the divorce. Dad had Ellen's and my hair chopped off when we came to live with him so he wouldn't have to deal with it. In my own mind, overnight I turned from a fairy-tale princess into a frog.

I sat in the chair, closed my eyes, and thought of England as the stylist washed, combed, cut, and blow-dried my precious hair – my one good feature. When I dared to peek at last, I thought she'd turned the chair and I was looking out the window at someone else. Someone way too chic for me. This person's hair swooped from a side part into feathery side bangs that framed her cheeks and then gave way to layered curls falling to the tops of her breasts.

Once I convinced myself I was indeed looking at my own reflection, the look began to grow on me. I'd always thought my face was ordinary, but this style made me look like Somebody. I could do justice to one of Morgan's Little Black Dresses with this hair.

Vicki clapped her hands. 'You look simply beautiful, Abby dear! Doesn't she?' She appealed to the whole salon.

Everyone, staff and clients alike, turned to look. Approving murmurs rippled around the room. The stylist smiled with brimming eyes. 'I do think this is one for the books. A real triumph. Can I take your picture, hon?'

My face was burning, but I couldn't say no when she was so proud of her work. She whooshed away the cape and straightened my collar, then whipped out her phone and took several angles.

'You're awful quiet, hon. Don't you like it?'

I turned to the mirror again and tried a little smile. 'I love it. It's the new me.'

Wanting to do justice to the haircut, I put on my second-best outfit for the evening (saving the best for Christmas Day; that was a Dad requirement). The rich brick color of the cowl-neck sweater brought out the auburn highlights in my hair and warmed up my pale skin. I even dashed on some lip gloss – not for the unknown Prince Charming I was due to meet, but for the absent Charles. 'I wish you could see me tonight,' I said to him in the mirror, blowing him an airy kiss.

Dad looked at me with visible approval when I came downstairs. 'I see you've made an effort, Abigirlie. My girl cleans up pretty good, doesn't she, Vick?'

'You look simply lovely,' Vicki told me with a smile.

I was grateful for Vicki's kindness, but I wished the little girl in me could cease to care what Dad thought of my appearance or any other aspect of my life. If he could exalt me with one word, he could crush me with another.

Prince Charming, aka Mark Fleming, arrived shortly afterward. He took a step back when he saw me, then held my hand rather than shaking it. 'Mr Taylor told me he had a daughter my age. He didn't tell me you were gorgeous.'

I felt myself blush as I gently pulled away my hand. Mark wasn't half bad himself – tall, reasonably fit for a teacher, with a cute, freckled boy-next-door face and a contagious grin. If I hadn't met Charles . . .

But I had met Charles. And I was going to be a lawyer in Silicon Valley, not a teacher in Bellingham. No matter what my father had planned.

The evening was pleasant enough, though I had a fine line to walk – trying to be friendly enough to pacify Dad without giving Mark too much false encouragement. He seemed like a nice guy; I was sorry to have to let him down.

After dinner and a rousing game of Scrabble – which I won, to Mark's admiration and Dad's blustering chagrin – I saw Mark to the door and stepped outside with him. I pulled the door shut behind me, and we stood in the porchlight watching the softly blowing snow. It could have been the perfect Hallmark moment – hardened city lawyer returns to her hometown and is surprised by the love of a simple local boy. Only this wasn't my hometown, I wasn't a hardened lawyer (yet), and I had no intention of falling in love.

'I've enjoyed meeting you, Mark. But before you ask, this whole thing was my father's idea, not mine. I'm dating someone at law school in California. We're pretty serious.'

His eyebrows shot up. 'You're in law school? Mr Taylor never mentioned that.'

'That's because he's determined to get me to quit and become a teacher. You were part of the plan, I'm sure. But he's not going to succeed. I've made my choice, and I'm sticking to it.'

'Well, good for you.' He gave a sad smile. 'Though I have to say, I'd consider going to law school myself if it meant having a chance with you.'

I smiled and let him kiss me on the cheek for Dad's sake. I knew he'd be watching through the crack in the living-room drapes. 'Goodbye, Mark. Merry Christmas. Have a nice life.'

Dad was smiling when I came back in. 'So you like Mark? I knew you would. When are you going to see him again?'

'Never,' I calmly replied.

The blood rose from the base of Dad's neck to his ears. 'What do you mean, never? That young man is perfect for you.'

This Dad – the face-about-to-explode-because-I-did-something-terrible Dad – had cowed me into submission for twenty-two years. I turned a corner when I insisted on going to law school in spite of him, but that didn't mean my stomach didn't clench or my hands go cold with the effort to stand my ground. But the thought of Charles sustained me.

'Dad,' I said quietly, 'I already have a boyfriend. A law student from a wealthy family. He's brilliant, charming, and handsome, and he loves me. I'm expecting him to propose any day.' That was a brazen exaggeration, but I had to make Dad take Charles's role in my life seriously. 'And there is no way you're going to stop me from becoming a lawyer.'

Much as he might want to, Dad could not control my education. He no longer held the purse strings. My schooling was paid for by a mix of scholarships, loans, and a life-insurance payout from my mother.

His face went white. 'What happened to honoring your father and your mother? I thought you were a good Christian girl.' Dad's religion was remarkably convenient – it could always be counted on to censure other people's conduct while justifying his own. My own faith, though weak and wavering, was at least honest: I knew I was as big a sinner as anyone else.

'I am honoring my mother's wishes – she wanted me to be happy. As for you – I'm sorry, Dad, but "honor" doesn't necessarily mean "obey." Not for a twenty-four-year-old, at any rate. You have to let me go and live the life I've chosen.'

His eyes narrowed dangerously, but Vicki materialized at his side and touched his arm. He took a long breath through flared nostrils, then turned and strode out of the room.

If it hadn't been holiday season with flights impossible to get, I'm sure I would have been on the next plane home. As it was, I stayed out the planned twelve days, with Dad doing his Iceman imitation the whole time. I had to feel for Vicki, trying to be nice to me and pacify him simultaneously. I would say it was the worst Christmas of my life except that there had been plenty of atrocious ones in my childhood. But I'd always had Ellen to lean on then.

When my sentence was up, Vicki drove me to the airport. She gave me a hug and said in my ear, 'He doesn't mean it, you know. Deep down, he loves you and wants the best for you.'

I appreciated her effort, but I wasn't buying it. 'He wants what *he* thinks is best for me. Not quite the same thing.' I gave her a grateful smile. 'Thanks for everything, Vicki. I probably won't see you again for a while.'

Or maybe ever. Dad was the past. Charles was my future.

# EIGHT

*Monday evening, February 26, 2018*

*Peter*

I look in on Abby one more time before leaving the hospital, but she's sleeping. I don't need the doctors to tell me sleep is what she needs more than anything. In the morning they'll begin whatever tests they'll do to pinpoint the cause of her blackouts – and, if necessary, begin treatment. That is, if the blackouts don't cease on their own now that the trauma of being an abused wife is over.

I examine the clothes they took off her. A little blood on the cuffs of her shirt, but nothing anywhere else. That's consistent with her finding the body, maybe checking to see if he was dead; if she killed him, I'd expect a lot more blood, and more spread out. Of course, she may have changed; but then why the blood on the cuffs? Forensics will have checked all the clothes in the house; I'll get that report in the morning. A nurse confirms they found no blood on Abby's body except under her fingernails.

I spend a minute in her room, watching her as she sleeps. She looks so small and vulnerable lying there, her unmadeup lashes soft and dark against her pale cheek, her lips slightly open and vibrating with her breath. I get a flash of my little sister Amy in the early stages of her leukemia – before she lost her hair to chemotherapy and her childish plumpness to the disease itself. My heart flips in my chest.

But this vulnerable young woman, this victim, may also be a killer. I can't lose sight of that, regardless of what her sister said. Regardless of what my own heart is telling me – that this is a woman who can only love, never hate enough to kill. I pray she'll wake up and remember exactly what happened. Maybe that will give me something to go on to exonerate her and find the real killer.

Meanwhile, I have a painful duty to perform – one I dread above every other aspect of my job: I have to inform the victim's parents that their son is dead. And I have the whole hour-long drive to Los Altos Hills to rehearse ad nauseam exactly what I'll say.

I get there about nine p.m. At least I won't have to roust them out of bed so I can shatter their world. Every time I do this job, I remember my mother's and father's faces when Amy finally left us for good. And they were prepared to lose her, as much as anyone ever can be. The news will hit these people like a runaway train.

The door is answered by a maid, a middle-aged Latina woman. I show her my ID and ask to speak to Mr and Mrs Crenshaw. The woman shows me into a formal living room whose rather sterile black-and-white decor is enlivened by a spectacular view out over the lights of Silicon Valley. In the daytime it must be stunning.

In a moment, I turn to see the couple enter the room – him about six feet, one-eighty, what they call distinguished-looking, the image of the rich and powerful lawyer; her maybe five-five, willowy, perfectly groomed, and wearing a dress so understated it smells of money – the image of the successful lawyer's wife.

'Mr and Mrs Crenshaw?'

He takes the lead. 'Yes. What is it, Officer?'

'Detective Peter Rocher. I'm afraid I have some bad news for you. You might want to sit down.'

Mrs Crenshaw puts her hand over her mouth and sinks into the nearest chair. 'It isn't little Emma, is it?' she asks in a small voice.

'No, ma'am. Emma's fine.' I shoot a questioning look at Crenshaw, but he gestures to me to get on with it. I guess he figures he can take whatever life might throw at him standing up.

I've learned from experience that a gradual lead-in doesn't help. 'I'm very sorry to have to tell you that your son Charles was found dead earlier this evening.'

Mrs Crenshaw draws in her breath in a loud gasp. Her husband sways slightly but remains standing.

'How did it happen?' he asks in a breaking voice. 'Car?'

'No.' People always assume a car accident when a young person dies suddenly. But the truth this time is far worse. 'He was found dead in his home. We're treating it as suspicious.'

Mrs Crenshaw finds her voice. 'Who found him? Not Abby?'

'I'm afraid it was Abby, yes. She was in a pretty bad state when we got there. She's in the hospital for observation now, but I'm sure she'll be all right.'

Crenshaw interrupts me. 'What do you mean, suspicious? You think he was murdered?'

'Oh, Charles!' his wife exclaims in horror. 'Surely not!'

I don't see much point in prevaricating. 'That does seem the most likely scenario at this point. But we don't have anything conclusive yet.'

'Cause of death?' Crenshaw demands.

I clear my throat and speak in a monotone, hoping vainly Mrs Crenshaw isn't listening. 'We have to wait for the ME's report to be sure. But it looks like blunt-force trauma to the back of the head.'

He grunts. 'Couldn't have been an accident?'

'That's possible. We'll know more after the postmortem and the forensics reports come in.'

Mrs Crenshaw gives a little cry that is half gasp. 'You mean they have to cut him up? Oh, my poor boy. My poor, beautiful boy.' She buries her face in her hands.

I soften my tone for her. 'I'm afraid we always have to do a postmortem in a suspicious death. But it's done as respectfully as possible.'

'You'll let me know when his body is released for the funeral?' Crenshaw says gruffly.

'Yes, sir. Although it's usual for the spouse to take care of that.'

He waves that aside. 'It's our responsibility. Abby won't be fit to handle it, anyway.'

I would stand up for her, but I suspect she won't be too disappointed not to be involved. 'Whatever you say, sir.' I take out my notebook. 'If you're up to it, I do have a few questions I'd like to ask.'

'Fire away.' Crenshaw takes a seat on one of the black leather chairs, hitching his trousers up at the knees to preserve their perfect crease. I take that as permission to sit down myself.

'First of all, were you both at home this evening, from about five o'clock on?'

'I was at the office till five thirty. My assistant can confirm. Then I headed home, got here about six.'

I look at Mrs Crenshaw. 'Ma'am?'

She flutters. 'Me? Oh, yes, I was at home. Yolanda was here with me.' When I look blank, she adds, 'Our maid.'

'Right. Does Charles have any brothers or sisters? Other close family?'

Crenshaw takes over the answering. 'No. Just the three of us. Our parents are dead.'

'What about close friends?'

'I wouldn't know. Colleagues. Maybe some buddies from school. Abby could probably tell you.'

'Do you know of anyone who might have any reason to harm your son?'

'Harm him? What, you mean like a dissatisfied client or something?'

'That, or anyone else. Anyone he'd injured or quarreled with? Anyone who might bear a grudge.'

Crenshaw exchanges a baffled look with his wife. 'No. Absolutely no idea. Unless . . .'

'Unless what, sir?'

'Unless Abby finally got fed up with him.' This in a reluctant mutter.

'Would you consider her capable of violence?'

Mrs Crenshaw speaks in a rush. 'No. Absolutely not. She and Charles may have had their . . . difficulties, but I'm sure it wasn't nearly as bad as that. For Emma's sake, at any rate, Abby would never have hurt her baby's father.'

I sense a bit of wishful thinking in that last remark, but I let it go. 'Other than a troubled marriage, are you aware of any stressful situations in your son's life recently? Financial problems, maybe? Anything that might have gotten out of hand?'

They both shake their heads. It looks like the numbness of shock is beginning to wear off, and I don't much want to be around for that. I close my notebook and stand.

'Thank you for your time. We'll be in touch.' I hand Crenshaw my card. 'Let me know if you think of anything that might be helpful.' I hesitate, then turn to Mrs Crenshaw one last time. 'I'm very sorry for your loss.'

# NINE

*December 2015–January 2016*

Charles and I had a date for December 29. I was finally back from the literal and emotional icehouse of my visit to Dad, and Charles had returned from his ski trip.

I opened the door to him, and he stopped cold. 'You look different.'

I smiled nervously. What if he didn't like it after all? 'It's my hair. I got it cut.'

He considered me with chin in hand, circling to get all the angles. 'I like it,' he pronounced at last. 'Makes you look more sophisticated. Good job.'

So something good had come of that trip to Dad's, after all. That is, in addition to me asserting my own will against him for the second time in my life.

'And perfect timing, too,' Charles said. 'We're invited to my parents' house for New Year's Day dinner.'

My newfound confidence ran out the ends of my perfect hair and dribbled on to the floor. 'I'm not sure I'm ready for that.' Visions of vast arrays of cutlery dedicated to arcane and unknown purposes danced in my head. I would have felt more comfortable if an Indian rajah had invited me to dinner – at least I'd have had an excuse for not knowing how to behave. 'What if I make a total fool of myself?'

'You'll be fine,' Charles said with the smile that mowed down all opposition. 'You'll be terrific. They'll love you.'

That possibility seemed as remote as Pluto, which I'd recently heard did not exist. Or wasn't a planet. Or something.

'What do you think you'll wear?' he asked in a casual tone. But it was clearly no casual question.

I froze. A whole new dimension of Abby-makes-a-fool-of-herself opened before me. 'Heck, I don't know. Would my Christmas dress do?'

I went to my closet and pulled out the emerald-green velvet dress I'd packed for Dad's house. It had been fine for Christmas dinner, but now I looked at the gathered skirt, puffed sleeves, and modest neckline through Charles's eyes.

It was hopeless.

His eyebrows went up, and a little smile played around his mouth. 'Tell you what. I'll take you shopping.'

The next afternoon we went to Santana Row, where shops like Gucci and Kate Spade New York lined the elegant lanes. I couldn't even afford to window-shop there. I was sure some alarm would go off the minute I stepped over one of those thresholds – *Intruder alert! Intruder alert!*

But I guess Charles's rich-person aura extended to me, because we were able to enter the first shop without causing security people to materialize and escort us out. He led me confidently toward a rack of cocktail dresses, prompting me to wonder how often he had shopped with, or for, his girlfriends in the past.

He pulled a dress off the rack and held it out to me. 'Try this one.'

I had no idea what the dress looked like – all I could see was the price tag. Surely it had too many digits. I blinked, but the digits didn't go away.

'Charles, I can't afford this. Any of this. Your parents will have to take me as I am.'

'My treat. Come on, try it on.'

*No* was not a possible answer. I made a supreme effort to focus on the dress itself. All I could see was black.

A salesperson materialized beside us, all white teeth and perfect outfit. 'Would you like to try it on?'

Charles handed her the dress, and she led the way to a changing room I would have been happy to exchange for my dorm room. I had the dress halfway on when a discreet knock came at the door, followed by, 'I thought you might like some shoes to go with it.'

I opened the door a crack to receive a pair of black heels, miraculously in my size. I refused to look at the sole for fear of being blinded by the price, but I couldn't help noticing the inner label – Manolo Blahnik. Morgan had several of those on her shoe rack. I slipped the heels on and felt as though I'd climbed the Eiffel Tower, my head spinning from the rarefied air at this altitude.

I channeled my inner contortionist to zip up the dress, then braved a glance in the mirror. I felt like Julia Roberts in *Pretty Woman*. In fact, I was nearly certain this was the exact same dress she wore for her first dinner with Richard Gere.

I stepped out into the shop, and Charles's eyes confirmed it. That was the way Richard looked at Julia when he saw her at the bar.

'That's the one,' Charles said.

My transformation into a young woman acceptable to the Crenshaw family was underway.

New Year's Day came far too soon. My outfit was ready, but I would never be. I barely slept the night before, dreaming of everything that could possibly or impossibly go wrong, such as all the Crenshaws turning into Zygons as we sat down to dinner and me being the main course. But I trembled my way into the Little Black Dress and the high black heels, and I managed to steady my hands long enough to apply a bit more makeup than usual, so I'd look less unbalanced. I also looked less like myself. Maybe I could get through the evening by being Abby playing the role of a proper girlfriend for Charles.

He greeted me with a kiss on the cheek so as not to smudge my lipstick. 'You look fabulous,' he murmured in my ear. The costume was working so far.

We drove up into the priciest part of Los Altos Hills, where an acre is considered a tiny lot and a house under four thousand square feet a starter home. Charles stopped the car on the top of a hill, in front of a house that couldn't decide whether to be modern or Mediterranean. We passed through a wrought-iron gateway into a paved courtyard surrounded by a colonnade, and from there through a vast foyer into a cavernous living room, where huge picture windows faced outward over a spectacular view. I had to remind myself firmly that the character I was playing would simply take all this in her stride.

Charles's mother, Jacqueline, greeted me with a gracious smile and a polished elegance I knew I could never match if I married a thousand Charleses. I couldn't put my finger on what made her so perfect; taken separately, neither her sleek blond French twist nor her understated jewelry nor her silver-gray silk dress was striking enough to account for it. In the end I concluded it must be simply the aura of money.

Charles's father, Charles Senior, did not emerge from the library on our arrival; I was taken in to meet him, no doubt so that he would appear to best advantage amid his glass-fronted bookshelves and leather upholstery. I would never have believed I could see Charles eclipsed by another man, but his father accomplished the feat. He was as tall as Charles and equally handsome, but with the added distinction of years – symbolized by a white stripe at the temple of his thick black hair – and the weight of a fortune he had augmented by his own labor.

Charles Senior took my hand and held it for a moment, looking me over boldly from head to foot. I prayed my perception filter would hold. At last he raised my hand to his lips, then let it go. 'You've done surprisingly well for yourself, my boy,' he said to Charles Junior, my Charles, as if I were not even there. 'She's quite a beauty.' But I could hear the subtext: *Now let's see how she behaves herself.*

During dinner, I kept a close eye on my hostess and matched her fork for fork, spoon for spoon, finger bowl for finger bowl. I have no idea what we ate, but I'm sure it was fabulous. All through the soup, salad, and main course, I fielded questions from Charles Senior: questions about my family, my upbringing, my studies. My answers walked a fine line between my own true backstory and that which belonged to my character for the evening. I didn't lie, but I was somewhat economical with the truth.

It seemed to work. As the dessert was served by a woman in a black cotton dress and white apron – maid or caterer, I couldn't be sure – Charles Senior said to his son, 'I think she's smarter than you are, my boy. You'd better watch yourself.' Then he turned to me with a smile that chilled my bones.

After we'd finished eating, Mrs Crenshaw said to me, 'Shall we retire to the living room for coffee, Abby? I'm sure the men have things to discuss over their port.'

I followed her, grateful to escape her husband's interrogation, even though I was fairly certain this old-fashioned postprandial separation of the sexes was intended purely to give her an opportunity to interrogate me herself.

'I like to see a young girl stand up for herself, as you did at dinner tonight,' she said after the coffee was served. 'In my day, we never did. We always went along with the men, humored them, tried to make them feel they were smarter than we were. They weren't, of course,' she added with a gentle laugh. 'But life goes more smoothly when they think they are.'

I was lost for a response. Was this truly a compliment to my assertiveness, or was it intended more as a warning?

But Mrs Crenshaw didn't wait for me to answer. 'I'm sure you're looking forward to your own career. I never had one, you know. Charles was born in the first year of our marriage, and his father felt it was important for me to stay home and care for him. And of course, I enjoyed doing that. He was such a delightful baby.' A gentle smile in my direction. 'I'm sure you'd love to have delightful babies of your own.'

I blinked. 'Oh, yes,' I said truthfully. I loved my niece and nephew and felt my hormones stirring whenever I spent time with them, but I had never consciously planned out how having children would fit into my life. 'I guess I haven't given it a lot of thought. How I'll handle babies and a career, that is.'

'It is difficult,' Mrs Crenshaw said in her gentle, monotonous voice. 'Either one alone seems all-consuming. I honestly don't know how women cope with "having it all." Especially those who can't afford any household help.'

I smiled. 'On a lawyer's salary, I don't expect affording help will be too much of a problem.'

'I suppose not.' She was silent for a moment, tracing a perfectly French-manicured nail along the woven pattern of a brocade pillow. 'But that situation could pose other difficulties. What branch of law do you plan to specialize in?'

'Family law. I want to protect children.'

'Charles's specialty as well.' A pregnant pause, and then, 'It's possible, you know, that you and Charles could someday end up on opposite sides of the same case. How would you feel about that?'

A black-and-white courtroom drama played out in my head, with a movie-star husband and wife sparring on behalf of their respective clients. Wasn't there a Tracy and Hepburn movie like that? I wasn't sure, but I had the feeling it had nearly ended disastrously. A man would need to have quite a resilient ego to be able to handle losing a case to his wife. I thought of the surfing trip and blanched.

Only then did it hit me that her question had assumed Charles and I would marry. Had he told his parents more than he'd told me? Yet another chasm opened before my feet. If I went along with the assumption, I could be seen as overconfident; if I contradicted it, she might assume I didn't want to marry her son.

I grasped at a noncommittal answer. 'I suppose we'll have to figure that out if the time comes.'

This conversation felt like a fathomless lake in which I could find no lifeline, no piece of flotsam to grab hold of. Just as I thought I would drown, the men came in. I shot Charles a look that was almost desperate, but instead of coming to my rescue, he sat next to his mother, and his father sat on the loveseat beside me. A little too close beside me, truth be told.

'You'll keep my son up to the mark, won't you, my dear?' he said, patting my sheer-stockinged knee and letting his hand rest there. So he was making the assumption as well.

I tugged at my expensive hem, but it wouldn't come close to covering my knees. 'I'll try my best, Mr Crenshaw.' That answer didn't necessarily depend on our marrying, did it?

'You do love him? Look up to him? Respect him? I know he's a bit of a disappointment, but it's a wife's job to make sure he doesn't feel that.'

I widened my eyes at him. How could he consider Charles a disappointment? 'Of course.' Finally, something Charles and I had in common, besides law school – we were both disappointments to our fathers.

'That's all right, then.' Charles Senior gave my knee a final pat and got up to pour himself a cup of coffee. I breathed for what felt like the first time that night.

As he drove down the hill later on, Charles loosened his tie and let out a long breath. 'Glad that's over.' He reached across to squeeze my shoulder. 'Good work, babe. They like you.'

I wondered what would have happened if they hadn't.

\* \* \*

The next weekend, Charles took me to a five-star French restaurant. I wore the dinner-with-the-'rents dress again, with all the trimmings. There was a frisson of expectation in the air, or maybe I imagined it. But the evening with his parents had felt so much like an interview for the job of Charles's wife that I couldn't help expecting some kind of sequel.

He kept me waiting all through dinner, giving me sly looks and patting his breast pocket from time to time. I pushed the food around on my plate, but the hundred-dollar meal was wasted on me; what I did get down, I didn't taste. If only he would get on with it! But I couldn't say that in case I had misread the situation completely.

At long last, after our dinner dishes were cleared and my stomach had tied itself into a knot Houdini couldn't have undone, Charles patted his pocket once more, then, in slow motion, reached into it and came out with a little square black velvet box. With a flourish, he placed it on the table in front of me. I stared at it, paralyzed.

'Open it,' he said.

I looked up at him and got an encouraging smile. Forcing my fingers to move, I pried open the box. Inside was a gold band topped by a cluster of diamonds that dazzled me with reflected candlelight. This was a ring worthy of Kate Middleton.

I caught my breath. 'Wow,' was all I could say.

'So put it on.'

I lifted the ring out of its cradle. It looked as if the band would fit me, but its mass might anchor my finger to the table. I turned it to catch the light, then looked Charles in the eye. 'Is this an engagement ring?'

'No, I go around giving out ten-thousand-dollar rings to every girl I date.' He smirked. 'Of course it's an engagement ring, silly.'

I hesitated, but this was one area where I was not willing to forgo what was my due. 'It's beautiful, but . . . isn't it traditional to ask the girl first?'

He rolled his eyes. 'You want me to do the whole down-on-one-knee thing?'

'I don't require that. But an actual question and answer would be nice.'

He made a big show of getting out of his chair and coming

around to kneel beside mine. Heads turned at neighboring tables, and I'm sure more than one phone camera was raised.

He took my left hand, since the right was still holding the ring. 'Abigail Taylor, will you do me the honor of granting me your hand in marriage?'

My heart flipped as I regarded him there at my feet – the tall, dark, handsome, brilliant, and (as icing on the cake) wealthy man of my dreams. In that moment, all the little doubts that had kept piping up in the moments just before sleep were silenced. 'I will.'

He took the ring from me and slid it on to the appropriate finger. Its weight was indeed alarming and the band a fraction too big. But the ring matched the restaurant, the dress, the man kneeling before me – they were all necessary ingredients in the fairy tale.

I leaned over and kissed him. 'My Prince Charming.'

He grinned. And the whole restaurant applauded. My life as Charles Crenshaw Junior's essential accessory had begun.


# TEN


*Monday evening, February 26, 2018*

*Peter*

I drive the long road home to my apartment in downtown Santa Cruz. Open the door and sigh. The upscale homes of the two Crenshaw couples seemed sterile to me, but my own apartment is just plain grim. I spend so little waking time here, I've never thought it worthwhile to paint the builder's-white walls or hang any pictures. What furniture I have is a mishmash of leftovers my parents gave me in college and stuff I've picked up at Goodwill. One IKEA bookcase. What's the point of spending good money on furniture when it's only for me?

And for Oliver. He's a partly reformed feral cat who adopted me a while back. I fed him once on my balcony, and he kept asking for more. Finally he condescended to come inside for an hour or two each day. He's a big tortoiseshell shorthair who loves to sink his claws into anything penetrable, including me. Another reason not to waste money on good furniture. He'd only claw it to death.

Oliver leaps up on the little table by the door for a head scratch. He won't let me pick him up, but he does have to have his daily scratch. After a few seconds he's meowing. I swear it sounds exactly like 'More?' Which, of course, is where he got his name.

I feed him and glance at the mail. Bills. Ads. A birthday card from Mom. I'd practically forgotten my birthday was coming up. The big three-oh, and what have I got to show for it? A drab apartment and a crazy cat for company. Decent job, I guess, for a guy my age. I am a pretty darn good detective if I say so myself. But on days like today, I'd trade this job for barista at Peet's. Not Starbucks. I do have my standards.

I trudge into the kitchenette and nuke myself dinner, then take it to the couch with a beer. Oliver plops down beside me. What this place needs is a woman's touch. No, let's be honest. What it needs is a *woman*. Someone who might answer when I gripe to her about my day – as opposed to Oliver, who merely purrs. Someone who would snuggle up to me on the couch and not put out claws to rip up my legs.

I've dated a bit here and there over the years, of course. But this is the kind of job where nearly everyone you meet is off-limits for one reason or another. Suspects and persons of interest are absolutely taboo, and dating coworkers is discouraged. Not that I've met any female coworkers who interested me in that way. Friends, yes, but no sparks. Maybe I'm too burned-out and exhausted for sparks. At thirty. That's sad.

I put on a DVD that has ads for a bunch of British shows up front. There's Tom Barnaby from *Midsomer Murders*, saying he doesn't believe the victim bashed in his own head. If only I could believe Crenshaw had. That would make it all so much easier.

Abby Crenshaw's face drifts into my mind, and my heart does a funny little jerk. I tell myself it's only her vulnerability that makes me react that way. Ever since my sister died, I've had a kind of knight-in-shining-armor complex, out to save the damsel in distress. I would never have made a doctor, so I guess that's why I became a cop. In ordinary life, most damsels don't seem to need or want saving.

I give myself a mental shake. Can't let this thing, whatever it is, take over, ruin my objectivity. Got to keep an open mind. All that damsel stuff might be an act. She could be a cold-blooded killer, and a damned smart one at that. Either way, I have to prove it beyond a shadow of my own doubt, or those eyes of hers will haunt me forever.

*Tuesday morning. February 27, 2018*

*Abby*

I awake in the hospital to a nurse bustling around my bed. I glance at the clock. Five a.m.

'I thought the point of my being in here was to rest,' I say.

The nurse smiles. 'Hospitals aren't great places for resting, I'm afraid. In your case, the main point is to find out what's been causing your blackouts. Then, when we've figured out how to treat them, you can go home and get all the rest you want.'

'With a nine-month-old baby. Right.' Then it hits me. *And a dead husband. Whom I may have killed.*

The nurse says, 'Well, all the rest you can, anyway.'

'So are the tests starting now? At five a.m.?'

'Not quite yet. I have to check your vitals and meds. The doctor will be here in a few hours to go over the plan with you. You can rest till then.'

She makes some notes on her rolling computer and pushes it out the door. I close my eyes.

They must have given me sedatives last night, because I don't remember dreaming, and I always dream. But now the images are coming thick and fast. Not coherent like a memory – just flashes, all convoluted and crazy, but with their own bizarre dream-logic to make me think they're real.

Charles alive, in a rage. I think he's going to kill both me and Emma. I grab her and flee. His anger follows me, like a dragon out for my blood. I can't get away from it. It swallows me.

Then I'm standing over his bloody body. Blood on the couch, the coffee table, the rug. Blood spreading from his head to fill the room, the house, my whole world. My mother is there, and the blood covers her, exactly as I found her all those years ago after she'd cut her wrists. It covers everything and everyone I know. I have Emma in my arms, and the blood starts to creep up on her, too. I can't stop it. I scream and scream and scream.

Then a hand is on my shoulder, gently shaking me. It's Charles, alive, standing up, still covered in blood. I shrink away, but the hand is still there.

'Abby? Abby, wake up. You're having a nightmare.'

The voice isn't Charles's. I struggle through to consciousness, and there's the nurse again. 'Are you OK? You seemed pretty distressed there.'

'Nightmare.' I start to rub my hands over my face, but the IV line pulls. 'Horrible.'

'You've been through some horrors, from what I hear. I'm going to give you a tiny sedative now so you can rest without any more dreams, OK?'

I nod. No dreams is good. She sticks a needle in my IV port, and I drift away.

# ELEVEN

*Spring and summer 2016*

I was sorry my mother was not alive to see me married – what girl wouldn't be? – but as far as the wedding planning went, it was probably just as well. She wouldn't have been allowed to do a thing. Jacqueline Crenshaw, in her quiet, unassuming way, made suggestions about everything that carried the force of commands. And since the Crenshaws were paying for it all – even for my dress – I could hardly object. What did I know about planning the kind of wedding that was expected in their world?

I found out, though, pretty quickly. The date was set six months out – a month after Charles's graduation, when I would still have a year of law school to go. Engraved invitations on paper that looked to be worth its weight in gold, with more enclosures than I could discern the purpose of, in envelopes engraved with the addresses. Hundreds of guests, of whom I was allowed to invite only my family and David (and I knew neither David nor my father would come). The venerable, impressive Santa Clara Mission Church for the ceremony, Filoli Mansion and gardens for the reception. Eight attendants each – Charles's friends and cousins were recruited to fill out my side, with Ellen as matron of honor. An entire florist's shop to fill the church and a bouquet so heavy I could hardly hold it. And the spread that was planned for the reception – well, let's just say there were a few items on the menu that I could pronounce.

And the gifts! When the gifts began to arrive and Jacqueline displayed them all in one of the lesser-used sitting rooms of their home, I felt as if I'd strayed on to the set of *The Philadelphia Story*. I'd never seen so much silver and fine china in one place. And I had never even set up a gift registry. That didn't seem to be the done thing in the Crenshaws' circle. People gave what they gave – the Soandsos always a silver champagne cooler, the Whatstheirnames their signature fish slice – and if you didn't like it, you could simply exchange it. No one would know or care.

I couldn't imagine living with any of these treasures, actually using them from day to day. At least one of these pieces would have to be exchanged for a set of everyday stoneware and some stainless-steel cutlery. That silver epergne from the Thingummies looked like a good candidate. It was so ornate as to be hideous, and what did one do with an epergne, anyway?

And then there was my dress. Jacqueline chose it while pretending to consult my taste. ('That one's very nice, dear, but don't you think something like this would be more appropriate?') Yards and yards of stark white satin (I look better in cream). The strapless bodice was molded to my torso, so rigid I could hardly breathe, let alone move. The skirt spread like an ocean of milk at least a yard to either side, with the train reaching halfway down the church aisle. And I was supposed to dance in this thing? In front of hundreds of people?

I looked at myself in the mirror during the final fitting and wondered who was looking back at me. I'd always thought I would make my own wedding dress – a Regency concoction of muslin and lace, perhaps, or, for a winter wedding, something medieval in creamy velvet with trailing sleeves. I'd marry the love of my life in a little homey church like the one in the town I grew up in, surrounded by close friends and family who would give me thoughtful gifts of more sentimental than monetary value. We'd hold the reception in the community hall, where our guests would dance the night away after my groom and I had gone on to spend our wedding night at a local inn. Friends would take funny and touching snapshots that my darling and I could laugh and cry over in the months and years to come.

I sighed as I played this scenario over in my head one last time. I could release the homemade dress, the intimate setting, the atmosphere of laughter and love. I told myself I was getting so much more than I had ever dreamed of – not only wealth and position, which I cared nothing for, but the love of a man any girl of my acquaintance would have died for. Little old mousy me, unloved by any man since birth, not only lovable but loved by Charles Crenshaw himself.

But what frightened me was that the face of the groom in my fantasy was not the face of Charles. It was a face I had never seen outside my dreams.

I got through the wedding somehow. In my eyes it had become nothing more than an ordeal to be endured before we could embark on our new life. Then, I hoped, my fairy tale could finally begin.

A job was waiting for Charles with his father's firm, but we had a month for our honeymoon – a month in Europe. I'd dreamed of touring Europe all my life. I would be in paradise – a week in London, a week in Paris, a week on a cruise along the Rhine, and a week in Florence. Charles had been to all those places before, and he knew what was worth seeing and what could be given a miss. My own list of must-sees was short: the Tower of London, the Champs-Élysées, a castle (any castle), and the Botticelli paintings in the Uffizi Gallery. Everything else would be gravy.

The first night, which we spent at the Clement in Palo Alto, was bliss. Charles was a masterful lover, and he showered me with endearments and gifts – a diamond bracelet, a negligée of gossamer ivory silk. Now I felt I was living in one of those escapist films from the thirties – a Fred-and-Ginger movie, perhaps, except that Charles lacked Fred's goofy sense of humor, I lacked Ginger's talent for disdainful quips, and we both lacked their flying feet.

The second night we spent on a plane, so it didn't count. The third was our first night in London. We stayed at the Ritz, and I kept pinching myself and humming 'Puttin' on the Ritz' until Charles said he'd move us to a different hotel if I didn't shut up. I changed into my gossamer negligée and sat at the dressing table in our suite to brush my hair with the silver-backed brushes Jacqueline had given me.

Charles came up behind me, moved my hair aside, and kissed my neck. He laid a gold-wrapped box on the table in front of me. 'I'd like you to wear this tonight,' he said in a husky voice.

I blinked in disbelief. What could be more wonderful than the negligée I had on? Would I end up with a whole wardrobe of them, like Ginger had, trimmed in feathers and fur? I pulled the ribbon and lifted the lid to see a mass of black lace. Oh dear. Black was all right for a cocktail dress, but it wasn't my first choice for bed. I pulled the garment out and saw it was a bustier with matching panties. Crotchless panties. Along with a pair of black fishnet stockings.

I'd stumbled into a different kind of movie now. The kind I didn't even want to watch, let alone act in.

'This . . . isn't really my style, Charles.' I'd never found an endearment for him that quite seemed to fit.

'You'll look fabulous in it, baby. And anyway, isn't it what I think that counts?'

As far as what would arouse him, I supposed he must be the authority. But I had hoped until now that I would arouse him simply by being myself, without any artificial accoutrements. And though I had never consciously considered the matter, I had assumed that our lovemaking would adapt itself to please us both.

I managed a smile and a kiss and went into the bathroom to change.

We toured the Tower of London, shopped and dined on the Champs-Élysées, and saw enough castles along the Rhine to satisfy even my thirst for them. But when the cruise was over, Charles calmly announced we were going to Venice instead of Florence. 'Venice is the city of lovers, after all,' he said with a smile and a caress.

'Oh,' I replied in a small voice. 'I'm sure it's lovely. But I did so want to see the Botticellis.'

'We'll see them another year.' Charles took my face between his hands. 'I want to kiss you under the Bridge of Sighs at sunset. Then you'll be mine forever.' He'd told me about this romantic legend earlier in our courtship. It seemed odd that a promise of undying love should be linked with a bridge that had once led across a canal from a prison to a place of execution, but history held stranger associations.

His kiss took the sting out of my disappointment, and the glories of St Mark's Cathedral nearly compensated for the loss of the Botticellis. But when Charles kissed me in the gondola as the bells of St Mark's tolled for the setting sun, all I could think about was the prisoners of days gone by, crossing the Bridge of Sighs to meet their death.

When we got back from our trip, we stayed at the elder Crenshaws' for the first couple of nights and then moved into our new home. I had known nothing about this home beforehand. Charles had insisted he wanted to surprise me. It might have been anything from a mansion to a travel trailer, located anywhere within a fifty-mile radius of campus. At the time, I'd thought it didn't matter; any home I made with Charles would automatically become my dream home.

But I didn't get the chance to make our new place a home. The house he brought me to was complete in every detail, all reflecting the same taste displayed in his parents' home. All our wedding gifts were stored in their proper places; all the clothes and books I'd left in storage had been unpacked and arrayed in closets and on shelves. But my few boxes of sentimental treasures remained unopened in the garage. There was no space for them in this house, where everything down to the last ornament reflected one style and was arranged with precise symmetry and balance. In fact, there was no space in this house for *me* – my things, my personality, my whims.

We finished touring the house and stood in the living room. 'Well? What do you think?' he said.

I felt my way, already cautious about how I spoke to him. 'It isn't what I expected,' I said. 'It's very nice, of course, but I thought I'd have at least some say in how it was put together.'

'This is the way it was always done in the old days.' He put his arm around my shoulders. 'It was the man's responsibility to make a home for his bride.'

'Yes, but this isn't the old days, Charles.' I turned to face him and put my hands on his chest. 'I was looking forward to creating our home together. This house is all you and no me. You haven't left a single thing for me to do.'

'We're one flesh now, baby. What's done by me is done by you.'

I was almost certain that was not what 'one flesh' meant, but it was pointless to argue with Charles.

And a bigger issue concerned me than that of being presented with a fait accompli for a home. The house was in Santa Cruz. It stood on a bluff overlooking the ocean – the view was incredible – but it was more than thirty miles of dense commuter traffic on a dangerous mountain road from Santa Clara University, where I still had a year to go to get my JD degree.

'Charles, I don't quite understand why we're living in Santa Cruz. It's lovely here, but it's such a difficult commute for both of us.'

'Oh, I won't be commuting. Our firm is opening a Santa Cruz office. I'll be working there.'

I froze. The fact that he hadn't told me, let alone consulted me, about something that would have so great an impact on our lives was bad enough. But it wasn't the biggest issue at this moment. 'I see. And you simply decided to favor your own convenience over mine. Without even giving me a chance to say yea or nay.'

'But baby, don't you see? You only have one year of school left. My career is for the rest of our lives. And besides, I may have to work long hours in the beginning to establish the practice here. You wouldn't want me falling asleep on Highway Seventeen coming home, would you?'

'Of course not, but I put in long hours, too. Studying.'

'Which you can just as easily do at home.'

I looked around the compact house, which consisted of living room, dining room, kitchen, two bedrooms, two baths, and a beautifully appointed study – for Charles. 'And where do you suggest I do that? At the dining-room table? Or maybe in the laundry room? Or I could prop my book on the kitchen counter and read while I stir the soup. In my apron and bare feet.'

He smiled and put his arms around my waist. I remained wooden. 'Now there's a pretty picture – you in the kitchen in nothing but an apron and bare feet. We'll have to try that sometime.'

In that moment, I was certain I would never want to try anything with Charles ever again.

# TWELVE

*Abby*

When I open my eyes, it feels like the very next second. But the nurse is gone, and a black-haired guy in a white coat is sitting on a stool at the foot of my bed, perusing an iPad.

'Are you the doctor?'

He looks up. 'Oh, you're awake! I didn't want to disturb you till I had to.' He gets up and comes to the side of the bed to shake my hand. He has lovely twinkling blue eyes. And he's not too tall, as far as I can tell lying here. Taller than me, but he wouldn't loom over me the way Charles did.

'Doctor Owen Elliot. Neurology. We're going to do some tests, see if we can pinpoint the cause of your blackouts. But first I have approximately one hundred gazillion questions for you.'

He grabs the stool and wheels it around to the side of the bed, then poises his stylus over his iPad. 'Ready?'

'As I'll ever be.' I glance at the water pitcher on the nightstand, and he pours me a cup. I down it in a few gulps, and he refills it. I do feel sort of rested now. The nightmares have receded. As long as he doesn't call them up again, I'll be OK.

Dr Elliot returns to his stool. 'Here goes. Do you have any history of epilepsy?'

'No.'

'Do you regularly overindulge in alcohol?'

'No. Glass of wine with dinner – that's about it.'

'Taking any medications or using any illegal drugs?'

'Only over-the-counter pain stuff. And allergy meds.'

'Have you traveled in any tropical places recently?'

'No. Unless Italy counts. That was over a year and a half ago, though.'

He smiles. 'No, Italy doesn't count. Are you diabetic or hypoglycemic?'

'No and no. At least not that I know of.'

'Any problems with low blood pressure or thyroid?'

'Still no.'

'Have you ever had a serious head injury?'

'I got hit in the head with a baseball once.'

'How old were you?'

'Ten.'

'And your blackouts started, what, a few months ago? I think we can rule out the baseball.' He grins. 'Anything else?'

'Not that I can think of.'

'Any headaches?'

'I get migraines from time to time.'

'Have they been getting worse lately?'

'Yeah, ever since I got pregnant. Which, in case you're math-challenged, is about eighteen months ago.'

He grins again. 'Got it. Can you describe the symptoms of your migraines?'

'Pretty typical, I guess. Before the actual headache starts, I get cranky and want to eat everything in sight. Then I yawn my head off and get a stiff neck. After that, the vision stuff – you know, flashing lights and all that. And then the vise tightens around my temples and I'm down for the count.'

'In the aura phase – when you see the flashing lights – are your other senses ever affected? Do you hear things, smell or taste things that aren't there? Feel tingling or numbness in your skin?'

'Now that you mention it, yeah. All of that. And it's been getting worse.'

'OK. That could be it, right there. People who have severe migraines sometimes suffer from transient global amnesia as well.'

'Transient what?'

That grin. I'm starting to like it. 'Basically, blackouts. Have you had a lot of emotional or physical stress in your life lately?' He glances at the iPad and goes white. 'I mean, before your husband's death. I'm so sorry.'

'Don't be. He *was* my stress.'

'I don't want to be intrusive, but were you having serious marital problems? Considering divorce?'

'I was planning to leave him. I hadn't quite gotten all the pieces in place yet.'

'Pretty major stress, then. OK. Now I have to ask some questions about the blackouts themselves.'

'You'd have to ask somebody besides me. They were blackouts. I don't remember them.'

'You don't remember anything that happened during any of them?'

'Well, a couple I do. The first few I remembered soon after.'

'Do you remember anything that might have triggered them?'

'I think the first one, I'd just had a fight with my husband. But that could apply to almost any time.'

He winces. 'Anything else?'

'One happened after a migraine, I think. Or started during one, maybe.'

'Uh-huh. Any others?'

'Oh, one came after I got off the phone with a divorce lawyer. I think he was a friend of my husband's, though I didn't know that when I called him. He made it sound like everything was my fault.'

The doc shakes his head in disgust. 'Lawyers.' Then he looks up. 'Oh, wait, you're a lawyer too, aren't you? Sorry.'

'It's OK. I've never practiced. Haven't even taken the bar exam. And with my head the way it has been, I doubt I could pass it at this point.'

'Don't worry. I'm making it my mission in life to see that you start getting better real soon.'

I could get addicted to that grin.

'Now. What happened during the blackouts you remembered? Anything unusual?'

'The first one totally freaked me out. I was at home in my kitchen, and what felt like the next second, I was knocking on my sister's door in San Jose. I must have driven all the way over the hill in a state of – what? I don't know. Semi-consciousness? It was pretty scary.'

'But you made it OK?'

'Yeah. Thank God.'

'How long ago would you say is the first blackout you never remembered? I mean never remembered what happened during that time?'

'Mmm . . . maybe a month or so?'

'And how often do the blackouts occur?'

'Every three or four days.'

'Do you know how long they last?'

'It varies, and I don't always happen to check the clock before and after. I've been watching TV and suddenly it's a different show from the one I started to watch. Or I'll be changing Emma's diaper and realize the last thing I remember was putting her down for a nap. I'd guess maybe an hour or two, most times? But a few a lot longer.'

'OK.' He drums his stylus against the rim of the iPad in some kind of rhythm, maybe a rumba. Then he looks up again. 'That's all my questions. Do you have any for me?'

'Only one.' One I've been dying to ask – but I dread the possible answer. 'Would I do anything in a blackout that I wouldn't do in normal life?'

He ponders with a little frown. 'That's a tough one. These things aren't very well understood. I think the best I can say is that it's a little bit like being hypnotized and a little bit like being drunk. Your inhibitions would be weakened, so you might do things you wouldn't ordinarily do. But you probably wouldn't do anything you didn't have at least a subconscious urge to do. I mean, your behavior wouldn't be totally random. And my guess is you wouldn't violate your own core principles – the things you govern your life by. So, for instance, if you're strongly committed to taking care of your baby, you'd still take care of her during a blackout, though maybe a little less capably. If you're strongly opposed to murder and you've never seriously considered killing anyone, you probably wouldn't kill during a blackout.' He looks me in the eye. 'Does that help?'

'Yeah. Thanks.' I smile, but the truth is it helps and it doesn't. Because yes, in principle, I'm strongly opposed to murder. But lately I have had fantasies of killing Charles. If I were outside myself, as it were, which would win – the principle or the fantasy?

I badly need to remember that crucial half-hour of my life. If I killed him, then my life will be over, because it would mean I'm not the person I always thought I was. I'll have to start over as someone completely new. Someone who has no business mothering a child.

Unless, of course, I killed him to protect Emma. I grasp at that straw with both hands.

'One more question. What are the chances I'll remember this

latest blackout – I mean, what happened when my husband was killed?'

He shakes his head. 'Impossible to say, I'm afraid. Something could trigger the memory in the near future. Or it could lie buried for years. Maybe forever.' The grin is half-hearted this time. 'We've learned a lot about the brain in the last few decades, but in some ways it's still a mystery. This is one of those ways.'

I try to swallow that, but it's like dry liver in my mouth. It won't go down. I *have* to remember. And soon. 'So where do we go from here?'

He flips the cover over his iPad. 'All around the hospital. You'll get the grand tour. We're going to give you some alphabet soup – an EEG, a CT scan, and an MRI to see what's going on in your brain. We'll take about a pint of blood to test for every conceivable substance or infection that's known to cause blackouts. And my guess is in all of that we won't find one thing that's abnormal. My guess is you've had recurring episodes of transient global amnesia related to migraines.'

I try to take all this in. 'So what causes that?'

He clucks his tongue. 'Here's one of those areas where Mother Nature still has medical science completely bamboozled. We don't know what causes either the amnesia or the migraines – we only know they sometimes go together. And – the bad news – we don't know how to prevent them, either. But the good news is I think in your case they're strongly connected with stress and/or with the hormones of gestation and lactation. Once you're through breastfeeding and past the stress of your husband – of this whole situation – I'd lay odds you'll start to feel a lot better.'

'Doctor Elliot—'

'Call me Owen.'

'Owen. That is the first entirely good news I've heard in a very long time.'

*Peter*

In the morning I check in at the station, then head over the hill to verify Mrs Stepanovich's alibi with her husband. She gave me his business card – he's a big shot at Apple. I call ahead for an appointment, then drive to Cupertino.

I've worn my best suit today, my most businesslike tie, but I walk into a hive of people whose style sense channels Steve Jobs – jeans, turtlenecks, lots of black. My clever plan to blend in has failed. The receptionist in the lobby calls ahead to verify my appointment, then directs me upstairs to Stepanovich's office.

His assistant, a pleasant-looking middle-aged woman, looks up from her computer as I approach. 'Mr Rocher? He's waiting for you.' She gestures toward the open door behind her.

The office is big but sparely decorated, with one unexpected feature – a large icon of the Madonna and Child on one wall with a candle burning in front of it. At least I assume it's the Madonna, but she sure looks different from other pictures I've seen – this is no fresh-faced, smiling girl, but a veiled woman who looks as though she's borne all the sorrows of the ages.

I tear my eyes away to give my interviewee the once-over. He rises from his desk with an unreadable mix of emotions on his handsome, broad-cheekboned face. He's got several inches on me, but he's lean, and his gait as he comes around the desk to greet me is springy like a cat's.

'Detective Rocher? Is that what I call you?' His Russian accent is faint but detectable.

I nod. 'Mr Stepanovich.' I shake his hand.

'Pavel, please. I hardly know my own surname anymore – nobody uses it here.' He directs me to a pair of comfy-looking chairs arranged around a small table. 'Coffee? Tea?'

I'll bet they serve good coffee in this place, and I haven't had my morning quota yet. 'Coffee, thanks.'

He goes to the door and speaks to his assistant, then comes back to sit catty-corner from me. 'How can I help you, Detective?'

My main goal is to verify his wife's alibi – and maybe his own as well – but I'll sneak that in later on. 'I'm trying to get a better picture of the events that led to your brother-in-law's death. What's your take on the Crenshaw marriage?'

He heaves a sigh, but before he can speak, his assistant comes in with two cups of coffee, a pitcher of cream, and a bowl of sugar cubes on a tray. He takes the tray from her with a smile. 'Thanks, Nancy.'

She smiles back and exits, closing the door behind her.

'Cream? Sugar?'

'Just a hint of cream, thanks.'

He pours it in – an actual hint, taking me at my word – and hands me the cup, then adds a good dollop of cream and two cubes of sugar to his own. I remember hearing somewhere that Russians tend to have a sweet tooth.

I sip. The coffee is in fact delicious.

Niceties completed, Stepanovich leans back in his chair and ponders my question. 'I disliked Charles. From the moment we met, actually, which is not a thing that often happens to me. He was arrogant, slimy, too charming for his own good. You know the type?'

I nod. My nemesis in high school fit that description.

'He was awful to Abby. Not violent, but with his words, with everything he did. A husband should cherish his wife, make her feel like the most wonderful woman in the world. Charles made Abby feel like dirt.'

'And how did that make *you* feel?' Sometimes a detective has to talk like a therapist.

He shakes his head. 'I was grieved for her. I made it clear that Ellen and I would do anything we could to help her get away, but beyond that, I could not interfere.' He pauses, sips his coffee, as if uncertain whether to say more. 'Charles would have cut Abby off from her family if he could. He resented Ellen's influence on her, and me . . .' He looks me in the eye. 'I had some reason to believe he was actually jealous of me. Though, of course, he had no justification for that at all.'

I chew that over a bit. Stepanovich didn't need to tell me about Crenshaw's jealousy; it's not likely anyone else would have mentioned it. Does this frankness mean he wants to be completely open with me, or is it a ploy to disarm me? *Look at me, I'm so transparent, I couldn't possibly be a murderer.*

Looking in his eyes, I can't help but think he really is transparent. 'What about Abby? What would you say her mental state was like the last few days?' He might have a more objective view of that than her sister does.

He frowns. 'She was distraught when she came to stay with us, of course. I wasn't privy to all the secrets she shared with my wife, but it was clear something terrible had happened. Something that went beyond Charles's usual boorish behavior. Abby had turned a corner. I think she was ready to leave him for good.'

'You say she was distraught. But was she stable emotionally?

Was she in a state where she might have acted irrationally, out of character?'

He shrugs with a reluctant grimace. 'I really couldn't say. All I know is that, in the normal way of things, Abby is as gentle a woman as I have ever met.' He grins, a twinkle in his eye. 'All the lioness traits went to her sister.'

That grin betrays a depth of affection for his wife that confirms my impression of his transparency. 'Thank you, Mr – Pavel. Just one more thing. Can you confirm that your wife was at home yesterday afternoon from five o'clock onwards?'

He nods. 'Yes, I left a bit early yesterday and got home at five. We were both there with the kids until Ellen got the call to go to Santa Cruz.'

I take a last sip of that excellent coffee, then stand, folding my notebook into my pocket. 'Thank you for your time. I'll be in touch if I need anything else.'

He shakes my hand – the dry, firm shake of an innocent man – and opens the office door for me. 'I'm happy to help, Detective. Anything we can do to make all this easier for Abby.'

I stop by the assistant's desk and ask her casually what time her boss left the previous day. She checks the calendar on her computer. 'Four forty-five,' she tells me with a smile. Enough time to get to his home in San Jose ahead of the rush; not enough time to get to Santa Cruz and kill Crenshaw before five thirty.

'Thanks,' I say with a smile. It's not her fault she's just eliminated two of the suspects with the strongest motives for this murder.

# THIRTEEN

*August 2016*

As the remaining weeks of summer passed, I used my own meager savings to surreptitiously replace some of the smaller items in the house with things of my own choosing. Dishtowels and potholders in a cheery green print took the place of the gray striped ones I assumed Jacqueline had chosen. They passed without comment, as Charles rarely entered the kitchen. I unearthed a few small sentimental objects – a picture of my mother with baby me, a lovely enameled box Ellen had brought me from Russia – and set them out on my dressing table, eliciting only a raised eyebrow from Charles. With plenty of time on my hands, I began knitting a colorful throw to liven up the black-and-white living room. Charles never paid attention to my needlework in progress, but it remained to be seen what he would say when the blanket was finished and became part of the furniture.

But what I seriously wanted – needed – was a desk of my own. It was mid-August – school would be starting in a week, and the dining table was not going to cut it as a study space. Charles insisted on eating there instead of in the kitchen – even for breakfast – so I'd have to clear away my things after every session. Ellen had offered me a desk that had been sitting unused in their garage since Katya was born. But where to put it? The living and dining rooms and our bedroom were arranged with such perfect symmetry and consistency of style that I knew I could never get away with moving things around to introduce a new piece. Besides, I'd have no privacy for studying in those rooms.

However, the second bedroom stood unused, sparsely furnished as a guest room for the moment. The bed and dresser there were castoffs from the family mansion, clearly intended to make way in due time for a nursery. Charles had no reason to enter that room, and we had yet to have any overnight guests. I might be able to sneak the desk in there without him noticing – or at least without him caring.

Pavel brought the desk and its accompanying chair to the house one day while Charles was at work and helped me move them into the room. Fortunately, the desk fit without our having to rearrange what was already there. It even blended reasonably well with the slightly worn walnut finish of the bedroom suite. I brought in a few of my most-used law books and arranged them at the back of the desk, then added my laptop. I felt like a student again.

I made Pavel a cup of coffee before he headed back over the hill. Pavel preferred tea, but not the way I made it; it had to be proper Russian samovar tea, which even Ellen had not perfected. We were sitting at the kitchen island, sipping the coffee and chatting about the kids' latest antics, when I heard Charles's car pull into the garage.

Charles hadn't seen Pavel or Ellen since our wedding. I'd tried to invite them for dinner several times since we got back from our honeymoon, and they had invited us; but every time, Charles came up with some reason it wouldn't work out. Inviting his friends was never a problem; we'd hosted Will and Melissa, Colin and Jennifer a couple of times, and gone to their houses as well. The other two couples had married during the summer and were living in Santa Cruz now, the guys working in Charles's office.

I'd hoped Pavel would have come and gone before Charles got home, so there'd be a chance he wouldn't notice the desk right away. But maybe it was better for him to find out about it while I had Pavel there to shield me from his potential wrath – figuratively, of course. Pavel was so calm and civilized, I couldn't imagine anyone displaying anger in his presence.

'Hey, babe,' Charles called as he passed through the mudroom. 'Brought you a present.' I knew from the tone of his voice what kind of present it was likely to be – the same kind he'd bought me in London. I was accumulating quite a collection. If I ever wanted to open a brothel, I'd have enough risqué lingerie to outfit all the girls. I hoped this one was well wrapped.

'Hi, Charles,' I said brightly as he stopped dead in the kitchen doorway, gold box in hand. 'Say hello to Pavel.'

Charles frowned. 'What are you doing here?'

Pavel blinked at this discourtesy and shot a questioning glance at me. He knew this was meant to be a stealth delivery.

I rescued him. May as well get it over with. 'Pavel came to bring me an old desk of theirs so I'll have someplace to study when school starts.'

'I see.' Charles's eyes darkened, but he kept his voice even. 'If you wanted a desk, babe, all you had to do was ask me. We don't need other people's charity.'

I tried to laugh that off, forbearing to mention all the times I had hinted that I needed a desk. 'Don't be silly, Charles. It's not charity when it comes from family. Why waste the money when Ellen had exactly what I needed sitting idle in her garage?'

He glared at Pavel. 'So is it now sitting in our garage? There's no room for a desk in the house.'

'We put it in the guest room. Nobody uses that room, and there was plenty of space. I have my own little study nook now. So I won't have to clutter up the dining room with all my books and stuff.'

Charles hadn't taken his eyes off Pavel. 'You've done what you came for. I'd like to be alone with my wife now, please.'

Pavel shot me a concerned glance as he slid off the stool. I nodded slightly. He couldn't stay forever, and Charles would only get angrier if he delayed.

'Thanks, Pavel. Give Ellen and the kids a hug for me, OK?'

'Of course.' He made a move as if to give me the customary Russian triple kiss on both cheeks but thought better of it. 'Goodbye, Abby. Goodbye, Charles. See you soon, I hope.'

Charles watched him out, muttering, 'Not if I can help it,' under his breath.

He turned on me. 'How *dare* you bring furniture – not to mention that *man* – into this house without my permission?'

I was flabbergasted. 'Charles – I don't understand what the big deal is. You knew I needed a desk to study on. This is my house, too – why do I have to have your permission to borrow something I need from my own sister? And Pavel brought the desk because he's strong enough to lift it. Ellen and I wouldn't have been able to handle it on our own.'

He snorted. 'Two strong girls like you? How big is this desk, anyway?' He strode into the guest room without waiting for an answer.

'It's solid oak,' I said, following him. 'It's heavier than it looks.'

'It takes up the whole goddamn room!' he blustered. Untruthfully – in fact, the desk's proportions fitted the room nicely. It wasn't even crowded.

'It doesn't, really,' I said in a conciliatory tone. 'There's still plenty of space to get around. And a smaller desk would hardly work for having books out, plus a laptop. You know what law studying is like.'

'I do.' He turned on me. 'I did it for three years so I could support a family. A wife who would keep my home and raise my children – not spend all her time hiding away in a spare room at a borrowed desk.' His fists clenched at his sides. 'So all I've done for you isn't enough. You have to go behind my back with that

Russian. My God, girl, I paid for our wedding, took you to Europe, bought you this house and everything in it. What can he give you that I can't?'

I was stunned. I'd expected him to be displeased about the desk, but this irrational jealousy of Pavel came completely out of the blue. 'I don't want anything from Pavel except the normal help of a brother-in-law. As for what I want from you – I want to be asked what I want, not told. I want to have my needs considered as I consider yours. I don't care about all the *things* you can give me, Charles. I just want . . . love.'

'I'll show you *love*, you ungrateful bitch.' He grabbed me by the arms and crushed his mouth against mine, bruising my lips against my teeth. Then he picked me up by my arms and threw me down on the pristine white coverlet of the guest-room bed.

What he did after that might go by many names, but *love* was not among them – not as I understood the word.


When Charles and I were dating, I never could have believed the time would come when I would shudder away from his touch, when his mere presence would revolt me. When to look in his eyes would bring not arousal but horror. When his dazzling smile would make my stomach turn.

In the next couple of days, I spent hours walking on West Cliff Drive above the ocean, my red eyes and swollen lips shaded by a wide-brimmed hat. I shied away from people, often sitting alone on one of the benches looking out to sea, leaving my eyes unprotected from the sparkle of sun on water as if punishing myself for having been blind for so long. What had gone wrong? What had I done, or failed to do, to turn Charles into such a monster? Or had he always been like that, and I'd been too besotted to see it?

I went over our whole relationship in my mind, again and again. Had there ever been a point before our marriage when I ought to have woken up and smelled the pending abuse in the air? When he teased me about not wanting to surf in October? When he chose an outfit completely out of my style or price range for me to wear to meet his parents? When he proposed without ever uttering the three crucial words, 'I love you'? When he failed to appear in my fantasy of the perfect wedding? When he took it for granted that his parents would plan and pay for our wedding, with no regard for what I might have wanted? When he let them buy and furnish a house in Santa Cruz without consulting me about a thing? But that last, of course, I hadn't known about until it was too late.

Too late for the deluded frog to jump out of the boiling water. Too late for me ever again to see Charles through the eyes of a glamour-struck girl. Too late for me to thrill to his touch without at least equal revulsion. Too late for me to love my husband as I longed to love him, ever, ever again.

And – given the fact that my period was now a week overdue – quite possibly too late for me to divorce him and make a new start unencumbered.

I never would have believed I could wish a possible child of my womb out of existence. But what kind of home would I be bringing that child into? How could my love alone compensate for a father who was unpredictable at best and, at worst, cruel? I wouldn't so much as form the word *abortion* in my mind; that was against everything I believed in as a prospective defender of children, against everything I had always desired for my life. But if I were to prove not to be pregnant – or if I were to miscarry – how much better and simpler everything would be.

Oh, God, what had Charles brought me to – desiring the death or nonexistence of my own child within two months of our marriage? The prospect of a baby ought to have been the crowning joy of my life.

Relationship status: *It's complicated.* That wasn't supposed to apply to an established marriage. But it certainly was beginning to apply to mine.

My lips were still swollen, and I still had bruises on my neck and arms when I met Ellen for lunch a few days after what I now thought of as the apocalypse. I tried to cover the bruises with makeup (it was too hot for long sleeves), but Ellen had X-ray vision where her little sister was concerned.

'Abby, what happened? You look awful.'

'I–uh–I ran into a post. Walking along reading a book like I always do, and, bam, there it was.'

'And it got your neck and arms rather than your forehead or your nose? You'll have to do better than that, sis.'

I stared into my coffee cup.

She slammed her hands against the table, sloshing our coffee. 'He hit you, didn't he? Charles.'

All I could muster was silence.

'I knew it. I knew he'd do something like that eventually. They don't come as controlling as Charles without some violence going with it.'

'He didn't hit me, exactly. I mean, not with his fists.'

Ellen stared. I watched the light dawn in her eyes. 'You're saying' – she hissed – 'he *raped* you?'

I nodded miserably. 'I guess that's what it amounts to. I mean, if it's possible for a man to rape his own wife.'

'Come on, Abby, you're the law student. Of course it's possible. Saying "I do" doesn't constitute blanket consent for sex any time, any place, any way the other partner happens to want.'

'I know,' I mumbled miserably. 'But I think I maybe drove him to it. I don't know.'

'Abby Taylor! Listen to yourself! Drove him to it? Didn't you go into law so you could defend the rights of women and children?'

A tiny, uncertain, 'Yeah.'

'And isn't rape the ultimate violation of a woman's rights?'

A louder and firmer, 'Yes.'

'And is there *ever* any justification for it?'

I sighed. 'No.'

'I'm glad we got that straight. Now tell me what heinous crime you committed that you think drove him to it.'

'I let Pavel bring me a desk.' Assuming Pavel had already related what happened while he was there, I started with his departure and told her everything up to the kiss that felt more like a punch. I couldn't talk about the rest.

Ellen was fuming by the time I finished. 'You need to press charges.'

I stared at her. 'Are you insane? Get up in front of a court and say all that? And they'd make me say . . . all of it. The part I can't even tell *you*.'

She sat back and folded her arms. 'In that case, I guess I'll have to put out a contract on him.'

'Ellen!'

'Kidding. But I am seriously tempted. How dare he do that to my little sister? At the very least, you've got to leave him.'

I crumpled again. 'I can't do that.'

'Why not?'

Another long silence. 'I think I might be pregnant.'

'Pregnant? I thought you were using birth control?'

'We were. Condoms. But the other day he left a box of them out on his nightstand. I went to put the box in the drawer and one of the condoms fell out. The wrapper was open. They were all open. I looked at one and it had a hole poked in the end.'

Now it was Ellen's turn to be silent. For about five seconds. 'Of all the unmitigated gall. He got you pregnant against your will.'

'Maybe. I'm not sure yet.'

'You better get sure. If you are, we'll take care of you. Pregnant or not, I want you out of there.'

Charles had worked late every night since it happened, crawling into our king-sized bed in the wee hours while I pretended to be asleep. But the evening after my lunch with Ellen, he came home early, with two dozen red roses in one hand and a box of Donnelly's chocolates in the other. 'Hey, babe,' he said, his tone as close to sheepish as I had ever heard from him.

I stood in front of a pot of pasta sauce on the stove, dripping spoon in hand. Speechless.

'Listen, about the other night . . . I'm sorry. I didn't mean to hurt you. I would never mean to hurt you.'

'You did hurt me. You hurt me very badly. My body and . . . my heart.'

He laid the flowers and chocolates on the table and came over to put his arms around me. I flinched away.

'I'm so sorry, babe,' he whispered in my ear. 'Let me make it up to you. Let me show you how much I love you.' He started to nibble my neck, and my stupid body, incredibly, wanted to respond. But I wasn't having it. I wrenched my head away.

'What, with more sex? Do you seriously think that's going to make everything OK?'

He looked honestly confused. 'You said you wanted to be loved.'

'Yes. Loved. Not lusted after. Loved as in respected, valued as a human being, treasured as your partner in life. Loved uncondi-tionally for who I am, not who you want me to be. Cherished with gifts and sacrifices that actually mean something to me.'

He backed away from me, his eyes hardening. 'God, you really are a demanding, ungrateful bitch.' He picked up the flowers and candy and threw them into the garbage can. 'Don't worry, you won't be getting more of the same from me. You make me sick.'

He turned and slammed out the back door. Thank God he wasn't going to take his anger out on me this time.

I turned off the burner under the sauce and covered it in case he came home hungry later. I'd lost my appetite. The pasta and tomato sauce smelled like so much gall and vinegar to me.

I went into the bathroom, got out the pregnancy test I'd bought on the way home from lunch, and peed on the stick.

The test was positive.

# FOURTEEN

*Tuesday morning, February 27, 2018*

*Peter*

The preliminary forensics reports are on my desk when I get back to the station – the house search, fingerprints, photographs. Lab results and the postmortem will take a few days, DNA a couple of weeks.

The house search yielded nothing unusual except a pretty extensive collection of risqué lingerie and sexual paraphernalia in the bedroom. Some women are into that stuff, I guess, but it seems out of character for Abby. I'd lay money it was all the husband's idea. For the rest – what you'd expect to find in any upper-middle-class family home. No bloodstained clothing stashed away or burned. A well-stocked liquor cabinet, none of the bottles gathering dust. No journals, diaries, or other private papers. Crenshaw didn't even have a computer in the house; he probably left his laptop at the office, maybe to keep it out of Abby's reach – he must have had secrets to keep. I make a note to apply for a search warrant for his office.

I turn to Abby's computer. The tech guys haven't gotten to it yet, so I make a stab at figuring out the password. Obvious choice – *Emma*. Nope. I find the baby's birthdate on Abby's phone calendar and add that to the end of her name. Bingo.

The browser history shows a lot of research into deafness in infants and something called cochlear implants. So that beautiful little baby girl is deaf? That helps explain why Abby found the prospect of single motherhood so daunting. The rest of her recent history centers on searches for jobs, housing, and daycare – confirmation of her plan to leave her husband. I also find a defunct GoFundMe page her sister created to raise money for the cochlear implants. A family as wealthy as the elder Crenshaws, you'd think they could cough up that cash. Cheapskates or uncaring? Or is it possible they didn't even know?

Abby's email exchanges with her sister betray a mounting frustration with her husband. Once or twice she says something to the effect of *I wish he would die. It would make life so much easier*, but she never makes any overt threat to kill him. None of her other correspondence is suspicious in any way – no secret affairs, no contracts with hit men. A few emails from way back with someone called David, but nothing romantic or suspicious at all. He might have been a brother or cousin, except the sister said there weren't any. Her Facebook page is likewise blameless, containing little other than baby pictures. I guess the real details of her life are not anything she'd want the world to see.

I look through her phone as well, and the results are similar. Her calendar features lots of medical appointments but not much else. She never got as far as interviewing for any jobs, apparently. Her texts are limited to brief logistical messages to her husband and conversations with her sister that resemble the email exchanges. But the texts *from* her husband – most of which she never answered – are something else entirely.

*Where's my dinner? You said home by 6. 6:15 and I'm starving.*
*Shut that baby up or I will.*
*Your cleaner is ripping me off. Wine stain by coffee table. UR a drunken slob.*
*Something special tonight. Come home horny. No spoilers, but starts with a D.*
*Saw you look at UPS guy. You wanted him, you slut. Burn in hell.*

If she did kill him, I'd be hard-pressed to blame her. What an absolute dick.

I look through Crenshaw's own phone records, too. Other than those texts, nothing stands out as being of particular interest. His bank records are a different story. He seems to have been skating on the edge of financial disaster. Lots of ATM-limit cash withdrawals. Not big enough for serious blackmail; more likely expensive pleasures he didn't want his wife to find out about. Her name isn't on these accounts. If she knew how precarious the situation was, would that have made her more or less likely to kill him? Probably depends on whether he had life insurance. I check the list of papers found at the house. A small policy on her, with Crenshaw as the beneficiary. No policy on him. Asshole.

I turn to the report on the actual crime scene. Forensics found traces of blood in the creases of the leather sofa and the cracks in the metal base of the coffee table, as well as in a large sponge that was left on the kitchen sink. It looks like we are dealing with the Mad OCD Killer after all.

Then I wonder: did Abby do the cleaning? The blood on her cuffs and under her fingernails would be consistent with that. But why? Of course, she was in something like a fugue state at the time, so her actions may not have been strictly logical. I think back to our earlier conversations. Several times she mentioned her husband's 'precious white carpet.' Maybe because he was a clean freak, she felt compelled to clean up what she could, even with him lying there dead?

Which still tells me nothing about whether or not she killed him. Except that the absence of any significant amount of blood on her clothing makes it seem highly unlikely.

Fingerprint patterns show nothing unusual. Three sets predominate – Crenshaw's, Abby's, a tiny set that must be the baby's. The cleaner probably wore gloves. A few scattered prints – none near the body – that likely belong to family or friends. Only the couple's prints on the outer doors of the house.

And nowhere in the house, yard, garbage cans, or immediate neighborhood did they find anything that looked like the murder weapon.

On to the house-to-house. No joy there. One neighbor noticed the UPS guy leave a package on the front step, but he didn't go inside. The same neighbor later saw a couple of young guys in suits – Mormon missionaries, most likely – knock, get no answer, and move on. But for some reason, this woman, who must live glued to her window, failed to see when Abby and Emma arrived home. Maybe she had to take a bathroom break right then.

One unlikely suspect and not a single other lead. I have a feeling this case is not going to constitute the high point of my career.

# FIFTEEN

*Fall 2016*

I didn't tell Charles about the pregnancy right away. For one thing, he didn't come home for several days after that blowup. And when he did sneak in finally in the middle of the night, I'd lost the impetus to tell him. Let him figure it out for himself.

Somehow – I never could understand how – we drifted back into some semblance of normality. We spoke to each other, not as two people who loved each other, but as people who at least did not hate each other. We even had sex – ordinary, unremarkable sex – usually in the middle of the night, when I was too far asleep to know I wasn't dreaming. The morning after, I would feel sickened by my own response to him, but then I felt sick every morning those days. I could hardly tell the emotional disgust from the gestational nausea.

For two full months I was horribly ill, morning, noon, and night. I couldn't keep anything down. And Charles never noticed. I even left the toilet unflushed with my vomit a few times, but he never said a word. It was only in the fourth month, when the sickness subsided and I began to regain the weight I'd lost and then some, that he finally spoke up.

'You're filling out, I see,' he said one evening as we were getting ready for bed. 'You were getting nice and thin there for a while, but now you're packing it on again. Better watch those desserts.'

I stopped in the act of pulling my nightgown on and stared at him. 'I cannot believe those words just came out of your mouth.'

'What? Doesn't a man have a right to want his wife to be desirable?'

'OK, that is wrong on so many levels. One, you found me desirable when you met me, and I'm about that same weight now. Two, desirability should be at least as much a function of love for the whole person as it is of a visual response to their appearance. And three, the reason I got skinny before and the reason I'm "packing it on," as you so charmingly put it, now, is that I'm pregnant.'

He gaped at me for a full ten seconds before jumping up to embrace me. 'That's fantastic! When did you find out? When is it due? Here, you should sit down. Can I get you anything? Oh my God! I'm going to have a son!'

'Or a daughter,' I said calmly. 'He or she is due around the middle of May. If she cooperates, I may still be able to graduate.'

'Graduate! Are you crazy? What's the point of finishing now? You're not going to be a lawyer. You're going to be a mom.'

'I'm going to finish this grueling education that I've already put two and a half years of my life into. What happens after that, we'll have to see.'

'No "we'll see" about it. You are going to stay home and be a mother to my son.'

'Or daughter. And that is not a decision for you alone to make. The baby is as much mine as yours, and the career I'd be sacrificing, or at least putting off, is mine alone.' I stared across the abyss of time at my past self, wondering how on earth she could have neglected to have this conversation before the wedding. 'I'm not your property, Charles. This is the twenty-first century, in case you hadn't noticed. Women no longer promise to obey.'

His nostrils flared and his fists clenched, the right one drifting up at his side. I tensed in response and glanced at the door, wondering if I could make it there ahead of him. Then, as I watched him, a deliberate calm came over his features, and his fist dropped.

'Let's sit down and discuss this reasonably, shall we?' He took my arm and gently led me to the bed.

That was almost scarier than the fist. Charles's idea of *reasonable* was as far from mine as my heart was now from that of the woman who married him. 'I am being reasonable. You're the one who's being reactionary.'

He smiled in a way that sent a chill through me – it reminded me of his father. 'You're not being consistent, though.'

'What do you mean?'

'You believe in the Bible, don't you?'

I scented a trap. I hadn't been a regular churchgoer in some time – law school had pushed everything else aside – but I hadn't abandoned the faith of my youth. I could give only one answer to that question, but I gave it warily. 'Ye–es.'

He pulled open my bedside drawer and took out my Bible. 'Look up Ephesians five.'

My stomach did a nauseating flip. 'I know what Ephesians five says. It was read at our wedding.'

'It says a wife should submit to her husband.'

I'd had this weapon wielded against me before, in a slightly different form – by my father. 'But it also says a husband should love his wife more than he loves himself.'

'But she has to submit first. How can he love her if she doesn't submit?'

'How can she submit if he doesn't love her? That would be suicide.' The word came out of my mouth before I thought about it. I'd meant it figuratively, but I was beginning to see that for me to submit to Charles could quite literally endanger my life. I couldn't leave him now, with his baby on the way, but I would have to hold my own against him.

He patted my hand. 'Abby, Abby. I'm afraid I'm going to have to tell your preacher on you.' The preacher I didn't have at this point. 'You just said obeying the Bible is suicide.'

'I did not! You're twisting my words.' Twisting my world, more like.

'I think you're the one who's twisting God's words.'

'What do you care about God's word, anyway? Except for our wedding, you haven't been to church in years.' The Crenshaws were Catholics in name but not in practice.

He slammed the Bible shut and stood. 'So now you think you're better than me – is that it? Miss self-righteous hyper-Christian bitch!'

I blinked. His about-faces were making me dizzy. 'I didn't say that. I just don't want you to turn my Bible against me.'

'There you go! *Your* Bible! The Bible is for everyone.'

'The word of God is a two-edged sword. If you misuse it, it will

turn on you.' I thought of the icon of the Archangel Michael in
Pavel's Russian Orthodox church. The angel carried quite an
impressive sword. If only he would turn it on Charles – to threaten,
of course. Maybe inflict a small wound to get his attention. Not
to kill.

'Well, now you're talking nonsense,' he said. 'I'm beginning to
fear for your sanity, my dear. You know, religious mania is a real
psychological disease.'

I stared at him in disbelief. *He* was accusing *me* of mental illness?
But it was obvious I could never win this argument; anything I
might say would only be twisted and used against me.

'Charles, I'm very tired. I need sleep if I'm to have a healthy
pregnancy. We're not going to sort this out tonight. Let me go to
bed.'

He sneered. 'Playing the pregnancy card already, are we? God,
you're pathetic. Fine, get your precious beauty sleep. There's no way
I can sleep now.' He grabbed his dressing gown and stormed out.

The next day, Charles was back to his normal self. As I dressed for
school, he came up and put his hand on my belly. 'Good morning,
son,' he whispered.

'Or daughter,' I said automatically, trying to pull on my shirt.

He slid his other hand around me and pulled my hips to his.
'That bump is kind of sexy. What do you say we make up for last
night?'

What the hell? I was used to Charles's mercurial moods by now,
but could he honestly think I'd want sex after he'd wrung out my
mind like a dishrag the night before?

I twisted away. 'I have class in an hour. I have to get going.'

He scowled. 'That damn class. School is eating up your entire
life. There's nothing left for me – for *us*.'

'We've already had this conversation. I've put a lot into my
education, and I want to get something out of it – even if it's only
a degree.'

He stormed out of the bedroom and disappeared until I'd
grabbed my decaf and bagel and was heading out the door. Then
he materialized in the mudroom.

'Hey, babe. I didn't mean it. Have a great day.' He gave me a
chaste peck on the cheek.

Whatever. I gave a mental shrug and headed out the door.

My day went well enough, although I felt as if the hormones of pregnancy were making my brain swell along with my belly; absorbing and retaining information was getting harder by the day. I headed home, exhausted, barely managing to keep my eyes open to navigate the traffic without caffeine. No caffeine, no wine – the sacrifices I was making already for this baby. And this was only the beginning.

But my grumbling was a token grumbling. I would have made much greater sacrifices than these. A love I'd never previously imagined was growing within me along with my child – a love so possessive, so protective, so tender, I honestly could not imagine putting my baby in daycare and going immediately to full-time work. But I was determined that would be *my* decision, not Charles's. And I *would* finish my degree, come hell or high water.

High water was a real concern these days; my area of California was gearing up for its wettest fall and winter in decades. Already in late November, mudslides had closed lanes of Highway 17 more than once, and the traffic crawled like elderly snails on sedatives. I needed all my alertness to keep the car on the road.

As I reached the summit of the pass, my little Mazda coupe began to make strange knocking noises. By the time I'd coasted into Santa Cruz and was taking the exit on to Highway 1, the engine was sputtering alarmingly, and the 'check engine' light began to flash. I'd planned to pick up some takeout anyway, since I was far too exhausted to cook, so I pulled over at the taqueria on Mission. I got the food and went to the car, but now it wouldn't even start. The 'check engine' light stayed solid red.

Blast, I would have to call Charles. I hated asking him for anything. Although he would usually do what I asked, he always made me pay for it – either with sex or by enduring his demeaning jabs about how stupid I was to have gotten myself into such a situation. Or both.

At least he was home. If he'd had to leave work to pick me up, the price would have been more than double.

'Charles? My car's dead. I need you to call triple-A and come get me.' I didn't have a AAA card of my own.

'Poor baby. Leave it to you to kill your own car. I've said it before – if you're going to drive a car, you ought to know enough to keep it running well.'

I took a few deep breaths. If I antagonized him now, I'd have to ride home in a tow truck, assuming I could even persuade the driver to take me – it would be well out of his way. 'That's as may be, but the point is it's dead. I have a feeling it ran out of oil, though I don't know how that could have happened. I had it changed at Oil-Can Benny's a couple weeks ago.'

'Stupid incompetents at those chain places. Should have taken it to a real mechanic. I'll have triple-A take the car to my guy. He'll do you up right.'

I didn't bother to explain that I couldn't afford his mechanic out of my pittance of housekeeping money. Anyway, I'd always gone to Oil-Can Benny's.

Half an hour later, we walked in our door, the Mazda on its way to the mechanic. Charles said, 'So what are you going to cook me for dinner?'

'I bought takeout. That's why I stopped at the taqueria.'

He grabbed the bag I held out. 'A cold burrito? That's all your knight in shining armor gets for rescuing you?'

'I did have a pretty rotten day. I'm completely exhausted.'

'And it serves you right for insisting on going to school thirty miles away while you're pregnant. You'll get no sympathy from me.'

I could feel the steam heading toward my ears, but I didn't have the energy to let it out full blast. 'Even though you're the one who moved us thirty miles away? That wasn't my choice, remember.' I hesitated, then threw caution to the wind. 'For that matter, getting pregnant right now wasn't my choice either. I found those punctured condoms, Charles. You deliberately put me in this position. You cannot blame me.'

He put on his hurt-little-boy face. 'I thought you wanted kids.'

'Sure, I want kids. But not *now*. I wanted to finish school first, practice for a couple of years at least. That's what we agreed on when we got engaged. But you decided to change the rules. Unilaterally, as always.'

The hurt look gave way to a haughty scowl. 'I am the man of the house, and it would behoove you not to forget it.'

How could I ever have found his domineering attitude attractive?

He was exactly like my father. And here I'd thought I was starting a completely new life.

'How can I forget it? You display the worst aspects of masculinity every minute of every day.' I got up quickly, before he could lunge at me, and headed for the spare bedroom. 'I've had it, Charles. I'm going to bed.'

# SIXTEEN

*Tuesday afternoon, February 27, 2018*

*Peter*

Tuesday afternoon I go to Crenshaw's office, search warrant in hand. His coworkers have gotten the news, and they all seem to be shocked but not deeply grieved. I speak with the senior partner, Daniel Hopkins. He looks to be cut from the same cloth as Crenshaw Senior – charcoal pinstriped all-season wool – but there's a trace of humanity in his eyes and around his mouth.

He invites me to sit in a leather club chair in his office and has his assistant bring in some excellent coffee. 'We're all deeply shocked by Charles's death, of course,' he says. 'Can you tell me anything more about it? Besides what was on last night's news?'

'Only that we're treating it as a suspicious death.'

'Murder or suicide?'

'Too early to say. Do you have any reason to think the victim may have been suicidal?'

'Not really. He certainly had not seemed . . . shall I say, at peace in recent months. I got the impression his marriage was not a great success. But in terms of his personality, I'd say Charles would be the last person to kill himself. He never took responsibility for his own mistakes. Everything was always someone else's fault.' He swallows, and his hand goes to his tie. 'I trust my comments will stay between us?'

'I won't pass them on to Crenshaw Senior, if that's what you're concerned about.'

He relaxes immediately. 'I wouldn't want to aggravate his grief by spreading disparaging remarks about his son.'

'Of course.' We understand each other. He's worried about his job. Though as a partner, surely he's safe on that front.

'Can you tell me what time Mr Crenshaw left the office yesterday?'

He frowns in concentration, then pushes a button on the intercom. 'Susan? Do you know what time Mr Crenshaw left the office yesterday?'

A slight pause, then his assistant's voice comes back. 'Four o'clock, sir.'

'Thank you.' He releases the button and looks at me.

I make a note. 'And what time did you leave, sir?'

'Six o'clock sharp.' This with the air of a man who is punctilious in fulfilling his responsibilities and has no time for anyone who isn't. Like Crenshaw.

'Did Mr Crenshaw have any particular friends here in the office?'

'Friends? I suppose it depends on what you mean by the term. He socialized with a couple of the younger men. Played golf and so forth. Drinks after work.'

'Which younger men would those be?'

'Will Melrose, Colin Murray. To some extent my son, Derek, though I think Derek tried to avoid Charles when he could.'

'I'll talk to each of them later, if I may. Do you know of anyone who might have wanted to harm Mr Crenshaw?'

Hopkins slowly shakes his head. 'Not seriously. I think we all wanted to kick him occasionally, but only in the seat of the pants.' He gives a small smile.

'No badly dissatisfied clients or anything like that?'

'Not to the point of murder. No.'

'Did he have any money troubles?'

Hopkins suddenly goes still. He's been playing with a fountain pen, uncapping and recapping it, but now he stops with the two halves in midair.

'Mr Hopkins?'

He slams the cap on to the pen and sets it down hard. 'To be perfectly frank with you, Detective, I've recently begun to suspect Charles may have been stealing from the firm.'

Here's a new angle. 'How serious were those suspicions?'

'I'd gotten as far as verifying that theft was definitely taking place. On a small scale, you understand – a hundred or two here and there. I had no clear evidence Charles was responsible, but . . . well, even the junior members of this firm are paid as much as any clean-living person needs for a comfortable life. The other members may have their little vices, but the only one I believe to be wildly extravagant was Charles.'

'Extravagant in what way?'

'I can't give you details. I've only heard whispers around the office. I expect Will and Colin could tell you more.'

I turn this over in my mind. Has Hopkins just handed me his own motive for Crenshaw's murder? But if an employee is stealing from you, you reprimand him, fire him, maybe prosecute him. You don't kill him. Especially if you're a stickler like Hopkins and you're not yet sure of your facts.

'All right.' I stand and put out my hand. 'Thanks for your time, Mr Hopkins. I'll need to search Mr Crenshaw's office now.'

'Oh, but there are confidential client files in there! I can't allow that.'

'I'm sorry, sir, but I do have a warrant. You can have someone watch while I search if you want. And I give you my word I'll ignore anything that isn't relevant. I'll also need to take his computer.'

Hopkins comes as close to wringing his hands as a dignified middle-aged lawyer can. 'There will be files on there pertaining to his current cases. Someone else will have to take them over. We need to get those off the computer.'

'You can send someone in to copy the files on to a thumb drive while I watch. I mostly need to see all his correspondence. In case anyone threatened him or anything like that.'

'Well – all right. I don't suppose I have any choice, do I?'

My smile says, *No, you don't.*

The physical search doesn't turn up much except a suggestion that Crenshaw spent a fair bit of his work time practicing his putting and tippling from his hidden whisky flask. The desktop computer is blameless, but the laptop tucked away in a drawer reveals less innocent pastimes, like online poker and a heck of a lot of porn. There's hardly a porn site known to cop-dom that he didn't visit at some point. Poor Abby.

He could easily have blown enough money on those sites to tempt him to steal. But what I don't find on this first cursory look is any indication of someone who might have wanted to kill him. Someone, that is, other than his long-suffering wife.

Young Derek Hopkins is out sick today, so I interview Crenshaw's pals Will Melrose and Colin Murray together. Will is a tall, blond surfer type; Colin is shorter with red hair and freckles. They both look uncomfortable, as if they think they should be sorrier than they are.

'Terrible business,' Will mutters.

Colin nods.

'How well did you both know Charles?'

'We hung out together since high school,' Colin says. 'But I'd say the two of us' – he gestures between himself and Will – 'are better friends than we were with Charles.'

'Yeah, Charles was a bud to do stuff with, you know?' says Will. 'But if I had a problem, I'd go to Colin, not to Charles.'

'So not the most supportive friend.'

They both shake their heads. 'It was pretty much all about him.'

'Either of you know of anyone who might have wanted to harm Charles?'

They exchange glances. 'Not seriously. No.'

'Not seriously? What does that mean?'

Colin clears his throat. 'Well, you know, he was the kind of guy who invites remarks like "I could kill you for that." Super competitive, not too careful about other people's feelings, kind of a user. But someone who would go so far as to murder him? I don't think so.'

Will adds, 'We were his best buds, so if we didn't want to kill him, it's not likely anyone else did.'

They exchange glances again, and I sense they're holding something back. Remembering what Hopkins said about his son, I take a shot in the dark.

'What about Derek Hopkins? Were he and Charles on good terms?'

Will's turn to clear his throat. 'Um . . . not really. At Colin's New Year's Eve party, Charles tried it on with Derek's wife. With Derek and Abby both right there in the room. Derek looked like he was about to explode. But he just took his wife and left, and nothing more was ever said about it, as far as I know. They just didn't speak after that.'

I make a note to track down this Derek. 'What about Abby? How did she react?'

Colin adjusts his tie, not meeting my eyes. 'She went stony-faced and turned away. I got the feeling it wasn't the first time she'd witnessed something like that.'

'So Abby and Charles were unhappy together?'

'Not for us to say,' Will says. 'We weren't inside that marriage.'

'But it looked pretty bad from the outside? That's the impression I'm getting all around.'

Colin relaxes a fraction. 'Yeah. I'd say it was pretty bad. Abby's a sweet girl, though. She might leave him, but she'd never kill him.'

'Besides, what would be the point of killing him?' Will puts in. 'Not like she'd inherit anything. He was broke.'

'I gathered that as well. But how did you know?'

Will shrugs. 'The way he threw money around. We knew we were all three making about the same, but Colin and I didn't have the kind of money Charles spent on drinking and poker and prostitutes. Plus he bummed stuff off us all the time. Stands to reason he was exceeding his income.'

I pick up on one point. 'Prostitutes?'

Fair-skinned Colin goes beet-red. 'He liked it – kind of kinky. Rough kinky. And he didn't care about consent. So he paid for it.' He grimaced. 'From the way he talked, I feel sorry for the girls.'

On a whim, not because it matters much to the investigation, I ask, 'Do you have anything good to say about him?'

Will ponders a minute. 'He could be generous. When he was flush with cash. And he could be good to his friends.'

Colin clears his throat. 'Will got the job here automatically – his dad's a partner. But they only took me on because of Charles.'

Not much of a legacy to leave behind. Sounds as if nothing in his life became him like the leaving it.

I ask them both what time they left the office Monday evening. 'Five thirty,' Will answers for them both. 'We went for a drink at Ninety-Nine Bottles. They know us there.'

On the way out, I check with the receptionist about everyone's time of departure. She confirms them all. I won't bother with the bar. These guys are clear.

Tally for today: relevant information about the victim, fifty points. Suspects: one, Derek, vaguely possible. But if he's crazy jealous enough to kill a man for hitting on his wife, why wait nearly two months to do it?

'Out sick' could be a euphemism for all sorts of things, including 'coming to terms with having just killed a man.' If that's the case, I don't want to give Derek Hopkins time to recover. I head to his house, hoping to catch him off guard.

He lives in the same neighborhood as the Crenshaws, a situation I suspect he would have avoided if he could. An attractive young woman in a baggy sweater, yoga pants, and a messy bun answers the door with a pink-clad baby on her hip and a curly-haired toddler clinging to her leg. Wife or nanny? I don't dare assume either way.

I flash my badge and introduce myself. 'Is Derek Hopkins available?'

The toddler yanks on the woman's pant leg. 'Just a minute, Danny, Mommy's busy.' Then to me, 'My husband's in bed. He's not feeling well today. Could it wait?'

'I'd really like to talk to him now, if that's possible.'

She sighs, blowing a stray strand of hair out of her eyes. 'Come in. I'll see if he's awake.' She turns to leave the room, then looks back. 'Is this about Charles?'

'Yes, ma'am.' I try to read her expression – is she glad or sorry Crenshaw's dead? But all I can see is a harried mom with one more thing to worry about.

She comes back shortly, the toddler now whining for a snack. 'He'll be right out. Can I get you anything?' She's already halfway to the kitchen, so I follow.

'Nothing for me, thanks. But can I ask you a couple of questions, Mrs Hopkins?'

'Monica.' She glances meaningfully at the toddler and the baby, who is now beginning to whimper in dissonance with her brother. 'You can try.'

'What time did your husband get home last night?'

'Six fifteen, as usual. I could set the clock by him.'

I wonder whether Derek takes after his father or is merely intimidated by him. Either way, six fifteen would have left him plenty of time to kill Crenshaw if he left the office early for a change. I'll have to call back there and check on that.

'And you? Were you home all afternoon?'

She opens the fridge and starts to rummage around in it. 'I had to take the baby to the doctor. We were there from four to about five thirty.'

That lets her out, assuming the doctor confirms. I jot down the practice's number from the emergency phone list magnetized to the fridge door.

'Were you friends with the Crenshaws?'

Pause while she finds the 'boo-beys' Danny's been demanding and pours some into a plastic bowl. She sits him down at the counter and straps the baby into a highchair with some blueberries of her own. Then she turns to me.

'I wouldn't say "friends" exactly. I like Abby – I'd be happy to be her friend, but it was tricky with her husband flirting with me right in front of her every time we met. I never encouraged him, but he just kept on. It seemed like he cared more about riling her up than about making time with me. I felt terrible about it, but there didn't seem to be anything I could do – short of slugging him or something.'

'What about your husband? Couldn't he do anything?'

She sighs again. 'Derek spoke to Charles about it, but he's such a diplomat, he never would come out and confront him in a way Charles would respond to. Charles was not one to take a subtle hint.' She turns away and rubs at a stain on the granite countertop with her finger. 'Honestly, I'm glad Charles is gone. For our sake, but even more for Abby's.' She looks back up at me with a little smile. 'Maybe now I can be her friend.'

I'm not getting a vibe that suggests Monica sees either herself or her husband as a possible suspect. She's simply getting something that's been bothering her off her chest with the first random stranger who's come along. Only I'm not random. I'm the police.

I turn at a noise from the doorway to see a disheveled man of medium height and build in a bathrobe open over striped pajamas, gazing at me through bleary eyes with a handkerchief covering his mouth. It looks like the 'out sick' excuse is literally true.

'Come into the living room, Detective,' he says. 'But don't get close to me. I don't want to pass this bug around. It's a nasty one.' He punctuates that with a chesty cough.

I follow him and choose a chair across the room from the couch where he collapses. 'Charles?' he says, presumably economizing on words to preserve his throat.

'Yes, sir. I need to know where you were between five and five thirty yesterday afternoon.'

He lifts his head off the back of the couch and stares at me. 'Where *I* was?' Then he lets his head fall again. 'I guess you heard about his siege of my wife.'

'Yes, sir. First from your colleagues, then just now from Mrs Hopkins herself.'

He utters something that starts as a grunt but morphs into a full-blown coughing fit. When he recovers, he says, 'I left the office early yesterday. But I didn't go to Crenshaw's. I went to urgent care 'cause I was feeling like crap.'

'What time exactly were you there?'

'Left the office at four thirty, so maybe four forty-five to just before six? Got home at my usual six fifteen, weirdly enough.'

'Which urgent care was that?'

He tells me, and I write it down. I'll verify it later, along with Monica's alibi.

'Your wife said you had spoken to Crenshaw about his behavior but not really confronted him.'

He squeezes his eyes shut for a minute, and when he opens them, tears glisten at the corners. 'Yeah. That's me. Always the negotiator. Never the shark who goes in for the kill. That role we all left to Charles.' He pulls his legs up and crouches there in the fetal position, coughing feebly, as miserable a specimen as I've ever seen.

Would he have had the strength – moral or physical – to attack a big man like Crenshaw in this state? It hardly seems likely. Nor is his present remorse consistent with having killed a man. It's much more indicative of him feeling he's failed his wife.

I stand. 'Thank you for seeing me, Mr Hopkins. I'll let you get back to bed now. I'll be in touch if I need anything else.'

He nods and waves a hand vaguely in my direction. He's a nice guy, probably a perfectly decent husband when he isn't sick. As I leave the room, I see Mrs Hopkins standing in the kitchen doorway and raise my hand in farewell.

Another family who will be much better off now that Charles Crenshaw is dead.

# SEVENTEEN

*December 2016*

T he next day I took the Highway 17 Express bus to school, which was a lot less expressy than it sounds. I had to catch a city bus from our corner to the transit center downtown, then wait twenty minutes for the express, since the Santa Cruz Metro schedulers had apparently slept through the class on how to make connections convenient for riders. At the end of the 17 bus line in downtown San Jose, I had to run through drenching rain to catch another city bus to get to Santa Clara (more sleepy schedulers). By the time I arrived at my first lecture, I felt ready for a nap and a hot bath instead of the grueling day of classes that awaited me.

Impatient for news of my car, I called the mechanic at lunchtime. 'Oh, hey, I already talked to your husband,' he said. Just like Charles to give them his own number instead of mine. 'You got a burnt-out engine here.'

'What?' I'd had literally not a spot of trouble with the car before yesterday.

'Yep. Ran completely out of oil. Engine froze up. Nothin' we can do except put in a new one. And that's gonna cost you big time. If it was me, old as this thing is, I'd scrap it and get a new car.'

My dear old Mazda. Gone to that great garage in the sky. How would I get along without her? And why did I have to?

'How could it run completely out of oil in one day? I'd swear it was fine two days ago.'

'Well, that's the funny thing about it. Looks like some joker's put a nick in your oil line.'

I froze as the implications of this played out in my mind. But I had to be sure. 'I had the oil changed at Oil-Can Benny's a couple of weeks ago. Could it have happened then? Accidentally, I mean?'

'Hard to say. How much you drive this thing?'

'Over the hill and back every weekday.'

'Oh, in that case, no way. Leak like this, oil woulda lasted maybe fifty, sixty miles tops.'

'I see.' And I did see – quite a lot.

'So, you want me to put in a new engine?'

'What did Charles say?' I hated having to depend on his decision, but I had no money of my own for either repairs or a new car.

'He said forget it. Told me to sell the car for scrap.'

'It's my car, not his. But if that's the way we can get the most out of it, I guess I'd have to agree. But be sure to make the check out to me, not Charles.'

'Gotcha. Too bad about your car. Kinda like losing a friend.'

More like losing a lifeline.

I got home pretty late that night, having navigated the reverse of the same route I took in the morning, and I didn't even have any takeout to show for it. I was dreading Charles's hangry reaction, but he met me at the door with a smile, covered my eyes with his hand, and said, 'Don't peek.' He led me into the dining room, where he removed his hand to reveal the table beautifully set – linen, fine china, flowers, the works – and a heavenly smelling dinner ready to be eaten. I was bowled over for about thirty seconds – until I remembered this was Friday, Consuelo's usual day to clean our house. I'd bet money Charles had paid Consuelo extra to do all this.

But what the hey, at least he'd made some kind of effort. A guilt meal, no doubt, to salve his conscience over wrecking my car. A year of such meals wouldn't make up for that treachery.

But I'd keep him sweet until the proper moment to plunge in the knife – which would be after I'd devoured this delicious meal.

'Thank you, Charles. This is wonderful. Riding the bus was quite an ordeal – it took me a full two hours each way. I'm exhausted.'

'Poor baby.' His face and voice were all concern, but I could hear the sarcasm lurking underneath. 'Sure you want to keep doing that for five more months? Sounds pretty grueling.'

'I was hoping we might be able to replace the car.'

He shook his head in mock sadness. 'I'm afraid not, babe. The budget won't cover it right now.'

I'd anticipated that answer. 'Then maybe I could use your car sometimes. It would be a lot easier for you to bus to work than for me.' Service from our house to his Mission Street office was practically door to door. For that matter, it wasn't a terribly long walk.

His eyebrows rose into his hair. '*My* car? I don't think you could handle it, babe. And I'm not about to trust my Porsche to someone who can run the engine of a Mazda into the ground.'

That was my breaking point. The dinner I'd eaten so far would have to do. 'My Mazda died because *you* cut the oil line. Don't even try to deny it. You cut it because you wanted me to be stranded here with no decent transportation so I'd have to quit school. I should sue you for the price of the car, not to mention reckless endangerment. What if the engine had frozen sooner, while I was still on Seventeen? I could have been killed. Along with your child.'

His face was a picture of outraged innocence. 'How can you say that? Do you honestly think I would ever put my son in danger?' I noted he did not disavow being capable of putting *me* in danger. 'It must have been those idiots at Oil-Can Benny's.'

'Your mechanic says not. He says the oil wouldn't have lasted more than one trip over the hill and back with that nick in the line. That means it was done between the time I got home Wednesday night and the time I left Thursday morning. When the car was parked in our locked garage. Nobody had access but you.'

'Ridiculous. You must have driven over some glass and it flew up into the engine and nicked the line.'

My knowledge of car anatomy made me highly doubtful that was possible, but it wasn't sufficient to allow me to refute the idea completely. I'd never get him to admit what he'd done. But neither would I give in. 'Whatever happened, you owe me another car, Charles. I don't care if it's new – it could be identical to my Mazda as far as I'm concerned. But I have to have something.'

He shoved away from the table. 'Well, you better get creative, because you are not getting it from me.'

The next day, Saturday, Charles went off to play paintball with his buddies, Colin and Will. The December storms were too fierce for even Charles to consider surfing.

I called Ellen and begged her to come over, if necessary with the kids.

'No problem,' Ellen said. 'You wouldn't believe how stir-crazy these two are, being cooped up inside with all this rain.'

'They can play in the guest room. I've already childproofed it and started stockpiling toys in there for when it becomes a nursery. It'll make a change from what they have at home.'

When Ellen arrived, three-year-old Nicky and one-year-old Katya flew into my arms, nearly smothering me. 'Whoa, one at a time, you two! Come on, you guys can play in the guest room while Mommy and Aunt Abby talk. Then later we'll have some pizza. OK?'

'Pizza!' Nicky threw his arms in the air, almost dislodging himself from my grasp. I set him down and carried Katya into the guest room. Ellen inspected it and gave it a childproof thumbs-up. Katya clung to me until Nicky started playing with a set of alphabet blocks, then she wanted in on the game.

'No, Katya, I'm playing with that one!' Nicky pulled a block out of her hand. Her little face began to pucker into a cry.

'Nicky, play nice with your sister. She's too little to understand,' Ellen said, no doubt repeating a mantra she uttered a thousand times a day.

Nicky grudgingly let go of the disputed block, and Katya's face cleared. Ellen gave me a wry grin. 'Sure you want to let yourself in for all that?'

'I hardly have a choice now, do I? But seriously, I'm looking forward to this baby. I just hope I can make it through law school first.'

I made tea, and we settled in the living room where we had a line of sight down the hall and through the guest-room door.

'So,' Ellen said. 'What made you so desperate for me to visit? Usually you like to come to me.'

I told her the story about the car.

Ellen put down her mug so hard the tea splashed on the coffee table and dripped on to the white carpet. Neither of us moved to clean it up. 'You're telling me he deliberately sabotaged your car? So you'd be stuck at home for your whole pregnancy?'

I nodded. 'Honestly, given the way he's behaved in the past, I'm hardly surprised. This is more extreme, but it's not a radical departure from his norm.'

'Abby, you have got to get away from this man. He's going to kill you one of these days – or at the very least, kill your spirit.'

'I can't leave now. Not while I'm carrying his child. Anyway, how would I survive? No one's going to hire a woman halfway through her pregnancy. With any luck, the baby will be a boy, and then Charles will worship the ground I walk on.'

'You think? I can see that happening for, oh, about the first ten minutes. Until the baby cries or poops or spits up on one of his starched Brooks Brothers shirts. Then it'll be back to business as usual, only worse, because everything the baby does will be your fault, too.'

I winced. The plausibility of this prediction was not lost on me. 'Even so, I have to give it a try. You know he'd find a way to leave me destitute if we split up.'

'But California has community property. You'd get half the house.'

''Fraid not. It's in his father's name.'

'Then we'll help you out. We have plenty of room – there's that whole empty apartment over the garage. And plenty of money to feed you until you're ready to go to work.'

I considered her offer. Seriously, I did. But Ellen as support person I could call on when I needed to and Ellen as a daily presence in my life, telling me what to do as if we were kids again, were two different things. Besides, I'd made vows to Charles, and I owed it – if not to him, then to God – to give the marriage the best shot I possibly could. And the clincher – for as long as I'd known I was pregnant, I'd been hearing my dead mother's voice in my head: *Don't give him a chance to take your child away from you. Anything is better than that.*

'I really appreciate the offer, El. And someday I may take you up on it. But not yet. I have to keep trying a while longer.' I pressed her hand. 'Charles can be sweet when he puts his mind to it.' *When he wants something* would have been more accurate, but Ellen didn't need to know that.

She huffed and threw up her hands. 'Abby Taylor, you are the stubbornest girl on God's green earth. But at least let me help out with the car. Pavel wants to replace his car – he needs something a little spiffier to drive bigwigs around in. I'm sure he'd be happy to give his old Prius to you. It's paid off. And it's reliable – should have plenty of miles on it yet.'

I gave my sister an impulsive hug. 'That's so generous of you, Ellen, and I'd love to accept. But Charles would only find some way to sabotage that one, too.'

'We'll keep the car legally in our name, on our insurance. Then he won't dare to damage it. He'll know *we* would actually sue.'

I hesitated, but in the end I gave in. After all, it was my only hope of finishing school – I knew I couldn't survive running for the bus for five more months, as my belly grew bigger and my feet slower. Whatever would I do without Ellen?

I didn't tell Charles about my agreement with Ellen until she and Pavel delivered the car the following Saturday afternoon. He knew something must be up when they pulled up in front of the house, Pavel driving the Prius and Ellen with the kids in their minivan.

'What are they driving two cars for?' he grumbled, peering out through the front blinds. 'Not bringing more castoff furniture, I hope? Because if so, they can turn right around and take it back.'

I swallowed, then opened my mouth to tell him. But I chickened out and pretended ignorance. The announcement would have more force coming from Pavel. And at least Charles would have to let them in the door. If I told him now, he'd likely lock it in their faces.

After the necessary greetings – warm on three sides, icy on the fourth – Charles cut to the chase. He addressed himself to Pavel. 'May I ask to what we owe the honor of you turning up here in this cavalcade, taking up the whole block?'

Pavel smiled blandly. 'We're leaving my Prius for Abby to use. Ellen brought the van to drive me back.'

I watched the blood rise from Charles's collar to his hairline. 'I'm sorry you've been put to the trouble, but we cannot accept this gift.' Possibly only I could hear the rage that trembled under the surface of his attempted courtesy.

'It isn't a gift, it's a loan. And it isn't for you – it's for Abby.'

'Abby can't accept it, then. It's too much of a responsibility. And you know how hard she is on cars. She destroyed a perfectly good Mazda last week.'

Pavel nailed him with a glare that said very clearly Charles was not going to get away with that particular ruse. 'I suggest you reconsider,' he said. 'Because if you don't, we may have to instigate an investigation into what *really* happened to that Mazda.'

Charles's face went from beet-red to pasty white in two seconds flat. Better acceleration than his Porsche. I could practically see the gears turning as he backtracked.

'A temporary loan, then. Until we get this new branch of the practice well off the ground and I can afford to buy her a new car.'

'That's all we're asking.' Pavel held Charles's gaze until Charles blinked, losing the staring contest.

'Won't you stay to dinner?' he croaked. 'Since you've come all this way.'

We all had what passed for a lovely evening, with Charles playing the perfect host. But when Ellen and her crew were gone, he said to me, 'I'm not sure it's a good idea for you to spend so much time with your sister.'

'Why ever not?'

'I don't think she's a good influence on you. And that husband of hers is definitely shady. Did you hear the way he spoke to me? I bet he's got the Russian mafia in his pocket. He'd order a hit on me in a heartbeat.'

'That is the most ridiculous thing I've ever heard. Pavel is a devout Orthodox Christian. He'd never have anything to do with a criminal organization. Besides, the Russian mafia doesn't exist outside Russia.' I wasn't sure that was true, but I hoped at least that Charles could not prove otherwise.

Charles gave a patronizing smile. 'Your naivety would be touching if it weren't so dangerous. At any rate, Pavel and Ellen are no longer welcome in this house. And I don't want you going over there, either.'

I faced him with hands on hips. 'If you think you can separate me from my sister – the only family, practically the only friend I have in the world – you are even more insane than I thought you were. Don't even think about it.'

Charles did not respond but skewered me with a gaze that chilled my bones. Regardless, I was determined: there was no way I'd allow him to cut Ellen out of my life.

# EIGHTEEN

*Tuesday afternoon, February 27, 2018*

*Abby*

T he nice detective drops by the hospital later that same afternoon. I'm in the middle of pumping milk for Emma. I turn away and cover up quick. He looks embarrassed. I disconnect and lie back on the pillows. I'm exhausted.

He sits on the edge of the bed, as if he were my brother or something. I would have liked to have a brother. 'Did you have your final exams today?' he teases. I didn't know policemen teased. It's kind of nice.

'I wish. Lots of exams, but I don't think any of them were final.'

'No results yet, I suppose?'

I don't have the energy to lift my head, so I turn it side to side on the pillow. 'Owen said they should know something tomorrow.'

'Owen?' There's a funny note in his voice.

'Doctor Owen Elliot. The neurologist who's handling my case.'

He kind of relaxes. 'Does he have any theories at this point?'

'Yeah, he thinks the tests will all be negative because it's stress- and hormone-related. Goes along with migraines.'

'I see.' He stares at the blanket, pleats it between his fingers. He's kind of sweet. Like he knows he ought to treat me as a suspect, but he can't quite bring himself to do it. 'You haven't remembered anything more?' He looks at me almost as if he's willing me not to remember. Or at least, not to remember it one certain way.

'Not to say remembered. Dreams, but nothing helpful.' I shudder, remembering those dreams. But then I think about what Owen said. 'I have this feeling . . .'

'Yes?'

'I feel like if I had killed him, I'd remember it. Or at least I'd *feel* as though I'd killed him. I don't feel that. I feel relief that he's gone, I feel horror at the thought I could have done it, but I don't feel guilt. And I would feel guilty about killing anyone, even a worm like Charles.'

His face brightens. 'Well, that's something. Not sure it would stand up in court, but it's something.'

I smile at him. He smiles back. I wish we could meet as something other than policeman and suspect. I think we might be friends. There's a kind of safe feeling about him that I like.

'Do you have any other leads? Suspects?' I ask him.

'I'm not supposed to tell you that. But I will tell you, it would sure help a lot if you could remember what happened when you first walked in the house.'

I sigh. 'I know. I would say I'll work on it, but Owen says that's not the way to go about it. He says to relax and not think about it, concentrate on resting and getting well, and the memories will come back in their own time.'

He pats my foot through the blankets. 'I'm sure the doctor's right. I'll come check on you tomorrow.' He stands. 'But you will call me right away if you think of anything? Anything at all.'

'All right, Detective.'

'Call me Peter.' He snaps his fingers, then reaches into his coat pocket and pulls out a folded sheet of paper. 'Almost forgot. I need you to sign this. HIPAA release so the doctors can talk to me about your condition and medical history.'

'Oh, sure.' I have nothing to hide on that front. Not anymore. I take the pen he hands me and sign the form on the bed tray.

He takes the form, thanks me, then hesitates, as if he doesn't want to go but can't think of any good excuse to stay. 'I'll see you tomorrow,' he finally says, and walks out.

*Peter*

Wednesday morning the captain calls me to his office. I go in nervous. He starts in on me, no preamble. 'Any progress on the Crenshaw case?'

'Not much, I'm afraid.' I sum up what we've learned so far.

'You have no other suspects besides his wife?'

'None that look viable. But I'm working on it.' The Hopkins' alibis checked out. I have yet to verify the elder Crenshaws'.

The captain runs a finger under his collar, which for him indicates extreme stress. 'I'm getting pressure from the chief on this. He plays golf with Crenshaw Senior, apparently. We need some action. Preferably an arrest.'

'That would really be premature, sir. We're waiting on the lab results, the autopsy, the DNA . . . We don't even know for sure it's murder. And the wife still doesn't remember what happened.'

He frowns at me. 'She could easily be faking that.'

'The doctors don't seem to think so.' Not that I've asked them. I should do that.

'How can they be sure? Can't be any medical way to tell. She could have them bamboozled, like she has you.'

My hackles go up. 'With respect, sir, she does not have me bamboozled. I just don't think she's guilty.'

'Why, because she's a cute young thing who looks innocent and vulnerable? You should know better than that. How long you been on the force again?'

'Ten years. And it's not because of . . . what you said.' Though, to be honest, it partly is. I can't get her face out of my mind. 'There's no physical evidence against her. Besides that, I have a gut feeling. And you know my gut has been right before.'

'Yeah, well, it's also been wrong.' He ticks off on his fingers. 'She was there. She was covered in blood. She won't say what happened. No evidence of anybody else at the scene.' He sits back, both palms spread. 'Face it, Rocher – she did it.'

'With respect, sir, she was not covered in blood – just a bit on her cuffs, which is easily accounted for if she checked for signs of life. That's actually a point in her favor. And we can't yet be sure there's no evidence of anyone else – not till we get the DNA.'

He waves a hand, as if to say *DNA, SchmeeNA*. I know his opinion – DNA should only be used for confirmation, not for detection. Mainly because it takes so damn long to get the results.

I drum my fingers on the arm of the chair. I'm out of excuses. 'Give me a little more time, sir. Please. There are some avenues I haven't had time to explore.' Yeah, the ones I don't know exist yet – but they've got to be out there. 'Give me at least till all the reports come in. If Mrs Crenshaw's memory hasn't come back by then . . . well, maybe the reports will give us something to go on.'

'I'll give you till the end of the week. Period. If we don't have an arrest by then . . .' He doesn't spell it out, but I know: his job will be on the line. And therefore mine as well.

Just what I love. A ticking clock. And this one is attached to a time bomb that could blow Abby's life apart.

I head to the hospital to check on Abby again. On the way to her room, I ask to speak with Owen Elliot, the doctor in charge of Abby's case. I find him in transit between patients, iPad in hand. He's a young, good-looking guy, blast him, but not as tall as I am.

'Doctor Elliot?' I flash my badge. 'Detective Peter Rocher. Can I talk to you for a minute? It's about Abby Crenshaw. And we do have her signed HIPAA form on file.'

He checks his watch. 'For a literal minute. That's about all I can spare.'

I choose my words carefully so as not to waste them. 'Do you feel Abby's memory loss is genuine?'

He startles. 'I hadn't thought to question it, frankly. But I'd say so. There's no test or anything we can do to verify it, if that's what you mean. But she seems sincere to me. I think in my job, as no doubt in yours, we learn to recognize when people are lying, to us or even to themselves. I don't get that feeling from Abby.'

'She hasn't mentioned anything that would give us a clue? Some memory slipping through without her realizing it?'

He shakes his head. 'No. As far as I can tell, that period of time is still a complete blank.'

'OK. Thanks.' I hand him my card. 'You will let me know if anything changes?'

'Sure thing.' He pockets the card and sprints off to his next case, his mind probably already full of that one and empty of Abby. If only I could get my mind to perform that trick.

# NINETEEN

*December 2016*

C harles waited until our next monthly family dinner with his parents to tell them about the pregnancy. 'I want to see the look on their faces,' he said on the way there, 'when I tell them they're going to have a grandson.'

'Or granddaughter,' I said to my window. The response had become automatic, but I didn't hold out much hope he'd acknowledge that possibility until he held a penis-free baby in his arms. For my own part, I was convinced – and immensely grateful – it was a girl. God forbid I should bring a Charles Crenshaw III into the world.

His father picked up on Charles's subdued excitement the minute we entered the house. 'What's got you looking like the cat that got the cream?' he asked.

'Is it that obvious?' Charles said with a foolish grin. 'I was going to save it for dessert. But since you've guessed – I'm going to be a father!'

Charles Senior's face lit up as I had never seen it. He thumped his son on the shoulder with his left hand as he pumped his right. 'Congratulations, my boy! This is indeed good news. Jacqueline, break out the champagne! We're going to have a grandson!'

'Or granddaughter,' I put in. I felt like a repeating echo of myself.

Jacqueline's face glowed. She took me by the shoulders and kissed me on both cheeks – real kisses, not air ones. 'That is wonderful news, dear. I'm so happy for you.' She whispered in my ear, 'And I hope it *is* a girl.' We exchanged a conspiratorial smile. 'Would you like to help me with the champagne?'

'Sure.' I followed her to the kitchen, which I'd never seen before. The maid, whom I now knew as Yolanda, was hard at work putting the finishing touches on our meal.

'Yolanda, Abby *está embarazada*,' Jacqueline said as she

opened the enormous refrigerator. How could three people need so much food?

Yolanda's face lit up as well. '*Muchas felicitaciones. Un bebé – que bendición!*' She came up to me and wrung my hand.

I smiled. I didn't understand the words, but the sense was clear. '*Gracias*,' I answered – one of the two Spanish words I knew that weren't food.

'Abby, will you open this while I get the glasses?' Jacqueline handed me a chilled bottle. A glance at the label made me start – the legendary Dom Perignon. What if I dropped it? With shaking fingers I peeled back the foil, unwound the wire holding the cork, and slowly twisted the cork free.

'Thank you, dear.' Jacqueline took the bottle from me and poured three full flutes, then two half ones. She handed one of the halves to Yolanda, who took it with a giggle. The other four flutes she put on a tray. 'Just a half for you, Abby dear. We have to be careful about the baby.'

'Of course.'

We rejoined the men, and Charles Senior raised his glass. 'To the continuation of the Crenshaw line!'

I sipped my champagne, adding silently, *Or to a granddaughter.* I wasn't surprised by Charles Senior's attitude, but it did make me even more concerned about what would happen when my little girl was born.

The Charleses drifted off, and Jacqueline and I sat down. 'You'll have to forgive Charles Senior, my dear,' she said. 'You see, he's an only son of an only son, and so, of course, is your Charles. They're eager for Charles to have a son to continue the family name.'

'I suppose that's reasonable,' I replied. 'But I have a strong feeling this baby is a girl. I hope they won't be too terribly disappointed.'

Jacqueline patted my hand. 'They'll get over it. Though possibly not until you have another baby – a boy.'

I didn't voice my response to that. A second baby with Charles? Fat chance.

*Winter and spring 2017*

After the car episode, Charles finally accepted the fact that I was determined to finish my degree. He made another U-turn and started treating me like a queen. 'Nothing's too good for the mother of my son,' he would say as he put a hassock under my feet and a pillow at my back at the end of a long day. I kept adding *or daughter* but learned to do it silently. I needed this pampering; I wasn't about to do anything to jeopardize it.

Although we couldn't afford a new car, apparently the budget could accommodate having prepared meals delivered every week. Charles proved he actually knew how to operate a microwave and, wonder of wonders, a dishwasher. He even made midnight runs to the store to accommodate my occasional pregnant cravings.

In the bedroom, he was more considerate of my needs though still just as demanding. He claimed he found my growing belly so sexy he couldn't resist it. During the second trimester, my hormones were favorable, and I didn't much mind having sex nightly with this new, thoughtful Charles, especially as every session began with a massage. But as month seven dawned, my hormones shifted along with my weight. I felt like a grounded, swollen-footed blimp, and sex was absolutely the last thing on my mind. Yet Charles would not relent. His favorite occupation seemed to be trying out new positions to accommodate my 'bump,' which was now more of a mountain.

Finally, with four weeks to go before my due date – and five weeks till graduation – I couldn't take it anymore. I'd been told that having sex in late pregnancy could bring on early labor, and that was something I had to avoid at all costs. I knew it would be useless to make that argument to Charles; he'd be delighted if I was unable to finish my exams. So I consulted Ellen and came up with a plan.

One Friday evening, I rose above my exhaustion to be especially sweet to Charles. But when it was time to head for bed, I dropped my bomb.

'Charles, you want me to have a healthy baby, don't you?'

His eyebrows peaked in hurt surprise. 'Of course I do. Why do you think I've been doing all this?'

'Well, I'm afraid I'm going to have to ask you for one more sacrifice. It's kind of a big one.'

He smiled and patted my belly. 'Anything for my son.'

Ultrasounds had revealed months before that my instinct was correct – we were having a daughter. But since Charles had never

accompanied me to a single doctor's appointment, I'd elected not
to tell him.

'You know Doctor Foster, my obstetrician, is in Palo Alto. So
I'll be going to Stanford for the delivery.' This choice had been at
Jacqueline's insistence – Dr Foster was 'the best.'

'Of course.'

This was where I had to depart from the truth a bit. 'He's getting
concerned about me living so far from the hospital. In case anything
goes wrong. He thinks the baby may come early, and he wants me
to stay somewhere closer until then.'

Charles pouted for a moment, then brightened. 'OK, fine. We
can stay with my parents. They won't mind.'

Oh dear. That would not suit my purposes at all. A fortuitous
fact came to my rescue. 'But, Charles, you know they're having
work done on the house.' Knocking out a wall to expand Charles
Senior's study into what used to be Charles Junior's bedroom.
'Doctor Foster said I must have peace and quiet. I thought I'd go
stay with Ellen.'

His brow grew thunderous. 'And you think her house will be
quiet? With all those kids?'

'They have a guest suite over the garage. I can have it all to
myself. It'll be perfect.' I had to spin this to his advantage somehow.
'And I know you must be worn out taking care of me. This way
you'll have a whole month to be a bachelor again. Your last fling
before the responsibility of parenthood closes in.'

I watched that sink in. I couldn't say I liked the smile that spread
over his face, but at this point I would buy my month of freedom
at any price.

'OK. Whatever you need, baby. No sacrifice is too great for
my son.'

What price I might have to pay for that sacrifice when he found
out he'd made it for a daughter, I would not think about now.
Sufficient to the day is the trouble thereof.

*May 2017*

During the last week of classes, I ran into David at the campus food
court. I'd barely seen him all year; he'd been studiously avoiding
me since my marriage. I'd texted a couple of times, but when he

didn't answer, I let it drop. Presumably he couldn't bear to see or think of me with another man.

I felt sorry for David; I'd always known he had a crush on me, but I hadn't realized his feelings ran so deep. I missed our old friendship. None of my female acquaintances had ever become such good confidantes as David had once been.

Pregnancy had altered my eating habits; salads no longer satisfied. On this particular day I craved pizza, piled high with all the toppings. I got my huge slice and turned from the line to come face to face with David.

He started and seemed about to duck away, then his eyes fell on my belly. At this point it was pretty hard to ignore. He pulled himself together with a visible effort.

'Hello, Abby,' he said in a voice that strove for indifference but didn't quite hit the mark. 'I'd ask how you are, but I guess that's kind of obvious.'

I glanced down. 'Well, part of it is. But that's hardly the whole story. Listen, I'd love to catch up properly.' I glanced around for an open table and nodded toward it, since my hands were full. 'I'll be over there. Come join me when you get your food.'

He made a noncommittal noise in his throat. I half suspected he would disappear on me, but he got his pizza and turned in my direction. He hesitated but then moved toward my table, jerkily, as if pulled by forces beyond his control.

He sat down and immediately stuffed the end of a slice into his mouth without speaking, so I took up the conversational gauntlet. 'So how have you been? I've barely seen you all year.'

He chewed a bit, then answered with his mouth half full. 'Busy. Big final project.'

David was finishing his degree this semester, too. But 'busy' didn't account for us never even running into each other.

'Going OK?'

'Wrapping it up this week. Then finals.' He glanced at me. 'You, too, I suppose.'

I gave a wry grin. 'Yeah, assuming I make it that far. I'm due any day.'

He looked me up and down. 'You're cutting it fine. Surprised you'd take that risk. Giving up on being a lawyer?'

I sighed. 'Not exactly. The pregnancy was not what I planned. I wanted to finish my degree and practice for a couple years before having kids. But now that this one's on the way, I'm going to take a year or two to be with her before I go to work.'

David's eyes drilled into me. I squirmed. Maybe pursuing this chance meeting had been a mistake. He always had been able to see right through me when he wanted to.

'In other words, the baby was Charles's idea, not yours.'

I grimaced. 'That's about the size of it.'

His eyes narrowed and his nostrils flared. 'I knew it. I told you that arrogant son of a bitch would run roughshod over you. But would you listen?' He shook his head and addressed himself to his pizza.

Had he ever voiced that insight to me? I honestly couldn't remember. I'd been in such a happy daze during the months of my whirlwind romance with Charles that David's warning could have rolled right off me, as Ellen's words of caution had done.

I spoke in a tiny voice, almost hoping he wouldn't hear over the noise of the crowd around us. 'If it makes you feel any better, I do wish now that I'd taken those words to heart.'

David turned toward me, his face suddenly all concern. He took my hand. 'Abby, are you seriously unhappy?'

I would have tried to deny it, but the tears that started to my eyes betrayed me. I nodded, eyes on my pizza, for which I now had no appetite.

'Then why don't you leave him?'

I looked up at him. 'In this condition?' I gestured toward my belly. 'I'm about to have his child. I can't get by on my own with a newborn. And maybe fatherhood will change him. Force him to think about someone other than himself.'

David snorted. 'It doesn't work that way, and you know it. A selfish bastard is a selfish bastard. A baby will only make things worse. I know – I saw it happen when my little brother was born. My stepdad went from bad to unbearable as soon as the baby started taking all my mom's attention.'

He leaned forward, covering our joined hands with his other one, which was greasy from his pizza. 'Abby, I'm begging you. Leave that dickhead. Let me take care of you.' He swallowed. 'I'll be a father to your baby. I don't care if it is his by blood. We'll raise it together.'

I stared at him in disbelief. From him cutting me dead to offering to help raise my child was a leap I couldn't compass in the space of ten minutes. 'David, think about what you're saying. This is crazy. How could you possibly take care of me? You live in a dorm room. You have no job.'

'I do have a job. I'm starting at SoftSell right after graduation at seventy K a year.'

I blinked. 'I'm so happy for you, David. But seventy thousand doesn't go that far in Silicon Valley, you know. You'll be looking at a studio apartment at best.' I shook my head. 'Anyway, that's not the real point.' The ultimate point was that I could never love David that way, but I couldn't say that to him now. 'The point is that I'm married to Charles. I made a vow before God. I have to give it my best shot, and I can't say I've done that until all hope of things getting better has gone.'

David dropped my hand and sat back, making a disgusted noise in his throat. 'Your optimism used to be one of the things I loved most about you, Abby. But now I'm beginning to think it's your fatal flaw.'

# TWENTY

*Wednesday morning, February 28, 2018*

*Abby*

New day. I think it's Wednesday. Time kind of blurs together here in the hospital.

Blood in my dreams again. Covering a prone figure that glitches between Charles and my mother. They told me Mom's suicide was not my fault – Ellen and the therapists told me that, over and over – but I know on some level it must have been, because otherwise the image of her swimming in her own blood would at some point have faded from my mind. And Charles must have been my fault, too. Regardless of what or who was the immediate cause of his death.

The IV ports are gone, so I shower, but I can't wash those images from my mind. Thank God, no tests this morning. Instead, the best possible thing to distract me: Ellen brings Emma for a visit. I've been aching for my baby, aching in my breasts, my heart, my bones. Nobody warned me motherhood meant that although the umbilical cord might be cut, an invisible, unbreakable cord would continue to bind mother and child just as strongly, if with a tad more physical space.

Emma reaches for me and plants her open rosebud mouth against mine in her version of a kiss. I hug her briefly, then she's tugging at my hospital gown. I pull the neck string open at the back so I can maneuver the gown off one arm and nurse her. Awkward, but worth it.

'Any chance you could swing by my house and get me a real night-gown?' I ask Ellen. 'These things are driving me nuts when I have to pump. Not to mention they're about as flattering as a camo tent.'

She laughs. 'What does it matter if they're flattering? There's only the nurses and me here. We don't care what you look like. And Emma certainly doesn't.'

I'm probably blushing. 'I do get other visitors, you know. Owen – the neurologist – and the detective. They're both kinda cute, in different ways.'

She raises one eyebrow. 'Your husband is barely cold, and already you're planning your next relationship? You might want to reconsider that. Not that anyone expects you to grieve, but you could use some time to heal before you jump into anything new.'

'I'm not jumping in.' Certainly not until I know whether or not I'm a murderer. 'I want to look like something other than a mental patient, that's all. What's wrong with that?'

'I do see your point. But I'm not sure if the police will let me in the house.'

'Did someone call?' A masculine voice at the door startles us both. Ellen grabs a baby blanket and throws it over my chest. I tuck it behind my shoulder.

It's Peter at the door. 'Well, speak of the devil,' says Ellen. 'We were just speculating on whether you'd let me into Abby's house to get her some proper sleepwear.'

'Fine, as long as I go with you,' he says. 'I'd like to talk to Abby for a minute, but then I'll be free.'

'Shall I leave?'

'You can stay if you promise not to interrupt.' He softens this with a smile. Ellen moves off the bed and into a chair in the corner.

Peter comes to stand beside the bed. 'I wanted to check on how your memory's doing today.'

I wrinkle my nose. 'No change, I'm afraid.'

'It's still early days. Don't worry about it. Have you by any chance thought of anyone who might have wanted to harm Charles? I know I asked you that before, but you weren't thinking too clearly at that point.'

'No, I still haven't. Charles treated other people a lot better than he treated me.'

He hesitates, as if he doesn't want to ask the next question. 'How much do you know about your husband's finances? Did he have any life insurance?'

I haven't gotten around to thinking about money yet. God only knows what kind of mess Charles left behind. 'I don't know how things stand in that department. Charles never shared anything like that with me. He just gave me a certain amount every month to buy groceries and stuff. I have a little bit I managed to save out of that, but it won't go very far.' I peek inside the blanket to make sure Emma's OK. She's falling asleep but still sucking. 'He didn't have any life insurance when we married, I know that. But I think his mother may have taken out a policy on him after Emma was born. She said something once about wanting to make sure Emma was provided for in case anything happened to Charles.'

'Do you have anyone who handles financial matters for you? Anyone who could give you advice?'

'Nobody official, because I never had any money of my own to handle. But Pavel, my brother-in-law – he's pretty good with money. He could help me figure things out.' I glance at Ellen, and she nods. I know I can count on Pavel.

'OK. That's it for now. Mrs Stepanovich, I'm ready when you are.'

Ellen comes up to the bed and reaches for Emma, but I hold her tight. 'Leave her until you get back. She's sleeping.'

Ellen looks a question at the nurse who's come in to check my vital signs or something. 'That's fine, as long as you're back by one o'clock. We have another procedure scheduled then.'

It's eleven now. Two whole hours with my precious baby girl. And then I can get pretty after the procedure is finished. This day is looking up.

*Peter*

I drive Ellen over to Abby's house and wait while she gathers up nightgowns, robe, and slippers, then adds some personal care products and makeup to the bag. So Abby wants to get pretty. Prett*ier*. For me or for that doctor? Maybe neither. I guess women need to feel pretty to feel good. And anyway, better get that thought out of my head. At least for now.

Ellen throws in a few books, picks up what looks like a knitting bag, and is ready to go. I drive her back to Dominican, then head over the hill once more. I want to check up on that life-insurance policy Jacqueline Crenshaw may have taken out on her son. I know I'm grasping at straws to think a mother might kill her own son, but straws are all I've got in this case right now. And I never did check Mrs Crenshaw's alibi with her maid.

I didn't call ahead, so I'm lucky to find both women at home. The maid – Yolanda, was it? – opens the door, so I grab the chance to talk to her alone first. 'Yolanda? Detective Rocher – remember me? I need to ask you a couple of questions.'

Her brown face goes pale. She clasps her hands to stop them shaking. She's probably illegal. They're always terrified of the police.

'It's all right. It's nothing to do with you personally.' Her eyes go even wider. I don't know how much English she understands. Or speaks. I pull out my high school Spanish. '*No se preocupe. No se trata de usted.*'

She relaxes her grip a little and nods.

'I understand you were here with Mrs Crenshaw on Monday afternoon. When young Charles was killed.'

Her eyes dart to and fro. I don't think she's getting it, and my Spanish isn't that good. '*Usted – aquí – lunes tardes? A las cinco?*'

Light dawns. She nods enthusiastically. '*Si, estuve aquí. Si.*'

'*Y la señora? Ella aquí tambien?*'

I'm afraid her head will nod off, she's so eager. '*Si, si. Estuvo aquí.*'

Mrs Crenshaw's alibi is confirmed. '*Muchas gracias. La señora, por favor.*'

She keeps smiling and nodding as she shows me into the living room. I hope she doesn't collapse once she's alone.

Mrs Crenshaw comes in, wearing black. Very elegant black. She's pale, but I don't see signs of tears.

'Detective. What can I do for you?' She indicates a chair for me and lowers herself gracefully into one opposite. The way she crosses her legs is a lesson in deportment.

'A few more questions, if I may.'

'Anything I can do to help.'

'It appears Charles did not have a life-insurance policy on himself, though he did have a small one on Abby. Is that your understanding?'

She nods. 'Yes. It was very remiss of Charles not to insure his own life, especially after Emma was born. But I could never persuade him to it, so I took out a policy on him myself. With Emma and Abby as beneficiaries.'

'So is there some sort of trust involved?'

'Yes. Half the money is Abby's absolutely; the other half is in trust for Emma until she comes of age, with Abby as trustee.'

'I see. You must have a lot of faith in your daughter-in-law.'

'I know she loves Emma more than her life. She'll take better care of her than anyone else could.'

'And what is the payout amount of the policy, if you don't mind my asking?'

'Two million dollars.' She gives me a tiny smile. 'Charles was young and healthy, so it wasn't as expensive as you might think.'

'And you paid for this out of your own money?'

'Out of my personal allowance, yes. My husband refused to contribute.'

'And did Abby know about this?'

'I told her I'd arranged for them to be taken care of if anything happened to Charles. I didn't mention the details.'

So the money wouldn't be a motive for Abby in itself. But knowing she'd be taken care of – that could be a reason to choose murder over divorce. Especially if she had some idea of how broke her husband was. 'It's good to know Abby and Emma will be well provided for. Thank you, Mrs Crenshaw. I think that's all for now. Unless you have anything else to tell me?'

She shakes her head. 'I'm afraid we're still mystified by this awful business, Detective. But I do hope you find the killer. For Abby's sake.'

She walks me to the door. 'Is Abby still in the hospital?'

'Yeah. They're doing tests to pinpoint the cause of her blackouts.'

'Blackouts?'

She looks shocked, and I realize I never mentioned Abby's memory loss to the Crenshaws. I guess it's not too surprising Abby hadn't told them herself – she wouldn't want to raise any questions about her fitness to care for Emma. 'She's been having blackouts for several months now. In fact, she had one when she found . . . the body. That's one thing that's making this investigation so difficult. She can't remember anything about it.'

Jacqueline clucks her tongue. 'Poor Abby. Could I visit her, do you think?'

'I don't see why not. Better call ahead to find out when she'll be free – they're doing a lot of tests. Best not to talk about the actual murder, though. She's still pretty raw.'

And I don't want you putting any ideas into her head, in case you had anything to do with the murder of your own son.

# TWENTY-ONE

*May 2017*

Thanks to the blissful peace of living in Ellen's guest suite (with daily covert forays into the main house to play with the kids), I made it through finals with baby in belly and with grades that would earn me a *magna cum laude* degree. I was certain that without the pregnancy brain, the commute, and the stress of living with Charles through most of the year, I could have made *summa cum laude*. But the main point was that I'd finished, despite all Charles's efforts to the contrary. I was hardly even disappointed to miss the actual graduation – my water broke the night after my last exam.

Despite his recent attempts at better behavior, the last person I wanted in the delivery room was Charles. He'd stopped going to childbirth classes with me after the first one, claiming birth was no job for a man. Ellen had offered to be my birth coach instead, which was fine with me. Given his lack of involvement, I was tempted not even to call and let him know I was in labor. But when I checked into the hospital, the admitting nurse made me feel so guilty about not having informed him that I asked Ellen to make the call.

My weeks of absence had turned him into pre-pregnancy Charles again. By the time he arrived, he was grumpy about having been awakened at four a.m., and finding that labor had barely begun, even grumpier about having gotten up and made the drive only to wait around in the hospital for hours on end. Ellen shoved him toward the cafeteria and told him to take all the time he wanted about getting breakfast. 'Most likely nothing much will happen for several hours, so there's no need for you to be in here,' she said. 'I'm sure there's a TV room somewhere.'

Ellen's prediction proved to be right. By ten a.m., I was only three centimeters dilated. 'It's going to be a long haul,' the labor nurse told us.

When Ellen conveyed this to Charles, he threw up his hands in disgust. 'I'm going to my parents'. Call me when she has an hour to go.' As if anyone could know that exactly.

The next few contractions were easier now that I didn't have his impatience to make me tense. But easier also meant less effective. The hours dragged on, and the pain grew so intense I began to rethink my determination to have a natural birth.

By the time I reached the transition stage of labor, it was midnight. Ellen called Charles, who grumped and grumbled about being deprived of a second night's sleep. 'I'll get there when I get there,' he said.

When my current contraction had passed, Ellen quipped to me, 'At least he didn't ask us to wait for him.'

The final phase of labor was as fast as the earlier ones had been slow. Half an hour after transition started, the baby crowned. By the time Charles finally sauntered into the birthing room, I held our perfect daughter, clean and blanketed, in my arms. I gazed into her unfocused eyes and found there a new reason for my existence – to love, nurture, and protect this tiny life, which both was and could never be separate from mine.

Charles strode up to the bed. 'He's here already?' he said, reaching for the baby. 'Let me hold him.'

I reluctantly handed over the little bundle that contained my world. 'She's a girl,' I said.

For one heart-stopping moment, I thought Charles was going to drop the baby on the concrete floor. Instead, he laid her roughly on the bed and began unwrapping her. 'I don't believe it. You're shitting me.'

'I promise I'm not. You won't find any penis in there. She's a beautiful, healthy, perfect little girl.'

Having removed the blankets – a print of white kittens on a pink background – to reveal the baby, clad in a pink undershirt and diaper, Charles paused as if almost ready to believe me. 'What the hell,' he growled, and unfastened the diaper.

I watched his face transform into a mask of utter defeat and despair. He spoke in a hoarse whisper. 'What the fuck am I going to do with a *girl*?'

I leaned forward and wrapped my beautiful baby up again. 'Love her, Charles. Just love her.' I said the words, but I had already learned the bitter truth that *love* was a word of which my husband had no comprehension. That capacity had been omitted from his makeup. His disability was less obvious than a missing arm or leg but no less real – and far more tragic.

I picked my baby up and cradled her against my shoulder. But Charles was still motionless, staring at the place where she had lain, when his parents walked in.

Jacqueline came up to me and kissed me. 'How are you, dear? Did everything go well?'

'Just peachy, Jacqueline. Isn't she beautiful?' I held the baby up for her grandmother to see.

'Oh, she is adorable,' Jacqueline cooed, taking her granddaughter gently in her arms. She turned to her husband. 'Look, Charles, isn't she perfect?'

Charles Senior had paused to shake his son's hand. The younger Charles had made an effort for his father's benefit and now wore a face that was a parody of a new father's joy.

'Let me hold my grandson!' Charles Senior bellowed, ignoring his wife's pronoun and holding out his arms. 'I bet he's a strapping young fellow.'

'Grand*daughter*, Charles,' Jacqueline said, softly but with emphasis. 'It's a girl. A beautiful baby girl.'

Charles Senior's face turned to stone and his arms dropped. He turned to his son. 'A *girl*?'

Charles Junior almost cowered. 'I know – can you believe it?' he said with a false laugh. 'The luck of the draw, right?'

His father's lip curled into a sneer. 'Useless,' he muttered. 'I might have known. You'd better get to work and make me a boy.'

Charles Senior left his son dumbfounded and marched out of the room. In a moment of blinding clarity, I understood – my husband had hoped to use a son to buy his father's elusive approval. Now that opportunity was lost.

I might have pitied him, but just then I had no emotion to spare – my love for my new daughter overwhelmed me. I would have to be everything to her as she was already everything to me.

Jacqueline held the baby a moment longer, touching her lips to the downy head. 'I love that new-baby smell, don't you?' she said to me as if nothing had happened. 'What do you think you'll call her?'

'I was thinking of Emma. After my mother. Maybe . . .' I had a flash of gratitude and compassion for my mother-in-law. She'd had to put up with her Charles for going on thirty years. 'Maybe Emma Jacqueline?'

Jacqueline's eyes went misty, and she leaned down to kiss my cheek. 'That is very sweet of you, my dear. I think Emma Jacqueline is a perfectly lovely name.' She blinked and set her jaw. 'And I will make sure those men of mine don't give you any trouble about it.'

She turned and glared at her son, who still stood gaping after his father, his shoulders sagging as if he had been the one laboring for the last twenty-two hours. 'Charles? I assume you have no objection to the baby being called Emma Jacqueline?'

He blinked as if coming awake. 'Call her what you want,' he said in a gruff, defeated voice. 'I don't care.'

He shuffled toward the door, then turned back. 'I'm taking you home first thing in the morning,' he said. 'Time to get our lives back to normal.' He closed the door behind him.

Jacqueline shook her head. 'Poor boy. He doesn't understand – neither of you will ever see pre-baby normal again.'

*Summer and fall 2017*

It was a good thing my love for Emma was so instant and over-whelming, because Charles gave me no help with her at all. Midnight feedings, diaper changes, rockings to sleep all fell to my lot. If I wanted to go anywhere, I had to take the baby with me. I felt as if I'd grown a new appendage. I could gaze into my Emma's face for hours, but more than once I wished her back in my womb just because she was so much easier to carry that way.

And sleep – sleep was like something I'd dreamed about (waking dreams, of course) but could hardly hope ever to attain. Emma didn't seem to know night from day, and she was never happy out of my arms. But Charles wouldn't hear of having her in the bed with us. In those early months, I spent more time dozing in the rocking chair with Emma in my arms than I ever spent in bed.

I talked to Ellen on the phone (being always too sleepy to dare the drive over the hill) about how exhausted and overwhelmed I felt, and her immediate reaction was 'Girl, you need to get some help.' Even with a supportive husband like Pavel, she'd found herself on the brink of a breakdown more than once with each newborn. The only way she saved her sanity was to hire someone to look after the baby a couple of afternoons a week.

I was sure we could afford such help and equally sure Charles would never agree to it. He was constantly mocking me for not being strong enough to handle the baby on my own. I needed some other excuse. Finally, about two months in, I found it.

I had always had migraines occasionally, but they'd grown more frequent with pregnancy. Now, with nursing hormones and no sleep, the migraines were becoming even more frequent as well as more severe. I worried they would interfere with my ability to care for Emma, so at last I asked Charles about hiring some help.

'Help? You have one tiny baby and you think you need help?'

'It's the migraines. I can hardly move when I have a bad one. I can't take care of a baby when I can hardly move.'

He surveyed me derisively. 'Fine. You pay for it out of the housekeeping money, and you can hire some help. But only during the day when I'm not here.'

So generous. As if he ever did help when he was there. Maybe if there were a true emergency, he would come up to scratch. With no practice, though, would he even know what to do for his own daughter?

I'd have to make do with calling a sitter when I felt a migraine coming on. That much I could squeeze out of what Charles allowed me for housekeeping.

For a while, I cherished an irrational hope that over time he might soften toward his daughter, that once she grew out of the always-sleeping-eating-or-crying stage and developed some personality, he would at least be charmed by her cuteness if not moved to genuine affection. When Emma first smiled at him – which wasn't till she was about five months old, since he interacted with her so little – Charles's face did indeed light up. And the first time she laughed in his presence, he couldn't help but laugh back. He poked her tummy and tickled her armpits until she went into such fits I was afraid she might hyperventilate.

From that time, although he still refused to take on any of the mundane duties of caring for Emma, he did warm up to her a bit. He began to show her off to his friends when they came over, and Will and Colin's admiration of her seemed to confirm for Charles that she might have some value for him after all – if only as another showpiece to add to his collection.

He started bringing her little gifts when he came home. One night he brought a toy that played electronic nursery-rhyme tunes when a button illustrating a given rhyme was pushed. He set it in front of the baby as she lay on her stomach on the floor.

'Look, Emma,' he said. 'Push the little lamb.' He laid her palm flat on the picture of Mary with her little lamb and pushed.

The tune played, but Emma did not react. She slapped at the next button, and the next, and the next, never waiting for a tune to finish before playing another one.

'Not like that, Emma. You have to play the whole tune.' He held her hands away from the toy until 'Baa, Baa, Black Sheep' was done. Emma whimpered and pulled at his hands, trying to reach the buttons. 'Cut it out, Emma. You're supposed to listen to the music.' She still wouldn't cooperate, and Charles turned away in disgust. 'Fine, then. Do what you want. Stupid kid.'

Looking on, I thought first that Emma was only displaying a normal baby's desire to touch things and did not understand the causal connection with the music. But when I saw her push the same button again and again, continually restarting the song, I began to wonder. I went up to her and clapped my hands loudly right next to her ear.

Emma did not flinch. She did not blink or interrupt her play for even an instant. She just kept pushing the same button until I thought I would go mad from hearing the first two notes of 'Mary Had a Little Lamb' over and over and over again.

Emma tired of the toy at last, and I put it away on a shelf. Then I took out my phone and called the pediatrician. At that moment, I didn't allow myself to feel or to think about the full implications, but I strongly suspected my precious baby might be deaf.

# TWENTY-TWO

*Wednesday afternoon, February 28, 2018*

*Peter*

While I'm over in Silicon Valley, I go to Crenshaw Senior's office. I never followed up on that end of his alibi.

He's out, but his assistant is in. She gives me a dazzling smile. Then I introduce myself and the smile fades. My guess, she took this job to meet a rich husband. A cop will never be that.

'Can you verify that Mr Crenshaw was here on Monday afternoon until five thirty?' I ask her.

'Let me check his calendar for that day.' She turns to her computer and clicks around for a few seconds with her long sparkly-red nails. I never could understand how women can type with nails like that. 'Monday afternoon. Yes. He had depositions here in the office that lasted until five fifteen. Then he answered some messages and left about five thirty.'

I expected no different but feel a certain disappointment nevertheless. And now that I'm here, I hate to leave with no more information than that.

'Did you know Charles Junior?'

'Of course. We went to college together.'

'Where was that?'

'Santa Clara, naturally. The rich kids' school.' She rolls her eyes. 'I went there on staff scholarship.'

'Were you fond of him?'

'Oh, all the girls loved Charles.'

'Loved as in . . . had a crush on? Or something more?'

She leans toward me, showing her cleavage through the gap in her red silk blouse. 'I would estimate Charles Crenshaw Junior slept with approximately half the girls on campus. Most only once.'

I can't resist. 'And what was your total?'

She smiles, her eyes hooded. 'I got him twice.'

I smile back, as if appreciating how special she is. 'What did you think when he married Abby?'

She straightens with a huff. 'That he'd decided to go slumming and got trapped.'

'Trapped? How? She didn't get pregnant before the wedding, did she?'

'Well, if you add up the months, I guess not. But she got her hooks into him somehow. I've never been able to figure out how.'

Maybe by being a kind, decent, intelligent, beautiful woman. Even a self-absorbed asshole like Charles might have recognized good wife material when he saw it.

I rest my palms on the desk and lean over it, all confidential. 'Did you ever try to – you know – get him back? After the wedding?'

She smiles a slow smile. 'You're putting your hands on the site of my victory right now.'

I jerk my hands away from the desk's surface and stare at them, as if the desk were covered in the aftermath of steamy sex at this very moment. My palms are dry, but I wipe them on my slacks nevertheless. 'So how do you feel about Mrs Charles Crenshaw Junior?'

'Obviously she didn't deserve him if she couldn't even hold on to him. I would have handled him a lot better, let me tell you.'

I bet you would. 'Do you think she killed him?'

The girl shrugs. 'That's for you to find out, isn't it? But I'd sure be tempted to kill any husband who cheated on me. Dating's one thing, but once that ring's on your finger, you have a right to expect him to keep it in his pants.' She smiles that slow smile one more time. 'Except in your bedroom, of course.'

I feel I can say quite sincerely, 'Too bad you didn't get Charles Junior. You two seem made for each other.'

She dazzles me again with her original smile.

'Obviously you took it well when he married Abby. But could there have been other girls who didn't take it so well?'

'Somebody jealous enough to kill him, you mean? I guess it's possible. But why would they wait so long? He'd been married over a year and a half.'

There is that. 'I bet in a big office like this, there are bound to be rivalries, jealousies. I'm sure a smart girl like you would know all about them. Any of the lawyers here have a grudge against Charles? Senior or Junior?'

She let out a hoot of laughter. 'Try all of them. Charles Senior is not exactly Mr Charm and Personality.' Yeah, I gathered that. 'Everyone in the office hates him like poison. But they wouldn't take it out on his son. I think most of them felt sorry for Charles Junior. The way his dad was always pushing him around. He was so relieved when they opened the Santa Cruz office and he found out he could work down there. Happiest day of his life.'

Struck out again. How did a man like Charles Crenshaw Junior go through life without making dozens of mortal enemies?

'Thank you, Ms . . .' I glance at her nameplate, but she supplies the name before I can read it.

'O'Hara. Scarlett O'Hara.'

Seriously? Her parents saddled her with that? Maybe she chose it herself – seems appropriate.

Well, frankly, Scarlett, I don't give a damn. 'Thank you, Ms O'Hara. Maybe I'll see you around.'

Back at the office, I subpoena Mrs Crenshaw's bank records. It's nearly impossible to believe that gracious woman could have killed her own son, and she does seem to have a solid alibi for the time of the murder. But she could have hired someone to do it. Could she have been that desperate to protect and provide for her grandchild? I've seen no evidence that Emma herself was abused by her father – neglected, yes, but his death won't solve that. Jacqueline's involvement is a slim chance, but it's the only chance I have for now.

I skim through the transactions in her personal accounts. The insurance premiums show up all right. Other regular expenses as you'd expect, for groceries, clothes, gas, restaurants, et cetera. She typically spends two or three thousand a month.

Then suddenly I come upon a check deposit and cash withdrawal for ten thousand dollars.

Ten thousand could pay a hit man. Those sleek silk sheaths of hers could be hiding a killer.

*Abby*

Wednesday afternoon, after the MRI, Jacqueline comes to visit. I'm beginning to feel like a pretty popular person in this hospital.

'Abby,' she says, greeting me with an air kiss as usual. 'How are you?'

'I feel like I should be asking you that. You're the one who's lost a son.' The grief I couldn't feel for myself now stabs my heart on Jacqueline's behalf. A mother can't help mourning a son, no matter how disappointing he may have been. And she doesn't know the half of it.

She tears up but keeps it under control. 'I don't think it's quite hit me yet,' she says. 'This investigation – it's as if we're on hold until it's finished. I don't think his death will quite sink in until we know how – and why – he died.' She looks at me with a question in her eyes, as if she thinks I might know something she doesn't.

'I kind of feel the same way. Only in my case, it's not simply a matter of finding out from some external source. Did Peter – Detective Rocher – did he tell you I've lost my memory?'

'He did. I guess I was hoping . . . well, that there was something, anything, you could tell me that I don't already know.'

'I'm sorry. All I remember is coming to after a blackout and seeing Charles on the floor, covered in blood.' I suppress the shudder that picture brings, will always bring. 'I have no idea how he got that way.'

Jacqueline stares into space for a minute. 'Abby . . . do you think there's any way he might have . . . well, threatened you or Emma? Made you so afraid that you lashed out?'

I quiver to my core. I've been hoping not to have this conversation with her, because that is my greatest fear. 'I really don't know. It's true that things had kind of . . . come to a head between us.'

She turns to stare at me, wide-eyed.

'I'm sorry. Of course, you didn't know. I'd been planning for some time to leave him, and then – well, something happened.' I couldn't tell her the details. 'It was getting pretty bad, Jacqueline. I was starting to fear for my own and Emma's safety. In a general way, that is – nothing immediate or specific. That I can remember.'

Her tears well up again. 'Oh, Abby. I knew Charles wasn't easy to live with, but I had no idea it was that bad. Did he . . . had he been . . . hurting you?'

'He never actually hit me. A couple of times I thought he might, so I left the house and took Emma with me. It was more – well, other things.' How do you tell a mother her son was a sexual predator and a narcissistic manipulator? Those are not words dear to a mother's heart.

She takes a ragged breath, closes her eyes, almost visibly stiffens her upper lip. 'I know you don't remember what happened, but do you have . . . any sort of feeling about it? About whether you could have . . . hurt him . . . in self-defense?'

I shake my head. 'Honestly, Jacqueline, I can't rule it out. But as I told Detective Rocher – I think if I had done it, I would feel guilty, even if I couldn't exactly remember. But I don't. And the doctor said it wasn't likely I'd do something in a blackout that was strongly opposed to my principles.'

I focus on her, willing her to look me in the eye. Finally, she does. 'I think if I did hurt him, as you say, it could only have been in self-defense. If I seriously thought he was going to kill me or hurt Emma. And like I said, there's no strong precedent for that.'

She bites her lip, fighting for control. I want to urge her to forget the control, let herself feel something for a change, but this probably isn't the time and place.

'I want you to know, Abby, if you did hurt him in self-defense, I would have no trouble forgiving you for that. Especially if it was to save Emma. She's my only hope for the future now. I think I would have chosen her over Charles myself.'

I reach out and squeeze her hand. I'm beyond words – that his own mother would feel that way about Charles is the strongest confirmation I could have that I wasn't imagining or overreacting to his treatment of me.

She blinks and pulls herself straighter. 'And one more thing I wanted you to know: I took out a life-insurance policy on Charles after Emma was born. You'll have a million dollars for yourself and another million in trust for Emma.' She gives me a small smile. 'A million isn't what it used to be, but I hope it will be enough that you won't have to worry about money, at least for a while.'

Now I'm tearing up for real. 'Oh, Jacqueline, thank you so much. I don't know what I'd do without you.' I hesitate, remembering my own mother and wondering what she would think of what I'm about to say. On balance, I don't think she'd mind. 'I want you to know, I feel you've been a real mother to me since Emma was born. I would never intentionally do anything to hurt you. And I hope we can stay close – maybe even be closer from now on.'

Her tears start flowing now, and she leans in to give me a real hug. 'Thank you, Abby. That means the world to me.'

# TWENTY-THREE

*October 2017*

I took Emma to Dr Chung, our pediatrician, the week after the incident with the musical toy. 'She never responds to lullabies,' I told her, 'and loud noises don't make her flinch. World War Three could happen next door, and she wouldn't wake up from a nap before it's time.'

Dr Chung glanced at me from under raised eyebrows as she skimmed through Emma's computer records. 'You didn't have a home birth, did you? Usually newborns have their hearing tested before they leave the hospital.'

'No, she was born at Stanford.' I thought back. 'We did go home early, though, at my husband's insistence. She was born after midnight, and we left later that morning.'

'That would explain it, then,' Dr Chung said drily. 'Let's have a look.'

She looked in Emma's ears, then put a baby-sized pair of headphones on her and fiddled with some dials. 'There is definitely cause for concern,' she said as she removed the headphones. 'I'm going to refer you to an ENT for further testing.'

Even though I'd had the clear evidence of my own senses that Emma's hearing was defective, I realized with those words I'd been cherishing a tiny, illogical hope that I was wrong. Now that hope was gone.

Back home, I called Ellen. 'I think Emma's deaf,' I blurted.

I could almost hear Ellen shift into big-sister-will-fix-this mode. 'What? Why? She seems perfectly normal to me.'

'I thought so too until last week.' I told her about the episode with the musical toy. 'So I took her to the doctor today, and she referred her to an ENT. She wouldn't have done that if there wasn't real cause for concern.'

'Not necessarily. You know they have to cover all the bases in case somebody decides to sue.'

'Yeah, I know, but you didn't see her face. I'm telling you, she thinks Emma's deaf.'

'Well, don't jump to any conclusions until you know. And if she is, we'll find a way to deal with it.'

That was Ellen. No problem too large for Super Big Sister. But what could she possibly do in such a case? You can't argue or cajole a baby into being able to hear.

The two weeks that passed before the ENT appointment were the longest of my life to date. I watched Emma constantly, on the alert for any sign that she might be hearing something, anything at all. But even with my wishful thinking tuned to its highest pitch, I could detect no grounds for hope.

When the day came, I carried Emma into the ENT clinic as if approaching a ritual sacrifice with the two of us as the victims. The tests were long and grueling, as befits such rites. But at last, the ENT, Dr Patel, called me into his office to give me the results.

He glanced at the empty chair beside me and frowned. 'Your husband should be here to hear this.'

I swallowed. I didn't want to admit that I hadn't yet told Charles about any of it. Or that he wouldn't have cared enough to come along if I had. 'He, uh . . . he couldn't get away from work. He never can during office hours.'

Dr Patel raised an eyebrow. 'Hmph. Well, Mrs Crenshaw, I don't believe in sugar-coating bad news. I'm sorry to have to inform you that your daughter has profound sensorineural hearing loss. In other words, she's completely and congenitally deaf.'

I heard what the doctor said, but I couldn't take it in. Not Emma. Not my perfect baby.

In that moment, I borrowed some of Ellen's indomitable spirit and became Tiger Mom. 'What can we do? How do we cure her?'

'There is no cure per se for congenital deafness,' Dr Patel replied. His face was kind, but his words cut to my core. My sweet Emma would never be able to hear me say, 'I love you.'

'But there must be something we can do. Hearing aids? Some surgery or something that can help her?' I refused to accept that Emma could be marred for life. Or that I could be destined to take on this burden with zero support from my husband. I wasn't really Tiger Mom – I couldn't cope with all that extra responsibility on my own. I was just me.

'There is one therapy we've had good success with in young children,' said Dr Patel. 'Cochlear implants. They don't exactly restore hearing; rather, they transmit the electrical signals of sounds directly to the brain. It takes some time and a lot of therapy before the patient is able to understand those signals as actual speech.'

A thread of hope. I grabbed on to it with both hands. 'I have nothing but time. I'll do whatever it takes. Let's do it.'

He held up a restraining hand. 'Hold on, Mrs Crenshaw. The implants and subsequent therapy cost an average of forty thousand dollars. And I already know your insurance won't cover it – we've dealt with them before.'

I gaped. I still had a Taylor concept of money, since so little of the Crenshaw finances had yet been at my direct disposal. '*Forty thousand dollars?* And why won't they cover it? It's not like having a facelift or something. Hearing is an essential sense.'

Dr Patel shrugged. 'I can't tell you why. Maybe they think it's still too experimental – the results are uneven in older children. But with babies and toddlers who are just learning language anyway, the success rate is very high.' His expression softened. 'Is there any possibility you could raise the money?'

'I don't know.' I didn't think Charles had that kind of spare change, and I was pretty sure he wouldn't spare it if he did. Forty thousand was close to the sticker price of the BMW X3 he'd bought me when Emma was born – whether as a guilt gift to make up for his lack of interest in the baby, or simply to keep up appearances now that I would be driving around Santa Cruz where his friends might see me, I neither knew nor cared. The car was a hulking beast that I would gladly give up. But, of course, I was fairly sure it was nowhere near paid for.

Then I thought of Jacqueline, who seemed to love Emma almost as much as I did. 'My in-laws are pretty well off. I can ask.'

'I recommend you do that,' said Dr Patel. 'Hearing loss is not the worst of disabilities, but this surgery could mean the difference between a normal life and a difficult one for your daughter – and for you. Keep me informed.'

I left the office in a daze. Before strapping Emma into her car seat for the drive home, I hugged her as close as I dared and whispered into her unhearing ear, 'We're going to fix this, sweetheart. You are my perfect baby, my sweet darling treasure, and I won't let anything stand in your way.'

I called Ellen again as soon as I got Emma home and settled for a nap. 'It's true. She's deaf. Completely and congenitally.'

Ellen took in a shocked breath. 'Oh, honey, I'm so sorry. How are you holding up?'

'I can't take it in. I'm just numb. How can I be numb?'

'You're in shock. It'll sink in all too soon, I imagine. What did the doctor say? Is there anything they can do?'

'There's something called cochlear implants. They have a good success rate with infants, but the whole process costs forty thousand dollars, and our insurance won't pay.'

She whistled. Ellen and Pavel were comfortably off, but, like me, she still had Taylor sensibilities when it came to money. 'Wow. Even for the Crenshaws, that doesn't sound like spare change.'

'Probably not. I wouldn't be surprised if our wedding and honeymoon cost that much, but that doesn't mean they could come up with it again. And honestly, I don't think either Charles or his dad would care enough to make the sacrifice.'

'Oh, Abby. Surely you're wrong. His own daughter? Granddaughter?'

'If she were a boy, they'd do it like a shot. But not for Emma.'

Ellen took a minute to digest this. 'What about Jacqueline? She doesn't feel that way, does she?'

'No, Jacqueline loves Emma. She's my only hope. The monthly family dinner is this Sunday. I'm going to talk to her then.'

'Good. I'll be praying for you. And you'll tell Charles in the meantime?'

I hesitated. 'I'm not sure. I have a kind of feeling I'd like to have one person in the family on my side before I brave his reaction.'

'Well, let me know how it goes. And don't worry – we will find a way to fix this, with Crenshaw money or without it.'

I didn't have much faith in Ellen's optimism, but I appreciated her support. It helped to fortify me against the ordeal of facing the Crenshaws on Sunday night.

When the time came, I could hardly eat the delicious dinner Yolanda had prepared, so nervous was I about the coming conversation. I'd have to wait till after the meal to talk with Jacqueline alone. She might not be completely *au fait* with the family finances, but she would likely have some idea whether coming up with forty thousand liquid dollars would be a piece of cake, or moderately difficult, or completely impossible for Charles Senior. And she'd be better able than I was to predict how he'd react to the request.

While Charles had softened into something resembling a normal father – at least, what would have been a normal father a couple of generations ago – his father had no time for Emma at all. He wouldn't allow her at the dinner table, claiming it was indecent to ask adults to eat with a slobbering baby. Either Emma would nap while we ate, or Yolanda would happily keep her in the kitchen until the meal was over. Then Yolanda would bring Emma to join me and her doting grandmother in the living room while the men went to Charles Senior's study for drinks.

When we were settled with our coffee and the baby, I began my campaign. 'Jacqueline, there's something I'd like to talk to you about.'

'Hmm?' she said, distracted by bouncing Emma on her knees and listening to her gurgle with pleasure.

'I took Emma to the doctor last week. And there's a problem.'

This got Jacqueline's full attention. 'A problem?'

'I've been concerned for some time now that Emma doesn't respond to sounds the way a baby normally would.'

Jacqueline looked puzzled. 'Really? I've never noticed that. Listen to her cooing at me now.'

'Yes, but she's responding to what you're doing with her, not to any sound you're making. Watch.'

I clapped my hands loudly right next to Emma's ear. She didn't flinch but went on smiling and gurgling as before.

'Oh my goodness. I see what you mean. Did you have her tested?'

I nodded and steeled myself to pronounce the dread words. 'It's profound sensorineural hearing loss. She's completely deaf.'

Tears started into Jacqueline's eyes. 'Oh, my poor darling . . .' She gathered Emma close to her chest and rocked her gently. Emma wriggled, wanting to go back to being bounced. 'There must be something they can do?'

'There is. There's a fairly new treatment called cochlear implants. If it's done young enough, it has a very high success rate.' I took a breath. 'The only problem is, the surgery plus the therapy afterward costs forty thousand dollars. And our insurance won't cover it.'

Jacqueline's mouth dropped open for a moment, then she snapped it shut. 'We'll pay for it. I'm sure Charles can afford that. And for his own grandchild, after all. He can't possibly refuse.'

I winced. From what I'd seen of Charles Senior's behavior toward his granddaughter, I thought the possibility of his refusal was very real.

As if reading my mind, Jacqueline patted my arm reassuringly. 'I'll take care of it. You'll see. Don't you worry about a thing.'

Nevertheless, I worried. Where either of the Charles Crenshaws was concerned, I had learned to take nothing for granted.

# TWENTY-FOUR

*Wednesday afternoon, February 28, 2018*

*Abby*

Jacqueline leaves my hospital room, promising to keep in touch. I'm feeling tired from all the tests and bad dreams and broken sleep, and I'm starting to drift off when my door opens again. For a second I think I'm dreaming. It's David.

I haven't seen him since before Emma was born. Now that we're both done with school, our paths don't cross, and the way we parted last time made it too hard to pick up the phone and say hi. How do you make small talk with a man who offered to take care of you and raise your useless husband's child, if that's the last thing you want?

But he's here now, so I'll have to find a way. I raise the head of the bed to a sitting position and try to force myself awake. 'David! I wasn't expecting to see you. How did you know I was here?'

He clears his throat. 'I, uh . . . I read about Charles's death in the newspaper.' I blink. It hadn't occurred to me that it would be publicized. He goes on, not looking me in the eye. 'You didn't answer your phone. So I called Ellen. She told me you were here.'

My phone. It must be around here somewhere, but I honestly haven't thought about it the whole time I've been in the hospital. 'Well, it's good to see you. Come on in.'

He shuffles up to the chair Jacqueline left next to the bed and perches on the edge of it. Why is he being so hesitant? Furtive, even. David's never been the most confident person, but he's acting as though he has no right to be here.

He glances up at me, then fastens his eyes on the blanket. It isn't that interesting, even as blankets go. 'So how are you? Why have they kept you in here all this time?'

'I'm basically fine now. I was pretty shattered right after . . . it happened. But I'm mainly in here for tests. I've been having blackouts the last couple months.'

He looks up sharply. 'Blackouts? Did that asshole drive you to drink?'

I shake my head. 'Not that kind of blackout. They think it was probably from migraines, but they have to wait for the tests to be sure.'

He examines the blanket again. Plain white, plain weave, perfectly clean. What's to examine? 'What are you going to do now?' he blurts out.

I blow out a big breath. David never was much of one for tact, and this is a question I haven't answered even to myself. 'I don't know. I can't go back to that house. Probably go stay with Ellen for a while till I sort myself out.' The only certain thing in my future is Emma's surgery and therapy, but I don't feel inclined to tell David about all that. Too much time has passed, too much has happened. We can't just jump back into our old closeness, even with Charles out of the picture.

He's silent a minute, then, 'Do they know yet who . . .' OK, so he has a little bit of tact. He can't bring himself to utter the words *who killed your husband.*

'No. They're working on it.' My turn to be silent. 'I had a blackout before I found his body. I can't be absolutely certain I didn't kill him myself.'

Now he stares at me, eyes wide. '*You?* No way. You could never kill anyone. The police don't suspect you, do they?'

I think about the way Peter acts with me and I can't believe he does suspect me, although there's no good reason he shouldn't. God knows I had motive. 'I'm sure they haven't ruled me out. Not till I can remember what happened, anyway.'

He grabs a fistful of blanket. 'They are not going to arrest you for this. I won't let it happen.'

I give a tiny laugh. 'How on earth could you prevent it?'

'I don't know. But I'll find a way.'

The only way I can think of would be for him to confess to the murder himself. Oh, David. At this moment, I wish I could love you. You're willing to put your life on the line for me. 'Don't do anything stupid, David. I don't believe I did kill Charles, but if I did, I'll have to stand trial like anyone else. If I did, it must have been self-defense – or defending Emma. They're sure to let me off easy for that.'

He shakes his head, but I'm not sure which part he's denying. 'Keep me posted, OK? You do still have your phone, don't you?'

Light dawns. 'Actually, I bet the police have it. That would explain why I haven't seen or heard it since I've been here.'

A voice comes from the doorway. Peter. 'The police do indeed have it. And we're returning it to you right now.'

He comes up to the other side of the bed and hands the phone to me, then turns to David, flashing his badge. 'Detective Peter Rocher. And you are . . .?'

David bristles at the presence of the person who could ultimately be responsible for depriving me of my freedom. But he forces his name out through gritted teeth. 'David Dunstable. Old friend.'

'David and I went to school together,' I explain. 'High school and Santa Clara. Not law school – he's a programmer.'

Peter looks David up and down with a face that says he could have guessed the programmer part. Only he would have said *geek*. 'Would you mind waiting outside? I need a few words with Abby alone, then I'd like to talk to you.'

David shoots me a look of concern, which I answer with a reassuring smile. He grudgingly takes himself out.

Peter watches till the door closes behind David, then turns to me. 'Everything OK?' Which I take to be code for *Was that guy bothering you?*

'Fine. David and I used to be close, before Charles. He was just checking up on me.'

'Close as in . . .?'

'As in friends. He may have wanted more, but I never did.'

I see Peter's shoulders relax a fraction. 'Seen much of him lately?'

'I haven't seen him at all since shortly before Emma was born. Things got . . . kind of awkward between us.'

'Awkward how?'

I sigh. I don't want to go into it, but if I say it's none of his business, I know what the answer will be: *Everything is the police's business in a murder investigation.* 'He knew things were bad with me and Charles. He offered to rescue me. I said no.'

Peter's eyebrows shoot up. 'Awkward indeed. He didn't pursue it at all?'

'No. I was pretty firm.'

He stares into space as if he's taking notes in his mind but doesn't want to pull out his notebook in front of me. Then he looks back at me. 'Any developments since this morning?'

'On the memory front? No. Nothing. It's been a busy day – I've hardly had time to think.'

'How about the tests?'

'Still waiting on results. Tomorrow morning, maybe.'

He nods. As he stands there, a tiny smile creeps on to his face, and I smile back. Then he kind of shakes himself. 'Better get going. You look like you could use some rest.'

'Yeah, I've had quite the parade of visitors today. I need a nap.'

He pats my shoulder and turns to go. 'See you tomorrow.'

I snuggle into the covers – which are not that snuggly, truth be told; I miss my down comforter – and pray for peaceful sleep. With no dreams.

*Peter*

I close Abby's door gently behind me. Dunstable's pacing a small oblong in the corridor. 'David? Let's go get a cup of coffee, shall we?' I don't want to talk outside Abby's room.

He hesitates, looking around as if for an escape route. But in the end he follows me.

In the cafeteria, I buy us both coffee and lead him to a table far from other diners. 'I understand you haven't been in contact with Abby for some time, is that right?'

He nods, not making eye contact.

'So what brings you here now?'

He shrugs. 'Thought she might need somebody.' He looks up at me, defiance in his eyes. 'A friend.'

I nod. 'Or maybe you're hoping to become more than a friend?'

He makes a dismissive gesture. 'Whatever. What's it to you, anyway?'

I choose my words carefully. 'Abby's personal life from this point forward is her own business, but anything that happened up to and including her husband's murder is my business. Any man who has designs on Abby is naturally a person of interest.'

'Designs!' He stares at me in disbelief. 'What kind of a word is that? I *love* Abby. Always have. I'd never do anything to hurt her.'

'What about something you might perceive as helping her?' Desperate for another suspect, I cut to the chase. 'Like getting her abusive husband out of the way?'

Dunstable scowls into his coffee. 'Maybe I thought about it. OK, fantasized about it at length. But I'm too much of a damn coward to do it for real.'

My gut is telling me this guy is genuine. He's clearly not a natural liar. But his whole manner suggests he's hiding something.

'Where were you on Monday afternoon?'

He blinks rapidly, looking over my shoulder. 'What time Monday afternoon?'

I still don't have the autopsy report with a more precise time of death, so I cut it wide. 'Between four and five thirty.'

He swallows. 'Must have been on my way home from work. Yeah, that's right. Did some errands on the way.'

'Where do you work?'

'SoftSell. Marketing software company in Cupertino.'

'And you live . . .?'

'South San Jose. Off Curtner.'

'And what time did you get home?'

'Uh . . . I don't know, I wasn't paying attention. Maybe five thirty, six?'

The difference between five thirty and six could be crucial, given the forty-five-minute drive from here to South San Jose. 'Can anyone vouch for your movements?'

He swallows again. 'Uh . . . somebody may have noticed what time I left work. We don't clock in or anything; people come and go, work from home sometimes. As for getting home . . . I share with two other guys, but neither of them was home when I got there, so I guess not.'

'What about the errands? Anyone likely to remember you? Store clerk, maybe?'

He shakes his head. 'Nah. I was in and out, here and there. One of a crowd.'

I raise a skeptical eyebrow, then pull out my notebook, flip to a blank page, and slide it across the table to him with a pen. 'Write down your contact info, please. Address, phone, email. Work and personal. Also the names and numbers of your housemates.'

He shoots me a look, then complies. His hand shakes a bit, and his writing is laborious, as if he rarely uses a pen. Makes sense for a programmer, I guess.

He slides the notebook back to me. Worst handwriting I've seen in a while that didn't come from a doctor, but I can make it out. Under the guise of entering his info into my phone, I sneak a snapshot of him so I'll have something to show to any potential witnesses. Not that I have any idea who they might be.

I skewer him with my omniscient-detective look, the one that says *You can't put anything over on me; I see right through you.* I slide the notebook into my inside breast pocket. 'I'll be in touch.'

# TWENTY-FIVE

*October 2017*

Having broken the news of Emma's condition to Jacqueline, I couldn't put off telling Charles any longer. When we got home from the family dinner, after I put Emma to bed, I found him in the living room pouring himself a neat whisky.

'Charles, I need to talk to you about something.'

'Can't it wait? I've been talked to enough for one day.' Charles Senior never missed an opportunity to harangue his son.

'I'm sorry, but it really can't. It's important.'

He sighed, downed the whisky in one gulp, poured himself another, then flopped on the couch. 'Fine.'

I perched on the opposite arm, my heart in my throat. 'You remember when you bought Emma that musical toy? And she wouldn't let a song play through?'

He grunted. I took that for a yes. 'I found out why. She couldn't hear the music. She's deaf.'

He stopped with his glass halfway to his mouth. 'She's what?'

'I had her tested. She has profound sensorineural hearing loss. She's completely deaf.'

Charles stared at his whisky for a moment, then threw his head back and poured it down his throat. 'Deaf. That's great. Just when I was starting to think maybe we could make a lawyer out of her after all, get her to stay a Crenshaw so Dad would have someone to carry on the line.' He slammed the tumbler down on the glass-topped coffee table so hard I was amazed neither of them broke. 'Who ever heard of a deaf lawyer?'

Putting aside my instinctive reaction to the idea that Charles had been planning to use Emma as a pawn in whatever sick game he and his father had been playing all his life, I forced myself to speak calmly and rationally. 'Deaf people do all kinds of things these days. Emma can be whatever she wants to be.'

Charles shot me a look of utter scorn and stomped off to his study.

That went well.

My neck began to ache and strange colored lights appeared before my eyes – the harbingers of a migraine. But I couldn't give in to it now.

After a minute, I composed myself and went after him. I opened the door without knocking. He sat at his desk, his chair swiveled to face the window.

'Her condition isn't irreversible. There's a treatment that has an excellent success rate with infants.'

He answered without turning around. 'What, some glorified hearing aid? So the whole world will know she has a disability?'

I flinched but kept it together enough to go on. 'No. It's a surgery. Cochlear implants. It translates audio signals into electrical signals the brain can interpret. Then there's some therapy to help the child learn to talk.'

'OK, so do the surgery. Anything to make her normal.'

I hesitated. 'The thing is, Charles . . . the surgery and the therapy afterward cost forty thousand dollars. And since it's still sort of experimental, our insurance won't cover it.'

At this he finally turned to face me. 'Forty – thousand – dollars? Do you think I'm made of money?' He held up his hand and pinched the base of his thumb. 'Ouch. Sorry, just flesh.'

My courage withered. 'I was hoping your parents might help. I asked your mother about it after dinner. She seemed to think there was some chance.'

Charles barked a laugh. 'With Dad? You are joking, right? He has no time for Emma. He won't part with a dime. And Mom doesn't have any money of her own.'

This only confirmed my own fears. But Jacqueline had been so positive. 'Don't we have any of it?'

Charles stood and strode over to where I was standing in the doorway. 'You want to know where my money is?' He picked up my left hand and wiggled the diamond cluster on my engagement ring. 'Here.' He pushed past me into the living room and swept his arm around to include all the furniture. 'Here.' He marched me to the garage door and opened it, pointing to my BMW. 'And here. Every penny of my salary is tied up in paying for the things we already have. Not to mention all the expensive crap you're always buying for yourself and the kid.'

That was a low blow. I'd never lost my Taylor attitude toward money. I spent little on myself and always shopped for the best bargains on Emma's clothes and equipment, often buying used. The only extravagances in our budget were those Charles himself insisted on, such as his plentiful supply of Macallan single malt.

'I'm not the one who spends a lot around here. That BMW wasn't my choice – we could sell it and buy a cheaper car.'

'And where would that get us? You seem to have forgotten we still owe as much as the car is worth.'

I wondered how I could be supposed to have forgotten something I had no means of knowing in the first place, since our finances – beyond my monthly housekeeping allowance – were a closed book to me. 'What about that?' I pointed to his Porsche. 'It's paid off, isn't it?' I didn't know much about car values, but I would have bet that Porsche was worth the full cost of the treatment plus the price of a more modest car.

Charles turned on me with a face so livid I shrank back instinctively. 'Do you seriously expect me to give up *my car*? The first thing I ever bought for myself? The symbol of everything I've achieved in my life?'

I stared at him in disbelief. Even for Charles, this was selfishness beyond the pale. 'But . . . it's for our daughter. For her only chance at a normal life.'

He leaned in until our noses were almost touching. '*Your* daughter. She's no good to me. *You* buy her a normal life.' He turned and strode back into the house.

That was when the first blackout happened. One minute I was standing in the garage with Charles's hateful words ringing in my ears. The next I was knocking on Ellen's door with Emma in my arms.

At first, I had no idea what had happened or how I'd gotten there. Ellen answered the door in her bathrobe, surprised at my visiting so late, and I made some excuse, hardly knowing what I was saying. She left me in the living room and went to make cocoa.

I cast my mind back to the devastating moment when Charles denied his daughter a normal future. I'd felt like a cartoon character who suddenly realizes he's walked off the edge of a cliff. The shock was nearly enough to send me unconscious again. But I pulled myself together and tried to reconstruct what had happened next.

I must have gone to the nursery, gotten Emma out of bed, picked up the diaper bag and my purse – I had them with me now – put them in the car, and strapped Emma into her car seat. Then I must have driven the hour from Santa Cruz to San Jose without being conscious of what I was doing. I shuddered to think what might have happened if whatever part of my brain had been operating the car had suddenly decided to shut down altogether in the middle of the highway.

Ellen returned with the cocoa. I laid the sleeping baby on the sofa beside me and took my mug gratefully in both hands, which had turned to ice.

'So what's up? It must be something to bring you here in the middle of the night.'

I glanced at my watch. 'It's only midnight.'

'That's the middle of the night when you have toddlers who wake up at six. And it's not like you to be up this late, let alone driving over the hill to see me.'

I sipped the cocoa, burning my tongue, but the pain was almost welcome. 'It's Charles.'

Ellen huffed. 'What has he done now?'

'I told him about Emma. The deafness. And the surgery. And he refused to do anything about it.'

'He refused to let her have the surgery?' Ellen's voice shrilled with disbelief.

'No, he just refused to pay for it. Any of it. He said she's my daughter and I can take care of it myself.'

Ellen sat back, her face frozen in shock. 'I can't believe it. He essentially disowned her?'

'He said she was *no use* to him. As if that's what kids are for.' I was still having trouble absorbing that myself. 'She's worth less to him than his precious car.'

Ellen slammed her palm against the couch, making Emma jiggle. I put my hand on the baby's belly to steady her.

'You've got to leave him,' she pronounced, sitting forward again. 'There is simply no other choice. You can't live this way, and neither can Emma. Imagine how scarred she'd be by growing up with a father who despises her.'

'At least she can't hear all his barbs,' I said bitterly. 'That's one mercy.'

'Not much of one. She can still perceive his attitude. And the older she gets, the worse it will be.'

The truth of this twisted my gut. 'But if I leave, how can I ever pay for the surgery?'

'How can you pay for it now? I don't see how leaving would make any difference.'

'It might make a difference with Jacqueline. I told her about it this afternoon. She's going to talk to Charles Senior.'

'And you think he'll come through? When his son won't?'

'There is a possibility. A slim one, granted, but he at least *has* the money. And if I left Charles, there'd be no chance at all.' Charles Senior would forget he'd ever had a granddaughter the moment the divorce papers were signed.

'So if he pays, wait till after she's had the surgery and everything, and then leave. Then he can't take the money back.'

'He'd probably find some way to sue me for it.' I sat back and passed my hand over my eyes, suddenly exhausted. 'I don't know, Ellen, I really don't think he's ever going to cough up at all.'

'So that leaves you right back where you started. What possible benefit can you get from staying married to Charles?'

I sighed. 'It's true he doesn't contribute much of anything positive to our lives except money to live on. And lately he's getting stingy with that. But with a deaf baby – how could I possibly cope? I could hardly go back to work if I can't get her treated. She'll need me every hour of every day.'

Ellen pounded the table. 'There has to be a way to pay for that treatment. Do you still have any savings of your own?'

'Less than a thousand.'

'We could sell off some of our investments. Let me talk to Pavel.'

I teared up at her generosity, but it wouldn't do. 'But that's for your retirement, your kids' college. I can't ask you to do that.'

'You're not asking. I'm offering. Give me a few days to see what I can talk him into.' She gave me a big, sisterly hug, which gave me the chance to hide my face, shattered by her love and support. 'Meanwhile, you start planning your Great Escape.'

\* \* \*

I couldn't wait until the next family dinner to find out how Jacqueline had fared. I gave her three days to talk to Charles Senior, then called her.

'Did you get a chance to ask him?'

'Oh, Abby, I'm so sorry.'

'That's OK, there's no huge rush.'

'No, I mean I did ask him. He said no.'

Although I'd expected that, I felt like the bottom had fallen out of my world. 'Does he not have the money?'

'Oh, he has it, all right. He doesn't think it's worthwhile to waste it on a *girl*. He doesn't believe in the treatment, either. I guess he heard about someone – a colleague's son, I think – who had it, and it didn't work. The boy never did learn to talk. So he says it's not worth wasting thousands on a girl who will never amount to anything.'

I sighed. 'That's basically what Charles said.'

We were both silent for a minute. The speechlessness of the Crenshaw wife, who despite repeated confirmations could never quite plumb the depths of her husband's profound selfishness.

'I wish I had money of my own, Abby dear. I'd give it to you in a heartbeat. Or if I had access to any of Charles's accounts, I'd take it in spite of him. I hope you know that.'

'Of course I do. And I do appreciate your efforts, Jacqueline.'

'Maybe you could do one of those online fundraising things. I saw one for an acquaintance who had cancer. Come Fund Us or something like that.'

'GoFundMe. I guess I could try.' A glimmer of hope, but it had its drawbacks. 'I hate the idea of exposing Emma's problem to the whole world that way, though. And Charles would have an absolute fit.'

'Maybe someone could do it for you. Anonymously. Your sister, perhaps? I'm afraid I don't have the technical smarts to volunteer for it myself.'

Of course. A way Ellen could help without impoverishing her own family – win-win. 'I'm sure she'd be willing. I'll talk to her.'

'I do wish you the best of luck. And maybe I could hit up some of my friends who have their own money.'

'Oh, but that would be so humiliating for you.'

'What does that matter when my granddaughter's hearing is at stake? Besides, I feel obscurely responsible. If I'd handled both

Charleses differently over the years, perhaps they'd be less intractable now.'

I'd had that thought myself from time to time, but I dismissed it as unworthy. What effect could Jacqueline's gentle tapping have had on the adamant that was her husband? And it was surely his fault, not hers, that his son was exactly like him. 'Not likely. Men like that are born, not made. At least that's my belief. Thanks for trying, anyway.'

'My very best love to you and dearest Emma. And we won't either of us give up.'

No. For my own sake, I'd sometimes been tempted to give up, shut down, and live out my half-life as Charles's Stepford wife. But with my daughter's future at stake, giving up was out of the question.

I called Ellen. 'No joy from the Crenshaws. But Jacqueline's not giving up. She suggested a GoFundMe, and she's going to canvass all her rich friends.'

'What a great idea! I could set up the GoFundMe for you.'

Good old Ellen – I didn't even have to ask. 'Can we make it anonymous? Charles would go through the roof at the publicity.'

'Theoretically we could, but a campaign is a lot more likely to be successful if it has names and pictures. People will look at Emma and their hearts will melt in a second. Followed by their pocketbooks.'

'Could you just use her picture and first name? Skip the Crenshaw?'

'I could do that. And when we share it on Facebook, we can block Charles from the posts. Of course, he might still see it through a mutual friend.'

'I guess I'll have to take that chance.' If Charles refused to do anything for his own daughter, he'd have to put up with a little public humiliation as I searched for alternative funding.

'While we're at it, do you want to go for a bit more than the forty thousand? Maybe round it to fifty? Give yourself a little cushion to start your new life with?'

Tempting, but I hesitated. 'That sounds like getting money under false pretenses.'

'Well, sometimes people keep giving after the goal is reached. Maybe you'll get some overflow that way.'

'That still seems wrong.'

'Abby, honey, give it a rest. Your scruples won't pay the bills. If you get more, it'll be because it's meant to be.'

'All right. How long will it take?'

'A typical deadline is thirty days out. Campaigns tend to lose traction after that. But I don't think we'll have any trouble reaching our goal in that time. And then some. I'll set the deadline for November fifteenth. Then you'll have the money by Thanksgiving, and maybe Emma can get the surgery before Christmas.'

'It's not that much of a rush. The doctor wants to wait till she's ten months old. That'll be March.'

'Still, we may as well do the fundraising now. Then you'll know if you need to pursue other avenues.'

Genuine hope thrilled through me for the first time since Emma's diagnosis. As long as I had Ellen, I would never be completely desperate.

She set up the page that evening and sent me a link. I saw my sister had sweetened the pot with a thousand-dollar gift of her own. I teared up at that. What a blessing that Ellen had married a tech exec who earned enough to fuel her natural generosity – and who cared enough himself to back her up.

# TWENTY-SIX

*Thursday morning, March 1, 2018*

*Peter*

Thursday morning. I only have one more day to come up with a suspect more promising than Abby. David Dunstable's looking good, but I'll have to find some way to place him at the scene. And I haven't ruled out Jacqueline Crenshaw with her mysterious ten thousand bucks. I'll deal with her first, then check on Dunstable's alibi.

Before I can head out, though, the lab reports come in. Not much useful. All the blood found at the scene matches Charles Crenshaw's.

No big surprise there. The glass that was on the coffee table held plain whisky. Can't get anything much from that.

Still waiting on the autopsy report. We had a spate of gang shootings last week, so the morgue is backed up. I tried to get this one moved to priority, but no luck. I call the medical examiner to check on progress.

'We've opened him up, and there's nothing we can see right off other than the obvious blunt-force trauma to the back of the head. But we're still waiting on toxicology. He had been drinking, I can tell you that, but I can't be sure how heavily.'

'Any guess what it was that hit him?'

'Something with a pretty sharp ninety-degree corner and straight lines. Couple inches thick. Doesn't fit any usual sort of weapon I can think of.'

No, it sure doesn't. But there is one thing it reminds me of: that glass coffee table. 'Did you find any bruising to his face? Or chest?'

'No bruising. Only the one big wound.'

That puts paid to my theory. 'Will you have the rest by end of day?'

'Maybe. Tomorrow morning for sure.'

'I'm running on a deadline here. Do the best you can. Please.'

I drive through intermittent drizzle back to Los Altos Hills. Pretty soon I'll be able to put the car on automatic pilot and have it get there on its own while I take a nap.

It's still fairly early in the day, and Jacqueline Crenshaw isn't quite as well put together as I've seen her before. I get the feeling she wasn't dressed when I arrived and threw something on. For a woman in her early fifties, she looks pretty good in yoga pants and a long sweater. These rich women have the time and money to live at the gym.

She asks Yolanda to bring in coffee, then sits down. 'What can I do for you this time, Detective?'

'I've been examining your bank records, Mrs Crenshaw. I see you made a check deposit of ten thousand dollars toward the middle of December and then withdrew the same amount a couple days later.'

She startles. 'What business is that of yours? And how did you get access to my accounts?'

'I subpoenaed them. It's standard practice for persons of interest in a murder case.'

'Persons of interest! Is that police code for suspects?'

I keep it bland. 'No, it just means people connected with the case.'

She collects herself. Yolanda appears with the coffee, and Mrs Crenshaw pours it out. '*Gracias*,' I say to Yolanda with a smile.

She grins her way out of the room. Mrs Crenshaw hands me my cup with a hint of cream. I take a sip. Delicious.

'So, about that ten thousand dollars. Where did it come from, and where did it go?'

She fiddles with her pearls. Even with yoga pants and a sweater, she wears pearls. 'You won't tell my husband?'

'Not unless I have to. If it's not relevant to the case, it won't go any further.'

She lets go of the pearls and drops her hands to her lap. 'I sold an old piece of jewelry. Something I inherited from my mother. I haven't worn it for years. If I'd had a daughter . . . but it wasn't Abby's style, and anyway she'd much rather have the money.'

'You gave the money to Abby?'

'Not directly. I contributed it to her fundraising account.'

'The GoFundMe for the cochlear implants?'

'Oh, you know about that? What am I saying, of course you do. Ellen set it up originally on GoFundMe. But they didn't get enough money within the thirty-day period. They only got about twenty-three thousand, and the cost is forty. So I gave the money to Ellen directly.'

'In cash?'

'I didn't want Charles to be able to trace it. Either Charles. I asked Ellen to meet me at the bank – we both use the same bank, fortunately – and I withdrew it and handed it over to her on the spot. She deposited it right away.'

I whistle. 'So Ellen is the custodian of all this money?'

'Yes. Abby was afraid if she put it in her own name, Charles might be able to get hold of it somehow.'

'This was back in December. But Emma hasn't had her implants yet?'

'No. I think they're still a few thousand short, and anyway, the doctor wanted to wait until Emma was ten months old. There's still about a month to go.'

This story is too plausible – if weirdly so – and too easily verifiable not to be true. 'Do you have a receipt from the sale of the jewelry?'

'Of course.' She goes to a small, elegant desk in a corner, unlocks a cubbyhole, and pulls out a slip of paper. 'Here you are.'

Handwritten receipt with date, description of item, and price paid. All in order. I'll check with Ellen Stepanovich about the money, but I'm sure she'll back up Mrs Crenshaw's story. I watch my promising suspect fly out the window.

I tuck the receipt into a small evidence bag. 'Mrs Crenshaw, I have to ask you a very uncomfortable question, but I need you to answer as truthfully as you can.'

She blanches. 'I'll try.'

This is one of those times when I hate my job. 'Your own grief aside, do you feel your family as a whole is better off for your son's death?'

She gasps, and her hand goes to her pearls again. They must be her safety blanket. 'What a question!'

'I know, but I have to ask.'

She stands, goes to the window, and looks out over the view as if drawing strength from it. 'Truthfully, I have to say yes, I do. Every one of us is better off. My husband found our son a disappointment; now that he's dead, he can delude himself that Charles would have shaped up one day. Of course, it does mean the end of the Crenshaw line, which is heartbreaking for my husband – but if Abby was leaving Charles, a son with her wasn't going to happen anyway.'

She turns back to face me. 'For Abby, the benefit is obvious. Dear little Emma will never have to experience her father's rejection of her again. And even for me—' She stops and makes a little choking sound. 'The fewer years he had on earth to make other people miserable, the less guilty I have to feel.' Her face goes stony. 'There. Are you satisfied?'

'I'm sorry, Mrs Crenshaw. I had to ask. Will you swear to me that you had nothing to do, in any way, with Charles's death?'

She draws herself up to the point that her flats seem like three-inch heels. 'In no way that I'm aware of, Detective. No. Acknowledging the mercy of my son's passing is a far cry from wanting, let alone causing, his death.'

What a woman. I'm not sure I'd want her in my family, but I

can't help admiring her. And something in me is relieved she didn't do it. 'Of course. Thank you, Mrs Crenshaw. I hope I won't have to bother you again.'

One suspect down, one to go. I'd give my badge for a bigger number. Let's hope Dunstable comes through.

I head first to his work. Office suite inside a big building. Door's on a keycard, so I have to buzz and wait to be admitted.

I flash my badge. 'Detective Peter Rocher. May I speak to the manager, please?'

The kid – well, he looks like a kid to me, probably fresh out of college – widens his eyes. I guess they don't get cops at the door every day. 'Uh, sure. I guess so. Follow me.' He leads the way through a bullpen of about a dozen open desks where every guy – and they are all guys – is glued to his own screen with headphones on. Who needs cubicles?

In the far corner of the room, a single large desk is set off by glass panels. A blond guy about my age – clearly senior to the rest of them – sits there in a Steve Jobs uniform of jeans and a black turtleneck. Homage to a hero, or delusions of grandeur? He alone of the whole bunch is not wearing headphones.

'Hey, Josh,' the kid says. 'Cop here to see you.'

Josh's expression mirrors the kid's initial one, but with a shade less of naive astonishment. He stands, and I flash my badge and introduce myself again.

'Josh Atkins,' he says, shaking my hand. 'What can I do for you?' He gestures to a guest chair in front of his desk.

I sit down. 'I'm checking on the movements of one of your employees. David Dunstable.'

More surprise. 'David? Is he a witness or something? Last guy I'd expect to be in any trouble.'

'It's just routine. He has a tangential connection to a case I'm working on in Santa Cruz. We have to check up on everyone.' Not all that routine, really, but I won't get him in trouble with his boss until I have to.

'I see. What specifically do you want to know?'

'What time he left the office Monday afternoon.'

'This past Monday? I have no idea.' He stands and looks out over the bullpen. 'He's not at his desk today. Must be working from home. I'll ask the guys.' He gestures to me to follow, then steps outside his glass box to a bank of switches on the adjacent wall. He flips one of them off and on a few times.

Must be a prearranged signal, because every guy looks up, pulling off the headphones. 'Listen up, gang. Detective Rocher here needs to know what time David left work on Monday. Anybody notice? Remember?'

Looks like the no-privacy culture here extends beyond the lack of cubicles. I wouldn't have chosen to expose Dunstable this way, but I guess the word would have spread pretty quickly even if I'd interviewed them all one by one.

They exchange baffled looks, some of them literally scratching their heads. After a minute, one guy pipes up. His desk backs up to an empty one I presume to be Dunstable's. 'Yeah, I think it was Monday – he left early, around four. Said he had an appointment.'

'You *think* it was Monday?' That was only three days ago. I need him to be sure.

'Uh . . . yeah. Definitely Monday. I remember because I was watching the clock myself – I had a date that night.' He blushes purple as a teasing 'oooh' goes around the room.

I make a note. 'Thank you. And you are . . .?'

He blinks. 'Gabe. Gabriel Muñoz.'

'Thank you, Mr Muñoz. Anybody confirm that?' I look around at a sea of blank faces. Apparently nobody notices much around here beyond his own screen. Can't say I'm surprised.

I turn to the boss, Atkins. 'That's all I need. Thank you for your time.'

'No problem. Glad we could help.' He turns to address the room. 'OK, guys, fun's over. Back to work.' Headphones go back on, faces snap back to screens. You have to wonder if these guys have any sense of time passing. Do they ever eat? Sleep? Talk to each other? Go to the john? My job's no piece of cake, but at least I get to move around, meet people, see more of the world than a computer screen.

I shut the security door behind me and think about my next move. Dunstable's non-alibi is confirmed so far. Leaving here at four, before the peak rush-hour traffic, would have given him ample time to drive to Santa Cruz, kill Crenshaw, and disappear before

Abby called 911. But not enough time to get back over the hill and home by five thirty. Six would have been pushing it, but possible. I need to talk to his housemates.

I check my watch. Ten thirty. Not likely they'll be home in the middle of the morning, but I have to try. I note the length of the drive from SoftSell to Curtner Avenue – roughly half an hour at this low-traffic time of day. Nothing there to make his story implausible, nor to prove it either.

His place turns out to be buried in a huge warren of identical condos that crawls up the side of a hill like a fungus. Takes me ten minutes to find the right number. I knock, wait a minute, knock louder. If anybody is home, he's probably glued to a screen with headphones on like all Dunstable's coworkers.

Finally, the door opens. Not Dunstable, but except for his darker hair and complexion, he fits the same basic description – jeans and nerdy T-shirt, a little overweight, a little unkempt, expression irritated at the interruption. 'Yeah?' he says. 'Make it quick. I'm in the middle of a game.'

I flash my badge. 'Is David Dunstable here?'

The housemate looks around vaguely. 'David? Nah.' He screws up his eyes. 'Probably at work. Or Starbucks – he calls it his second office.'

Dunstable's absence suits me for the moment. I make a guess at which of the two housemates this might be. 'Are you Mr Sanjit Chatterjee?'

He nods.

'I'm sorry to interrupt, but I'm going to need a few minutes of your time.'

'Oh, hell. I guess you better come in.' He leaves the door open, walks over to a shiny new laptop lying on the ratty old couch, hits a couple keys and shuts it. Sits down. He doesn't offer me a chair, but I find one at the table and pull it around to face him. 'What's this about?' he says.

'I'm checking on the movements of David Dunstable on Monday afternoon, February twenty-sixth. Nothing to worry about, just routine.'

He makes a baffled face. 'Monday? I don't know. He goes to work – or Starbucks – he comes home. So do I, so does Sung. We don't keep track of each other.'

'Were you here on Monday between five and six p.m.?'

He runs a hand over his hair. 'Monday . . . No, I think I was out. That's right, Sung and I grabbed a beer and a bite after work. Didn't get home till about . . . seven, seven thirty?'

'And was David home at that time?'

He looks at me like I'm from another planet. 'How should I know? His door was shut. He didn't come out and say hi, but then he wouldn't. We're not buds. Sung and I hang out together, but David just rents a room.'

'You didn't see him come home any time later that night?'

'Nah. But Sung and I went to our own rooms right away. I watched the tube for a while, then went to bed.'

'You didn't hear him come in or move around at all?'

'My room's upstairs and David's is back there.' He jerks a thumb behind him. 'Plus I had earphones in. He could have brought an army through and I wouldn't have heard.'

'And I suppose the same applies to Mr Li?'

'Sung? Yeah, for sure. He likes action movies and he plays them loud. He wouldn't have heard a tornado.'

I stand. 'All right. Thank you for your time, Mr Chatterjee. I'll let you get back to your game.'

He pulls the laptop on to his lap and opens it, already lost to the world. I show myself out.

# TWENTY-SEVEN

*October 2017*

With the fundraiser rolling – if slowly for now – I had some hope that Emma's deafness would eventually be cured. I began to think seriously about leaving Charles. I was sure he would use every trick in his divorce lawyer's book to make sure I left with nothing, but with Emma so young and with the evidence I could bring of Charles's neglect of her since her birth (such as his non-attendance at birth classes and at every medical appointment beginning with my pregnancy), I hoped I'd at least get out of it with custody and the statutory minimum of child support. Beyond that, I didn't care. No amount of property or alimony could compensate for what I'd gone through as Charles's wife.

Ideally, I'd leave shortly before Emma's surgery. I didn't want to risk her ever hearing and understanding a word of her father's scorn. We'd have to live with Ellen for a while at first, because I wouldn't be able to go to work right away. Emma would need constant attention, someone speaking to her every waking minute, if the implants were to do their job and help her brain translate the electrical impulses of human speech into actual communication.

After the therapy was done, if I could pass the bar exam and land a junior position with a law firm, I might barely be able to afford a tiny apartment and a full-time trained nanny. Leaving Emma in order to work long hours would be heartbreaking enough – no way would I dump my precious daughter in a group daycare or with some young girl who would spend all day playing on her phone or talking to her boyfriend.

Finances would be a whole lot easier if I could move to a less expensive area. But that would mean leaving my only support system – Ellen and Jacqueline – behind. Of course, I might lose Jacqueline anyway, in leaving Charles, but my feeling was that her love for her granddaughter would prove stronger than her loyalty to her son.

My biggest concern about the whole plan was my migraines – and especially that recent blackout. How could I hold down a job and care for a baby on my own when I was incapacitated every few days and might occasionally lose whole chunks of my life? I didn't dare consult a doctor. Word might get back to Charles one way or another – through the old-boy network, which I was sure superseded doctor–patient confidentiality – and if he knew, he might fight me for custody of Emma. Not because he would genuinely want custody – he'd probably dump her on his mother – but merely to hurt me in the deepest way possible. My only hope was that once I was free of the stress of living with Charles, the migraines would cease on their own. Of course, I would then have the stress of being a single working mother, but surely that could never be as bad as what I was going through now.

One afternoon in late October, when the GoFundMe account had reached nine thousand, six hundred dollars, I left my laptop open on the kitchen table while I went to get Emma up from her nap. I'd minimized the browser window, but the tab for the fundraising site was still open – along with tabs for job searches and housing options. When I came back into the kitchen after changing Emma's diaper, Charles was there. I hadn't heard him come in.

He wasn't standing by the laptop, but he had the air of having just darted across the room, and the look in his eyes made me wary. I decided to pretend nothing had happened. Casually shutting the laptop with my free hand – and noting the browser was still minimized – I said, 'You're home early. Everything OK?'

He shrugged. 'Felt a little off-color. Might be coming down with a bug.'

'Why don't you lie down and rest? Can I get you something? Ginger ale? Chicken soup?'

'Uh, no, thanks anyway. I think I'll lie on the couch in the study and watch some golf. That's pretty soporific.' He grinned, something resembling the old smile that had captivated me what seemed like eons ago – in actuality, it was only about two years – when we first met. Could the world have turned on its head in such a short time?

'Fine. Let me know if you need anything.'

He was acting too nice, too innocent. I suspected he wasn't ill at all but had simply used that excuse to come home early and catch me out – doing what, in his perverted imagination, I had no idea. Having sex with the delivery guy on the kitchen table, perhaps.

I sat down to nurse Emma and reopened the laptop. I brought up the browser – it was still open to Facebook, where I'd left it. The GoFundMe link did not appear on the screen, but one of Ellen's daily links to the site showed up when I scrolled down. I sighed. No way to know what, if anything, Charles might have seen, but he would undoubtedly begin punishing me for it soon. I would have to be more careful.

That evening, Charles claimed a miraculous recovery and insisted on a three-course dinner. I was tired before I even started cooking, as Emma had had a fussy afternoon with teething and the beginnings of a cold. By the time I'd put her to bed and cleaned up the kitchen, I could feel the migraine coming on. That meant sleep was going to be impossible. I took a hot bath, then went into the living room to watch Netflix until the visual and aural stimuli became unbearable.

I started watching an episode of *Father Brown* that I'd seen a couple of times before – the one where he first encounters Flambeau. Halfway through the episode, I blinked, then came to with a jerk and found myself at the end of a different episode in the next season. I assumed that, contrary to expectation, I'd fallen asleep, but there on the coffee table in front of me were the remains of a bowl of ice cream and a cup of hot chocolate – which had definitely not been there before. As far as I knew, sleep-eating was not in my skill set.

A long shudder went through me. Another blackout. I'd cherished some slim hope the first one had been a one-off. Was this going to become another regular feature in the horror show that was my life?

What if Charles had awakened and found me in the middle of it? Would he have realized anything was wrong? I had no idea, beyond the slim evidence of the snack dishes, how I might have acted, whether I would have seemed normal or robotic and glassy-eyed, whether his usually unperceptive self would have caught on to what was happening.

I turned off the television, cleaned up the dishes, and went back to bed. Charles appeared to be fast asleep beside me. I could only hope.

*November 2017*

Over the next month, I watched the tally in the GoFundMe account rise with frustrating slowness. If I'd felt safe sharing the page myself, so that my own friends could see it, it would no doubt have fared better. But Ellen's and Jacqueline's friends were one step removed, and the friends they shared it with were removed even further. So it wasn't surprising that most of the gifts were small.

At the end of the thirty days, Ellen came by to commiserate with me over the news: we had raised only twenty-three thousand dollars. A little more than half what was needed.

'One ear's worth,' I said bitterly. 'Of course it doesn't work that way. How will I ever find the rest of the money?'

Ellen stroked my back as we sat on the couch, watching Emma playing happily on a blanket. 'We'll find a way.'

Her words rolled off me. 'I'll never be able to leave Charles,' I wailed. 'Emma is going to need me every minute until she's an adult. I'll never be able to go to work and earn enough money to live on.'

Big-sister indignation overcame Ellen's optimism. 'This would be the perfect time to bump him off for the insurance money,' she growled.

'What insurance money? Charles isn't insured. At least, not that I know of.' I was shocked that this was my first thought, rather than *I could never kill anyone.*

'Holy crap. How does he get away with that? You can't even say you're better off with him dead than alive – I mean, not from a monetary point of view.' She drummed her fingers on her knee. 'Does he have any savings? Investments? Retirement accounts?'

'I suppose he must have at least some retirement. But he's only been working a year and a half, remember. It can't amount to much yet. I have no idea about the rest of it. He never tells me a thing about money.' I shot Ellen a sharp look. 'Besides, you can't be serious. We can't actually bump him off.'

Ellen heaved a sigh. 'No, I suppose not. And I have a feeling praying for his death would not go over well with the Man Upstairs. But we can at least pray for a miracle for Emma.'

'You do that. I'm all prayed out.' Any faith I retained from childhood had been burnt out of me by my travesty of a marriage, by the fact that my daily prayers that something would change for the better were going, to all appearances, completely unanswered. I had no hope left.

I'd had a stiff neck all day. After Ellen left, the phantom lights and noises began. It was Charles's night to go out with the guys, but my babysitting budget for the month was exhausted. I got Emma to bed as quickly as possible, then went to bed myself. If I blacked out again, maybe I'd simply stay there and not do any harm.

I came to myself in daylight. It had been twilight of a November evening when I went to bed. Now I wasn't in bed. I was in the nursery, getting ready to change Emma's diaper.

In a way, this was reassuring. It suggested I could continue to function somewhat normally while I was blacked out. Whether I always did so was a question I couldn't answer.

I pulled the old diaper off and gasped. The skin of Emma's bottom was red and raw, and the diaper was full to bursting with urine and mushy brown poop. How long had it been since she was changed?

There was no clock in the nursery, and I didn't have a hand free to check my phone. Hastily I cleaned Emma's bottom, applied diaper cream and powder, put a fresh diaper on her, and changed her sodden pajamas for a clean shirt and pants. By this time she was wailing for milk, so I sat in the nursery rocking chair and offered her the breast. At last I had a hand free. I pulled out my phone.

Ten a.m. I'd been out for about sixteen hours.

Much of that might have been normal sleep. Could a blackout begin while one was asleep? What would be the difference? How could anyone tell? Maybe the dreams of sleep would be noticeably weirder than any semi-consciousness during a blackout. I thought back, trying to capture any dreams from the night before, but I came up blank.

And what about Charles? When I didn't get up this morning, had he assumed I was just sleeping in? Or did I get up and make him breakfast without knowing it, but still neglect Emma? Surely not that; if I'd been capable of doing anything, I would have cared for Emma first. Or had Charles never come home? He'd been known to stay out all night before.

Thank God Emma was not yet capable of climbing out of her crib. Only think what could have happened if she'd been roaming free around the house.

With a rush of belated fear and relief, I hugged my darling baby to me so closely that she broke away from the nipple and glanced up at me in confusion. I relaxed my hold and stroked her hair. 'I'm sorry, sweetheart. I'm just glad you're OK. You go right back to nursing. I'm so, so sorry I neglected you for so long.' A mother's instinct to talk to her baby could not be inhibited by anything so trivial as deafness. I was convinced that in some mysterious way she could still understand.

When Emma had finished nursing, I took her into the kitchen. I needed some breakfast myself.

I put the baby in the highchair with a teething toy and took a carton of eggs out of the fridge. It felt strangely light, and I opened it to find it empty. This carton had had ten eggs in it the day before; of that I was absolutely certain. Charles never ate more than three eggs at a time, and anyway he refused to cook for himself; if I wasn't around to feed him breakfast, he would grab something at Starbucks along with his coffee. I had previous evidence that Blackout Abby was prone to the munchies – but *ten eggs*? And if I had somehow managed to eat all those eggs, even if it was in the middle of the night, surely I wouldn't be so hungry now.

I looked around the kitchen. No dirty frying pan or spatula. No dirty plate in the sink or dishwasher. No clean ones in the dish drainer either. I checked the garbage. No eggshells. No whole eggs. The disposal was broken, so that wasn't an option.

Either a thief had broken into the house and stolen most of a dozen eggs – and nothing else that I could see – or I myself had left the house in order to dispose of them. The first was ridiculous, the second too bizarre to contemplate.

I glanced down at my clothes. I was wearing a sweater, jeans, and sneakers, whereas last night I'd changed into a nightgown before going to bed. I checked the soles of my shoes. Clean. I went into the bedroom and checked my slippers. Also clean. I went into the garage and checked the big garbage bins. No eggs or shells. And none lying around in the yard.

There was only one explanation. I must be going out of my mind.

# TWENTY-EIGHT

*Thursday morning, March 1, 2018*

*Peter*

Most of a morning checking up on Dunstable has gotten me precisely nowhere. I change direction and head back to Santa Cruz. If I can't prove he was or wasn't in San Jose at the time of the murder, maybe I can prove he was in Santa Cruz.

I drive to the Crenshaws' block and look around. The house-to-house turned up nobody who saw anyone around the house at the crucial time. But that doesn't mean someone couldn't have been hiding. If Dunstable, for example, had been lying in wait for

Crenshaw to get home from work, he would surely have found a concealed location to lurk in.

The house to the left of the Crenshaws' has a *FOR SALE* sign at the curb. Could mean it's unoccupied. I go to the door, knock, get no response. Casually peek in the windows – no furniture. It's empty, all right. I try the door – locked tight. But the yard is surrounded by a high hedge – piece of cake to hide behind it, with no one in the house to know or care.

I pace the length of the hedge where it borders the street and turns to run alongside the Crenshaws' property. Opposite their living-room window, there's a gap around eye level, big enough to see through without being seen. And right below the gap, in the dirt, is a pull tab from a soda can. It's lying on top of the ground, clean. Bingo. I photograph the tab in place, then bag it. Probably too small to get a fingerprint from, but it's worth a try.

Somebody was here within the last few days – we had rain over the weekend, so if the pull tab had been there then, it would have been beaten into the mud. Now all I have to do is find out who. My money's on Dunstable, but I haven't ruled out the possibility of a Mr X who hasn't appeared in the case yet. Or a Ms X – sounds like Crenshaw may have made more female enemies than male in his short life.

Time for a second house-to-house with a slightly different focus. May as well start with the nosy neighbor – the one who stays glued to her window. I check my notes – Mrs Ravenscroft, right across the street. Perfect.

I knock, and she answers right away. Probably been watching me. Little old lady with piercing, squinty black eyes. 'Hello, Officer,' she says before I can pull out my badge. My car's not marked, either – does she remember me from the other times I was on the street?

She smiles brightly. 'How can I help?'

'Mrs Ravenscroft? I'm Detective Peter Rocher. I'm following up on your interview with Officer Spinelli the other day. May I come in?'

'Of course.' She stands aside. I walk into a room that could have been lifted from a seventies issue of *Better Homes & Gardens* – the 'rustic' look with brown plaid plush upholstery and embroidered sayings framed in rough wood on the walls. My grandmother's house looked like this when I was little, but she finally got around to redecorating about twenty years ago.

Mrs Ravenscroft motions me to one of the plush chairs. It sags alarmingly in the middle, so I sit on the edge of it, hoping it will bear my weight. I'm not especially heavy, but I must have fifty pounds on her – she's not much bigger than the bird she's named for.

'Would you like a cup of coffee? It's fresh.'

I'd die for one, actually, but I don't want to distract her. Besides, I'd be willing to bet she makes Folgers or Maxwell House in a percolator. 'No, thank you.' She perches on a chair across from me, bird eyes bright.

'Your statement to Officer Spinelli was very helpful. But I want to ask you to think on a larger scale.'

She blinks rapidly, smiling. She's in her element. 'Anything I can do.'

'I'd like you to think back over the last, say, couple of weeks. Have you seen anyone on the block who doesn't belong here? Not a resident or a delivery person or anything like that – a stranger, kind of hanging around?'

She puts a coy finger to her chin. 'Let me see . . . Oh, yes, there was that one young man who kept coming by to check on the Hawkins house. That's the one that's for sale, next to the Crenshaws'. He wasn't dressed like a real estate agent – too scruffy. And he didn't have any tools with him, so I don't think he was a gardener or a workman. He didn't even have a truck.'

This sounds promising. 'Did you notice what he was driving?'

'Bless you, no. He wasn't driving at all. He always came on foot. Around the corner from Miller Street.'

Probably parked his car where it would be out of sight, at least from the Crenshaws'. Or he could conceivably have come by bus.

'How many times did you see him?'

'Goodness, I don't know. Quite a few times. Once or twice a week since the Hawkinses moved away – that's a couple of months now. I guess the real estate market must be slow for the house to be on the market so long.'

Sounds like a stalker to me. 'And what did this person do, exactly?'

'He'd go in through the gate and come out again an hour or two later.' She frowns. 'I couldn't see any more past that unsightly hedge of theirs. I do hope the next owners will trim it down. It's quite an eyesore.'

*And quite a hindrance to your surveillance*, I add to myself. 'Can you tell me what the man looked like?'

'Oh, yes. He was about medium height, on the heavy side. Brownish hair, kind of scruffy-looking, you know – hair a little too long, always looked like he forgot to shave that morning but not a real beard. Glasses . . . always wearing jeans and a gray – oh, what do they call those things? Like a sweatshirt with a zipper and a hood on top.'

I suppress a smile. 'A hoodie?'

'That's it. I knew I'd heard it on the television.' She smiles triumphantly, as if this one fact would seal the case. 'A gray hoodie.'

Dunstable to a T. I pull out my phone and find the surreptitious photo I took of him. 'Is this the man?'

She takes the phone gingerly, as if afraid to break it, and peers at the screen. 'Yes, that's him. I'm sure of it.' She hands the phone back to me. 'How clever of you to already have a picture of him! Is he'– she leans forward and speaks in a stage whisper – '*known to the police?*'

I ignore that and make a business of putting my phone away. 'Did he always come at the same time of day?'

She nods. 'Around twilight. Five or five thirty. I didn't always see him leave – I generally turn on the television at seven o'clock. And it's dark by that time anyway, this time of year.'

This woman's as good as a security camera. Maybe better.

'That's very helpful, Mrs Ravenscroft. Now, I want you to think carefully for me, please. Did you see this man on Monday? The day Mr Crenshaw was killed?'

She widens her eyes. 'Oh, yes. I remember perfectly. He came early that day, before five. But after the police cars showed up, he left. He seemed in a bit of a hurry – looking around like he didn't want to be seen.'

I make a note, trying not to show my irritation. 'Mrs Ravenscroft, why didn't you mention this to Officer Spinelli at the time?'

She widens her eyes in hurt surprise. 'He didn't ask. He only wanted to know who had come to the Crenshaws' house. I never saw this hoodie man go as far as the Crenshaws' – only into the Hawkinses' yard, as he always does.'

Right. I don't know whether to be ticked off at Mrs Ravenscroft or at Spinelli for being so narrow and literal. But at least I have the info now.

'Has this hoodie man been back at all since Monday?'

'Oh, no. Not that I've seen.' She smiles brightly. 'I expect all you policemen scared him away.'

That, or he no longer has any reason to come now that the Crenshaw house is empty.

I stand. 'Thank you for your time, Mrs Ravenscroft. You've been extremely helpful.'

She stands, too. 'Oh, must you go so soon, Detective?' As if we'd been having a friendly chat. She must be starved for company.

'I'm afraid so. I'll be in touch if we need anything else.' I give her my best nice-young-man smile.

She walks me to the door, then stands there waving as if sending off a favorite grandson. I almost wish I could stay and keep her company for a while. The chorus of 'Eleanor Rigby' runs through my head.

But I'm a cop, not a social worker. I head back to the Hawkins yard for one more look around.

If Mrs Ravenscroft didn't see Dunstable leave through the front gate until after we showed up on Monday, there must be some other way from the Hawkins yard into the Crenshaws' – a gap in the hedge or a gate in the back yard. Either that, or Dunstable is not my man. But I won't think about that quite yet.

I examine the length of hedge that separates the two properties and see nothing like a gap that a man could fit through. The hedge continues along the side of the house, but in the back it stops and is replaced by a board fence of about the same height that goes all the way around the yard. No gap between hedge and fence, unless you're a rabbit. No gate.

It wouldn't be easy to climb this fence – it's just flat boards over here, with the horizontal supports on the Crenshaw side – but it might be possible. I give it a running jump and barely manage to scramble to get my elbows over the top, then drop back down. And I work out. The only parts of his body Dunstable appears to exercise are his fingers and his mouth.

Nevertheless, I'm not pronouncing death on this lead yet. I'll get the forensics guys to go over the yard with a microscope. He could

have used a ladder or something to give him a boost, though I don't
see any indentations in the ground to suggest that. But if they find
a fiber of his sweatshirt on this fence, he's dead meat.

*Abby*

Late Thursday afternoon, Owen comes in for the first time since
Tuesday. I'm glad I had the chance to shower and freshen up. I'm
wearing a nightgown and robe I chose myself, a modest ivory nylon
set with lace.

'Got some results, finally,' Owen says. He pulls up a stool next
to the bed and fires up his iPad.

'The CT scan and the MRI yielded absolutely nothing abnormal.
Just as I thought. The EEG showed some patterns we typically
associate with migraine sufferers. So it looks like I was right after
all.' He grins.

'What about the blood work?'

'Negative on any substance or infection known to cause blackouts. You're in the clear. So the good news is, the blackouts are
migraine related, not due to something more serious like epilepsy
or meningitis.' He makes a face. 'The bad news is, we don't have
any idea how to treat them.'

'But you said they'd probably get better on their own, right? I've
definitely felt better since – well, for the last couple days.'

He nods. 'There's an excellent chance they will. Although I know
single motherhood can have its own kind of stress.'

'Yeah, but at least I won't feel like I'm going crazy all the time.
Like everything that's wrong is all my fault somehow. I don't think
anything could be as stressful as that.'

He looks me in the eye, head cocked. 'Tell me more about feeling
like you're going crazy.'

'It was the blackouts. The weird things that happened. Like one
time, I seem to have somehow evaporated most of a dozen eggs.'

'Evaporated? What do you mean?'

'I went to make breakfast after a blackout, and ten eggs were
missing from a carton. I'm absolutely positive they were there the
night before. And Charles has never cooked a thing since Emma
was born. I looked all over, and I couldn't find any trace of them.
No shells in the garbage, nothing. I knew I couldn't have eaten them

all, because I was still ravenously hungry. So I must have made them vanish somehow.'

'Hmm.' He gets that concentrated kind of frown. 'I don't think blackouts give you magical powers. There must be some logical explanation.' He winks at me. 'Maybe that detective friend of yours can figure it out.'

'Peter? Have you met him?'

'Briefly, the other day. Seems like a nice guy. For a cop. Pretty concerned about you. And not just as a suspect.' He gives me a sly little grin.

So I'm not imagining the softness in Peter's eyes when he looks at me. That sends a little wave of warmth all through me.

'Is that all?' Owen says. 'I mean, is that kind of thing all that makes you think your mental state is fragile?'

'Yeah, pretty much.'

'Based on that, I don't think there's anything wrong with your mind. But if it would make you feel better, I could refer you for a psychological evaluation. In fact, talking to a therapist wouldn't be a bad idea in light of everything you've been through. Post-traumatic stress is a real possibility.'

Those dreams. If anything could stop me having those dreams . . . 'Yeah. I think that would be good.'

He scribbles on his iPad. 'I'll have Doctor Georgiou come in and see you this evening. Then, if you want, you can continue on an outpatient basis. Since all the tests are done and you seem to be doing well physically, we can't justify keeping you cooped up in here any longer. I'm ordering your discharge for tomorrow morning.'

'Wow.' I'm a little stunned. This hospital room is all the home I have, for now. I can't go back to that house, even if the police would let me, which I doubt. I guess I'll have to impose on Ellen for a while. Till I figure out what I'm going to do with the rest of my life.

But I'll finally be with my baby again. It doesn't matter where I am, as long as I can be with her.

Owen says goodbye – with a handshake, like *really* goodbye. I'll have to do without that grin from now on.

# TWENTY-NINE

*November and December 2017*

The Thanksgiving holiday seemed liked black irony to me. What did I have to be thankful for? Emma and I were still alive. Period. I wasn't even allowed to spend the day with Ellen and her family, which would have made it bearable. No, Charles and I had to go eat with his parents.

Which would mean an entire afternoon and evening of listening to Charles Senior disparaging his son, daughter-in-law, and granddaughter, and to Charles lamely trying to defend himself (not Emma or me). Which in turn would lead to a night of Charles taking his frustration out on me.

Lately, I'd begun almost to wish he would go ahead and hit me instead of devising ever new forms of emotional and/or sexual torture. At least I'd have bruises to show for it. I could go out in the world with a purpled face, and somebody would be bound to ask, 'Did your husband hit you?' I could say a tearful yes, and the kind stranger would take me to the police station, where I could describe what had happened and get sympathy and action instead of shame and disbelief. I could press charges against Charles and get him put away once and for all.

But I could never describe, even to Ellen, all the twisted tortures he actually put me through. I didn't even have the words.

At least, I thought as I dressed in my best for Thanksgiving dinner, I now had Jacqueline on my side. Perhaps she would even stand up for her son this time and help him to come home less defeated, less humiliated, less full of blind anger that he had to pour out on someone else because he could never express it to his dad. I almost pitied him at moments like these – at least, until he drew his invisible weapons on me.

The dinner, at any rate, was fabulous, catered by a highly exclusive restaurant so Yolanda could have the day off. If only I could have become temporarily deaf like Emma, I might have enjoyed it.

And Jacqueline and I did get several hours to ourselves while the guys watched the obligatory semiannual football game in the den.

Jacqueline smiled down at Emma as she played on a blanket on the immaculate carpet of the living room. 'She gets more precious every day, doesn't she?' she said to me. 'Who do you think she looks like?'

'Well, she seems to have your hair,' I said tactfully. 'I think she has my mother's eyes. For the rest, I'm not quite sure. I don't think she's going to be anybody's mini-me. She'll just be her own sweet self.'

Jacqueline dangled a plastic chain for Emma to grab at, like a kitten. 'How's the fundraising going?'

My momentary good humor vanished. 'It isn't.'

She looked up sharply. 'What do you mean?'

'The GoFundMe page had a time limit, and it expired. We've only raised twenty-three thousand dollars.'

'Oh, Abby!' Her distress was genuine. 'I'm so sorry. I was sure we could do better than that.' She pondered for a minute, then stood. 'Come with me.'

I scooped Emma up from the floor, and Jacqueline led me into the master bedroom. From her dressing-table drawer, she took a long blue velvet box. She laid it on the table and opened it to reveal an ornate, old-fashioned necklace sparkling with sapphires and diamonds. I caught my breath at its loveliness.

'This belonged to my mother, and I had planned to give it to you or Emma one day. It's valued at ten thousand dollars. Would you rather I sell it and give the money to the fund?'

No contest. Beautiful as the necklace was, I couldn't imagine wearing it, and no mere thing could compete with Emma's hearing. 'But are you sure you want to part with it? I mean, it is your heirloom.'

'I haven't worn it since my debutante ball, thirty-odd years ago. I think the setting is rather hideous, truthfully, though the stones are lovely, of course. I'd be much happier to see its value do Emma some real, permanent good.'

I gave Jacqueline an impulsive hug. Tears sprang to her eyes as she hugged me back.

'Thank you, Jacqueline. That is the most generous thing anyone has ever done for me. Now maybe I'll' – I stopped myself. I'd been about to say, *Maybe I'll be able to leave Charles after all.* But I didn't feel sure enough of my ground with Jacqueline for that. Instead, I finished, 'Maybe I'll be able to find the rest of the money.'

'Yes, of course, you'll still have seven thousand dollars to go. And I don't dare sell anything Charles has given me – though I have plenty of jewels I never wear. He'd be sure to decide to inventory them or revalue them or something, and then there'd be hell to pay.'

I nodded, understanding exactly what she meant. 'I can't expect you to do everything. I'm sure we'll find the rest somehow.'

I was already seeing one miracle. Maybe it was possible to believe there could be another.

One night in December, I went to bed early with a migraine. Charles had let me know he wouldn't be coming home that night. I didn't ask why; his absence was always a relief, and I didn't want to jinx it by questioning.

I woke up groggy at eight thirty a.m. and stumbled to the nursery in a panic. Emma normally awoke no later than seven. I couldn't understand why she wasn't crying her head off by now.

I opened the nursery door. The crib was directly in my line of sight – and it was empty.

'Emma!' I cried, coming fully into the room. I whipped my head around in terror, certain my baby had been kidnapped.

Then I saw her. She was sitting on the floor, surrounded by dirty clothes and blankets, tossing them gleefully about. She'd managed to pull the hamper over.

I ran to snatch her up out of the laundry, sobbing her name over and over. I hugged her tight as my mind raced through all the disastrous things that might have happened but didn't. She could have fallen while climbing out of the crib and hit her head. She could have gotten into something dangerous instead of merely the odd pee- and poop-stained pair of pajamas. She could have become tangled in the laundry and smothered herself. She could have been in a frenzy of fear and hunger instead of playing happily alone.

But the biggest question of all was, how on earth had she gotten out of her crib? And why was she not crying with hunger? I held her a little away from me to take a better look. She was dressed in daytime clothes, though I had definitely put her to bed in pajamas the night before. I felt her diaper. It was dry.

Emma was seven months old. She could sit on her own and had begun to creep a bit, but she had not yet pulled herself to standing. I couldn't believe she might have the strength and coordination to climb safely over the high bars of the crib and lower herself to the floor. And to change her own diaper and dress herself? Maybe in an alternate universe. I screwed up my scrambled brain to remember what day it was. Tuesday? Maybe Wednesday. But definitely not Friday, so it couldn't have been Consuelo who got her up.

Could Charles have come home earlier in the morning, to shower and change, perhaps? He never lifted a finger to care for Emma, so I couldn't imagine he might have gotten her up, changed and fed her, then left her to play while I slept. And if he had by some miracle managed to get through her morning routine, surely even he, undisputed holder of the Useless Father of the Year award, would have known better than to leave her on the floor unsupervised for who-knew-how-long until I awoke.

The only possible conclusion was that I had done it myself, in a blackout. I must have gotten up, changed and fed my daughter, then left my own precious baby to play alone on the nursery floor while I went back to bed.

Blackout Abby was clearly not to be trusted. How could I leave Charles and care for Emma on my own if I was capable of something like this?

# THIRTY

*Thursday afternoon, March 1, 2018*

*Peter*

The captain OKs the forensics team for the neighbor's yard immediately – no doubt he sees the chief's face looming over him, demanding results. They do their thing in record time and report back to me as I'm about to leave for the day.

But this report does not make me happy. I had them check both yards, to be sure. No signs of a ladder or any other aid being used to climb the fence. No fibers from a gray hoodie, jeans, or a magician's robe. It seems Dunstable would have had to be a magician or something like it to get over that fence.

Nevertheless, I'm not giving up on him yet. There's still a chance he could have escaped Mrs Ravenscroft's beady eye and simply walked out the gate of the empty house, down the sidewalk a few paces, and in at the Crenshaws' front door.

I call Dunstable's cell to let him know I'm coming over the hill to talk to him. He suggests we meet at a Starbucks near his house – probably the same place he's been working all day. Fine by me. Although I would have chosen Peet's.

He's waiting at a corner table when I arrive, coffee in front of him, looking at his phone. I'm starved, having missed lunch, so I grab a plain coffee and one of those boxes of fruit and cheese bites before joining him.

He looks up as I sit down, takes a last swipe at his phone, and puts it away. 'Detective,' he says, trying to be casual, but I can tell he's wary. But then most people are when they talk to the cops. Everybody has some guilty secret, even if it's only parking in front of a fire hydrant.

'David. I have a few more questions for you.'

'So you said.'

His tone says *duh*, but I ignore it. 'It's come to my attention that you've been stalking Abby for the last couple of months.'

He looks genuinely shocked. 'Stalking! What gave you that idea?'

'You've been spending a lot of time in the yard next to hers, keeping surveillance on her house. In my book, that constitutes stalking.'

He gapes, then shuts his mouth and swallows. 'How do you know?' His voice croaks, and he takes a sip of his coffee.

'We have a witness. A highly observant and reliable witness.'

He's pulled himself together now and gets belligerent. 'Well, all right, I was there, but I wasn't *stalking* her. I was keeping an eye on her. A friendly eye. I knew that husband of hers was a jerk, and I wanted to be sure she was OK.'

I pierce him with my patented truth-extracting glare, but he doesn't flinch. That's how he honestly sees it.

'How far would you have gone to be sure she was OK?'

He starts. 'Wh–what do you mean?'

'I mean, suppose you'd actually seen Crenshaw abusing Abby. Would you have gone over there and confronted him?'

He pulls at the front of his hoodie, not meeting my eyes. 'I–I don't know, honestly. I never saw him raise a hand to her, so it didn't arise.'

Is he lying to avoid admitting to murder, or is he simply embarrassed that he's too much of a physical coward to confront Crenshaw in person? Crenshaw had a few inches on Dunstable and was in much better condition. I know who I'd have put my money on if it had come to a fight. I'm guessing he's embarrassed.

Dunstable may not be a viable suspect – just my rotten luck – but at the least he's an eyewitness to what went on inside the Crenshaw house. The first one I've found. 'All right, let's leave that aside for a minute. According to my witness, you were there looking through the hedge at the time of the murder.'

He stares at his coffee. 'Yeah. I guess I must have been.'

'Must have been? You don't know?'

'Well, I didn't actually see anything. I mean, I got there a few minutes before five, and I saw Crenshaw come into the living room. He must have already been home – I didn't see his car. I saw him moving around, pouring a drink, I think. But it was getting dark, and he didn't turn on any lights or come close to the window, so I couldn't see much after that.'

'Did you see anyone else come to the house? Or anyone already there?'

'Only Abby. I saw her car pull into the garage at about a quarter after five.'

My heart does a flip. Quarter after five. Enough time to kill her husband, theoretically, but not so much as to make the timing of her 911 call seem suspicious.

'Did you see Abby through the window at all?'

'After a couple minutes, I saw her come up to the window and close the blinds. Then the lights went on. That's all I saw.'

I screw up my eyes and try to remember the scene as I entered it. The lights were on, of course, but I'd have to ask the first responders whether they were on when they got there. But the blinds – what about the blinds? Did I even look at the windows, or did I focus first on the body, then on Abby?

Got it. I did survey the room when I first arrived. I call that up and replay it in my mind. Yes, the blinds were closed.

Back to Dunstable. 'Did you hear anything from inside the house?'

He frowns. 'Like what?'

'Like a loud argument? A thud? A scream? Anything.'

He thinks, then shakes his head. 'I've never heard much when I've been there. Double-glazed windows, I guess, and the hedge is a pretty good sound barrier.'

'But surely you would have heard it if Abby screamed. As she probably would have done when she found the body.'

He shrugs. 'I don't know. Maybe.' He looks me full in the face for the first time, eyes wide. 'You don't think *Abby* killed him, do you?'

I slip and speak as man to man rather than cop to suspect/witness. 'It's a possibility. Not one I much like, but it's there.'

He sits back and slaps the table. 'No way. Abby is absolutely incapable of murder. You must realize that.'

I play devil's advocate, since that is what I want to believe myself. 'Anybody's capable of murder if they're desperate enough. And you have to admit, Abby was pretty desperate. Stuck in an abusive marriage with a deaf baby, thousands of dollars short of the cost of her surgery—'

'Yeah, I saw that on Facebook. I gave all I could, but I haven't been working long. Haven't been able to save much yet.'

'Anyway, for most people, I'd say that was desperate enough to kill.'

He shakes his head. 'Not Abby.' Then he draws himself up, and his face sets, his eyes turning to steel. He grips the edge of the table and takes a deep breath.

'I know Abby didn't do it. Because I killed Crenshaw myself.'

For one brief shining moment, I believe Dunstable's confession. I want to believe it, anyway. But I have to be sure.

'Walk me through it.'

'H–how do you mean?'

He's stalling, making up a story. Damn. 'When did you enter the house? And why?'

'Uh . . . it was after Abby got home. I lied about her closing the blinds. I saw Crenshaw start to hit her, so I ran over there and punched him in the face. Then, uh . . . he fell and hit his head.

And he was dead. I didn't mean to kill him – so it's just manslaughter, right?'

He's brave enough to confess in order to save Abby, but not brave enough to face life in prison. Or he's starting to realize what his confession could mean.

He has it partly right, anyway. Crenshaw did die of a head wound, to all appearances. But as for the rest of it . . . 'You ran in through a locked front door.' Abby had said her husband always kept the doors locked.

His eyes go wide. 'Uh . . . no, I tried the front door, but it was locked like you say, so I went through the garage. Abby left it open when she came in.'

The garage door was closed when I arrived. But someone on my team could have closed it before I got there. Ditto the blinds. Although if that happened, I'd be having a word with that person.

'Crenshaw didn't have any bruises on his face. Neither did Abby.'

He licks his lips, eyes darting. 'I didn't say he actually hit Abby, only that he looked like he was going to. And as for him . . . I misspoke. I didn't hit him in the face. I shoved him in the chest and he fell.' He looks at me again, but the certainty in his eyes is gone.

'A shove would have left bruises on his chest. There weren't any.'

'It wasn't a hard shove. He was off balance.'

I raise one eyebrow. 'Where exactly did he fall? What did he hit his head on?'

'Uh . . . I think it was the coffee table. Yeah, he fell in front of the coffee table.'

Close, but no cigar. I shake my head with a pitying smile. I wish to God he'd been for real, but he's not. 'Sorry, David. Nice try, but that's not the way it happened.'

Of course, he could be making a deliberately falsified confession to disguise the fact that he's actually guilty. But given that he confessed at all simply to save Abby, it's hardly likely. He must be a smart guy to do what he does for a living, but I don't think he's that devious. He's incapable of telling a convincing lie.

His face falls and he buries it in his hands. 'Oh, God, I can't do anything right. Can't even save the woman I love. Useless, useless, useless!' He bangs his fists against the side of his head.

I can only hope I never get that pitiful.

I lean over the table. 'Look, David, you gave it your best shot.

It's not your fault you don't have ESP to know how it really happened. I wish to God I did.' I close my eyes for a second and take a breath. 'But man to man, between ourselves, I don't believe Abby did it, either. I just can't find anybody else.'

He looks up at me, eyes between hope and despair. 'Nobody?'

I shake my head. 'On your own showing, you were watching the house during the time of the murder. You saw Crenshaw come in, and you didn't leave until after the uniforms showed up, when he was dead. And you saw no one enter the house except Abby. And the baby.'

He perks up briefly. 'Somebody could have come from the other direction and gone in through the garage. I wouldn't have seen them that way.'

'That's true. I'd expect the witness who saw you would have seen that, but it is barely possible.' I heave a sigh up from my toes. God, I'm tired.

I skewer Dunstable with one last look. 'I could arrest you, you know. For withholding evidence, impeding an investigation, wasting police time.'

He buries his head in his hands again. 'I know. And I deserve it. I should have spoken up in the first place. But I didn't see anything, so I told myself it wouldn't matter.' He holds out his hands, wrists together. 'I guess you better take me away.'

I manage half a smile. 'Not today, David. It would be a bigger waste of my time to book you. But for God's sake, do better next time. If there is a next time. Which I hope there never is.'

He sags back in relief. 'Thank you, Detective. I promise I will.'

I stand to go, and he stands with me. 'How is Abby?'

'I haven't seen her since yesterday. I'm heading over there now.'

'Give her my . . . well, tell her I said hello, will you?'

I shake his hand. 'Yes. I will.'

*Abby*

At the end of the day on Thursday, Peter comes to see me. Everything about him is sagging, from his eyelids to his shoulders to his shoe-laces, untied and dragging on the floor as he walks in. I have this crazy urge to stroke his head and say, *There, there, it'll be all right.*

'How are you doing?' he says. 'Any news?' He sinks into the chair by the bed.

'I'm doing great. I got the word from Owen that all the tests have come back negative. Which means the blackouts were probably migraine related and they'll most likely go away. He's kicking me out tomorrow morning.'

'That's great news.' He smiles. He has a pretty nice smile himself, though it's got a lot of sadness behind it. But my life has a lot of sadness, too. 'Just one thing – do you have a place to go? Your house—'

'Yeah, I know, it's still a crime scene. I don't want to go back there anyway. It was always Charles's house, not mine. I can stay with Ellen, I'm sure. Till I figure out what I'm going to do.'

'You were researching stuff before, weren't you? Jobs and whatnot? Any good leads?'

'A few, but the situation's different now. With the insurance from Jacqueline, I might not have to work full-time. And if I don't have to, I don't want to. Not till Emma's older.' With the thought of Emma, the milk starts to swell in my breasts. I don't want to leak in front of Peter. I pull the blankets higher.

He nods, looking a little abstracted. 'I have to ask . . . any memories yet?'

I shake my head. '*Nada*.' That's the other non-food Spanish word I know.

He sighs. 'I'm getting desperate here. I don't exactly have suspects crawling out of the woodwork on this case.'

Which means all he has is me. 'So is this where you start to eye me narrowly, wondering whether my memory loss is all a front and I'm really an ingenious hardened killer after all?'

He gives an even sadder smile, as if he'd like to laugh but can't. 'I suppose theoretically I ought to. But when I look at you, I don't see an ingenious hardened killer. I see a woman who's been through hell but come out of it with her humanity intact. I see—'

Maddeningly, he stops there. If I could produce a killer for him by wishing, I'd do it in a heartbeat. If only to hear him finish that sentence.

'I wonder if there's any way we could trigger the memory.'

He grimaces. 'The only thing I can think of would be to take you back to the scene. Maybe stage a reenactment of several possibilities of how it might have played out. And I'd hate to put you through that.'

He might as well ask me to relive one of my blood-soaked dreams. 'No, I don't think I'm ready for that yet. Let's keep it for a last resort.'

He stares at his undone shoelaces. 'Abby—'

'What is it, Peter?' I'm hoping he'll go back and finish that sentence about how he sees me.

'We're pretty close to needing that last resort. The captain said by end of day tomorrow, I'm going to have to make an arrest.' He doesn't say it, but I can see in his eyes the person he'll have to arrest is me.

I blanch. 'Isn't that . . . kind of rushed?'

'Yeah, a bit.' He bends down and ties one shoe. 'He's getting pressure from the chief. Who plays golf with your father-in-law.'

I should have known I wasn't rid of Charles Senior yet. But I'm damned if I'll let him get me arrested for something I didn't do. Assuming, that is, that I really didn't do it. I have to be sure – for my own sake as much as the law's. Dreams or no dreams.

'How about this? Tomorrow when they discharge me, you pick me up and take me to the house to pack up some things. Not to reenact anything, but maybe being there will trigger some recollection.' I have a horrible thought. 'I guess it hasn't been . . . cleaned or anything?'

'No.' He gives me a searching look. 'Are you sure you're up for that?'

'No.' The mere thought of it gives me the heebie-jeebies. 'But it's better than going to jail.'

# THIRTY-ONE

*Christmas 2017*

After the GoFundMe was over, Ellen and I transferred the money into an account in her name so that Charles wouldn't be able to get hold of it. But the total still fell short by five thousand dollars. I went on Facebook and shamelessly begged anyone who felt inclined to give a Christmas gift to either me or

Emma to contribute to the fund instead. But there was hardly anyone to appeal to. My father hadn't spoken to me since I married Charles. His wife, Vicki, did keep up a Facebook connection and had expressed sympathy for Emma's condition but gave only a small gift. I didn't blame her – knowing my father, she wouldn't have any disposable income of her own. David gave a few hundred, bless him, which I was sure was all he could afford.

I scoured my meager personal belongings for anything that could be sold. If only I could sell my engagement ring – that would make up the difference and more, all by itself. But I couldn't provoke Charles by doing that until I was ready to cut ties with him permanently. At that point, the ring's value would provide a nice nest egg for Emma's and my future.

The only other thing I had of any value was a mink stole that had been my mother's. I'd kept it through the years solely as a link to her – I couldn't bring myself to wear real fur in a climate that didn't demand it. On Christmas Eve, I got out the fur, gave it a last loving stroke, wrapped it carefully, and locked it in the back of my car to take to a shop that dealt in used furs. The shop was in San Jose, and I was planning to stop there before dropping off my gifts for Ellen and her family. Once again, I was not to be allowed to spend a holiday with the people closest to my heart.

Charles came in as I was wrapping the last of the presents. His firm was taking a holiday from Christmas Eve until after New Year's Day. I could hardly imagine how I would survive being with Charles in the house all day for ten days straight. I prayed for good weather so he could spend most of his time golfing.

He pawed through the wrapped packages as I gritted my teeth. 'More junk for your sister's brats? Don't they have enough toys already?'

'I'm giving them books. A child can never have too many books.'

'They can't even read yet!'

'No, but their parents can read to them. Ellen and Pavel love to read to their children. It's good for their development.'

'So how come you never read to Emma?' He struck his forehead. 'Oh, right, she can't hear you!'

I clenched my teeth and leaned hard on my hands to stop them from flying up and strangling Charles of their own accord. Not that they'd be strong enough to do that, but I would try.

'If you can't be supportive of my efforts to get our daughter's hearing restored, at least you could refrain from making cruel jokes at her expense. And before you make your next brilliant observation, the fact that she can't hear your jibes is completely beside the point. *I* can hear them, and she can sense your hostility. Look at her.'

I was working at the kitchen island, and Emma sat in her high-chair at the far end. She'd been playing with some Cheerios and occasionally putting one in her mouth. But when the air began to sizzle with our anger, she started to whimper and reach for me.

I put down the package I'd finished taping and scooped Emma into my arms. 'It's all right, baby girl. It's all right. Mama's here.' She might not be able to hear my words, but she could feel the comforting motions of my body and maybe the vibrations of my speech as her head nestled into my neck.

Charles made a disgusted noise and walked out. One-handed, I stacked the wrapped gifts in a shopping bag. Then I changed Emma's diaper, put on our coats, and took Emma and the bag of presents to the car. I set the bag on the floor behind the driver's seat and strapped Emma into her car seat behind the front passenger seat.

The drive through heavy rain and Christmas Eve afternoon traffic took over an hour, and I was frazzled by the time we reached the used-fur store. At least it wasn't in a main shopping area – all those must have been completely mobbed. I found a parking place near the shop and opened the back of the car to grab the fur before getting Emma out of her seat.

The fur was not there.

I moved the few items in the back around, checking behind and under each one. No fur. I checked the back seat and the floor there, then the front, although I knew the front was empty. The cotton bag containing my mother's mink stole was nowhere to be found.

I felt ready to tear my hair out. I distinctly remembered placing the bag right there, in the back left corner of the cargo space. It could have shifted, but there was no way it could have slipped into a crack or fallen out of the car altogether. If it had slipped anywhere, it must have been into another dimension.

There was only one rational explanation. I must be going mad.

But whatever had happened, with no fur to sell, my current errand was pointless. I shut the car and drove the couple of miles to Ellen's house.

With Emma on one arm, my bag of gifts weighing down the other hand, and a Santa hat perched rakishly over my hair, I rang Ellen's doorbell. 'Ho, ho, ho!' I said when she opened the door, the kids crowding around her feet. 'Merry Christmas!' Merry was the last thing I felt, but I tried to summon a semblance of gaiety for the children's sake.

'What did you bring us, Auntie Abby?' they chorused, though in Katya's case it was more like 'Wha bing, Aun-ie?' Katya had only just turned two.

'That's Auntie Santa to you,' I replied. I handed Emma to Ellen and led the children into the family room, where a nine-foot spruce reached up toward the cathedral ceiling. 'You have to put these under the tree for now. No peeking till tomorrow morning!'

I doled out the gifts, reading the tag on each one. Nicky stacked his neatly at the front of the pile of gifts already waiting under the tree, while Katya tossed hers or dropped them in any random place.

'Careful, Katya! You don't know what's in those. Something might break.'

I'd doled out all the packages for Ellen and the kids. I reached into the bag for the last gift – Pavel's – but came up empty.

I upended the bag and shook it, although the box for Pavel had been too big to get stuck in a corner – it contained several T-shirts from his favorite nerdy-humor T-shirt company. 'What the heck? I had one in here for Pavel. I know I did.'

'Maybe it fell out in the car,' Ellen said, bouncing Emma on her knee in the changing rhythms of 'This is the Way the Lady Rides.'

'I don't see how – it was at the bottom. But I'll check.' I went out to the car and scoured it one more time. Again nothing.

'It's gone,' I said as I came back into the house. I was on the verge of desperation. 'Completely gone. And that's the second thing that's disappeared today.' I told Ellen about the fur.

'Mom's mink stole? Oh, Abby, I'm so sorry. But you know, it probably wouldn't have fetched much anyway. It was at least twenty-five years old, and furs don't last forever.'

I crumpled into a ball on the couch. 'It isn't just losing it that worries me,' I wailed. 'It's the fact that I don't see how I could have lost it. I distinctly remember putting the fur in the car inside the locked garage and locking the car. Like I remember putting

Pavel's present in the bag. And I haven't had a blackout today – I remember every minute of the day, no gaps. I must be going mad.'

Ellen sat up straight, startling Emma, who gave a little cry. Ellen resumed her bouncing. 'Did you say *blackout*?'

I cringed. I hadn't meant to tell Ellen about the blackouts. She would only worry without being able to do anything to help.

'You said you didn't have a blackout *today*. That implies you have had them other times. Lots of times?'

'A few. One or two.' As usual, I minimized the problem to keep my sister from overreacting. 'And always after something horrible happened with Charles.'

'But Abby – that's serious. People don't have blackouts unless there's something very wrong. You haven't been drinking, have you? Not that I'd blame you, under the circs.'

'No, of course not. I mean, never more than two glasses of wine.' I was a little offended she would even raise that question, but I knew overindulgence in alcohol was the most common cause of blackouts. 'But I have been having a lot of migraines, and the blackouts always seem to go along with those.'

'Surely something can be done about that. You need to see a doctor.'

'Yeah, I know. But my doctor's a friend of Charles's. I don't trust him to keep it confidential. And if Charles found out, God knows what might happen. He could use it against me if it came to a custody fight.' I shuddered at the mere prospect.

'You can see my doctor, then. She can be trusted, and she knows her stuff. I'll set it up for after the Christmas break.'

I didn't argue. When Ellen decided to do something, arguing was pointless. With any luck, the doctor would be booked up for months, and then I could always conveniently forget the appointment.

The truth was, I didn't want to go to a doctor because I was afraid she would confirm my worst fear: that I really was going mad.

That evening, Emma and I tagged along with Ellen's family to the Christmas Eve service at their Russian Orthodox church. The service was long – luckily, Emma slept through much of it – but it was beautiful and calming. The candlelight and incense created an atmosphere of hushed otherworldliness, while the chanted prayers, hymns, and scriptures washed over my soul in a cleansing tide. Although my faith at this point was tenuous at best, I still felt Christmas was a time for worship. I returned home feeling a core of peace within myself that I hoped would give me strength to endure the coming days of Charles's vacation. Beginning with Christmas Day at his parents' house.

Charles was waiting when we got home. 'That was a long visit.' His voice was casual on the surface but held a warning edge. 'Surely it doesn't take six hours to distribute a few gifts.'

His look was peculiar, as if he were waiting for something. I ignored it and spoke lightly. 'We went to church with them and stayed for supper. The Russians have a unique tradition for Christmas Eve. They spread hay on the table, to symbolize the stable, and serve special foods. You should come some year. It was fun.'

He sneered. 'Sure, lots of fun to eat like animals with hay in your food. No thanks.' The waiting look returned. 'Everything go OK?'

I pushed past him toward the nursery, my arms aching with the weight of the sleeping baby. 'Sure. Why wouldn't it?' No way would I mention the missing gift and fur. I would never reveal my mental troubles and give him ammunition to use against me, either now or at some future date when we might be battling for Emma in court.

Charles shrugged. 'Oh, you know. Wet roads and all.' The roads had indeed been wet and treacherous, but it was unlike Charles to express any concern for our safety.

He leaned on the doorjamb as I laid Emma in the crib and covered her, keeping my hand on her belly for a minute so she wouldn't wake. When her breathing was slow and steady, I gradually withdrew my hand, then tiptoed to the door. But Charles stood there, immovable.

'Come on, Charles,' I whispered. It was instinctive with me to move and speak quietly when Emma was sleeping, even though consciously I knew no noise would awaken her. 'Let's let her sleep.'

Charles straightened and put his hands on my waist. 'Sleep is the last thing on my mind,' he said in the tone I had come to dread. 'I've got an early Christmas present for you. I want to try it out.'

Oh, God. That could mean only one thing. One type of thing, anyway. Some new sex toy to torture me with. As if having ordinary sex with my husband – merely being touched by him – were not torture enough. All the holy peace I'd retained from the service drained instantly away, and I was left with only revulsion and shame.

There was no point in refusing. It would get me nowhere and would make him angry, leading to something even worse than what he had originally planned. I slipped from his grasp and trudged down the hall to our bedroom.

Why couldn't I have a blackout now?

On Christmas morning, after a late breakfast, we drove to Charles's parents' house. The house was decorated to perfection inside and out – sterile perfection, everything matching in a blue-and-silver color scheme. The identical balls on the lifelike fake tree were placed at precise intervals; the lines of small white lights ran in regular rows from the top of the seven-foot tree to a foot from the bottom. On the lowest tier of branches, Jacqueline had varied the pattern and hung unbreakable ornaments – a set of cloth Nativity figures and some carved wooden symbols of the season. 'For Emma,' she murmured to me as we surveyed the tree. 'In case she crawls under the tree.'

I smiled my gratitude. I had not been looking forward to keeping my curious crawler away from the fragile ornaments all day.

Yolanda served coffee and eggnog – homemade and liberally spiked – and we set to opening our gifts. Jacqueline's gifts to us all were lavish, as usual, but also tasteful and thoughtfully chosen. For me, a cashmere pullover in a rich forest-green that complemented my complexion, along with a Mont Blanc fountain pen and a beautifully tooled leather journal. For Emma, a dozen different toys, all of the highest craftsmanship and precisely calibrated to her level of development – none of which made artificial sounds.

The mohair beret and cowl I'd knitted for Jacqueline seemed a pale return for all this bounty, but she exclaimed over them as if they were the rarest treasures. 'Oh, Abby, they're lovely! And the perfect color, too – I love periwinkle. Did you really make these yourself? How clever you are! I could never make anything half so beautiful.'

Charles Senior opened his own gifts quickly, bestowing a mere 'thanks' on the slipper-socks I had knitted for him, and then buried his face in the newspaper. Charles Junior ripped through his own gifts, then interrupted his mother's raptures to thrust a small gold box under my nose. 'Here. Open this.'

I gave him a sidelong look, somewhat surprised he had bothered to get me a real gift in addition to the farce of the night before. I pulled off the ribbon and opened the box to see a pair of diamond earrings, each stone nearly the size of the main one in my engagement ring.

I was too stunned to speak. Charles wouldn't cough up a dime for his daughter's surgery, but all the time he had thousands to spend on diamond earrings?

'I–I don't know what to say,' I managed through a strangled throat. In fact, I knew exactly what I wanted to say, but I couldn't say it in front of his parents. It was all I could do not to throw the earrings in his face.

'Put them on,' Charles insisted.

'I don't know if I can,' I temporized. 'I haven't worn earrings in so long, I think my holes have closed up.' That was true – Emma had started pulling on my earrings when she was tiny, so I had stopped wearing them.

'Here, let me help you,' said Jacqueline. I held out the earrings and turned to face her. We exchanged a glance of complete under- standing. Jacqueline gently pulled on each earlobe until the gold posts slid through. 'There. Lovely.'

She led me to a mirror that hung on one wall. As we both pretended to admire the earrings, Jacqueline whispered, 'Wear them a couple of times, till the holiday parties are over – then maybe you can sell them and he won't notice. At least not until the surgery is done.'

I gave the mirror-Jacqueline a radiant smile. Aloud I said, 'They're beautiful, Charles. Thank you.' I turned and accepted his embrace although inwardly I was still quivering with rage.

'Only the best for my beloved wife,' he said with a proud smile.

I gaped at him. Could he be so oblivious to his own hypocrisy? Was it possible he had no idea that what passed for love in his mind bore not the slightest resemblance to the genuine affection and self- sacrificing care a husband ought to bestow on his wife? Or was this all just a show he put on for his parents' benefit? *Look at me, the perfect son with the perfect wife and the perfect marriage.*

Only not the perfect child. What a shame that Emma had ruined his carefully constructed façade. No wonder he resented her so much. But if that was the way he felt, why not pay to make her perfect?

There was no hoping for consistency in a mind like Charles's. He'd put Emma into a box labeled *Problem*, and problems were to be ignored.

# THIRTY-TWO

*Thursday evening, March 1, 2018*

*Abby*

Thursday, after what passes for supper – hospital food, and not nearly enough of it for a nursing mom – I get a new visitor. A short, plump, dark-haired, middle-aged woman with a kind smile and laugh lines around her eyes. Like a friend's nice mom who welcomes you with milk and cookies after school.

'Abby?' she says, coming up to the bed with outstretched hand. 'I'm Doctor Georgiou.'

Nice mom-cum-shrink. OK, I guess I can deal with that. 'Oh, hi. Owen said you'd be coming.'

'May I sit down?'

'Of course.'

She pulls the chair up to the bed and sits, takes a legal pad and pen out of her bag. 'Don't mind the notepad – it's just my abominable memory. There's nothing legal or official about this chat. It's an opportunity for you to talk about your experiences, maybe get a neutral perspective on everything that's happened.'

'Everything?' I blow out a breath. *Everything* is a lot. 'That could take way more than an hour.'

She smiles. 'We don't have to cover it all tonight. If you want – if you find this helpful – we can continue to meet after you leave the hospital.'

I nod. I like this being open-ended. 'Where do we start?'

'That's up to you. We could start with your husband's death and how you feel about it. Or we could start farther back. Doctor Elliot told me you had some concerns about your mental health. You could tell me about that if you like.'

The picture from my dreams – Charles lying in all that blood – flashes into my mind. I shudder. Not ready to go there yet. 'Farther back would be good.'

I tell her about the blackouts, the weird things that happened, the things going missing, and all the rest of it. She doesn't speak but nods and makes a note here and there.

When my words run out, she looks up at me over her half-glasses. 'And this type of thing is what made you feel as if you were going mad?'

I nod, swallowing. I feel as if my fate is in her hands.

She gazes into my eyes – into my soul, I think – for a minute, then says, 'Mental illness is roughly defined in layman's terms as not having a good grasp on reality. People who are losing touch with reality don't generally speak as lucidly as you've been doing. Also, they tend to create explanations for their own behavior that lay the blame on someone or something else – extraterrestrials and international conspiracies are popular choices.' She gives a little smile. 'As I see it, you've done the opposite. You've assumed the blame for things that someone else has done.'

I'm confused. 'Someone else? But who?'

She doesn't answer directly. 'Are you familiar with the term *gaslighting*?'

'I've heard it. People seem to use it in different ways. I'm not sure I understand what it means.'

'People do throw it around rather carelessly these days. The word is taken from the 1940s movie *Gaslight*. It's about a man who tries to make his wife believe she's going mad – by doing exactly the kind of things you've been describing. He hides things so she'll think she's lost them, tries to convince her that she's ill, separates her from anyone who might support her, and so forth. The character in the movie ultimately wants to get his wife put away in a mental institution so he can claim her fortune. But when the term is used today, the culprit is generally a person – often someone with narcissistic personality disorder – who simply wants to control his partner by blaming her and making her feel helpless.' She looks into me again. 'Does any of that sound familiar?'

The light dawns – and now I can't believe it didn't dawn sooner. 'You mean *Charles* was doing all those things? So I would feel like I couldn't get along on my own? So I wouldn't leave him?'

She nods. 'It certainly sounds that way to me.'

I lie back on the pillows, feeling as if an enormous weight has been lifted from my chest and I can breathe again. I go back over each incident in my mind – the disappearing eggs, the missing fur and gift, finding Emma playing alone in the nursery. I can't find a single case where it doesn't make sense that Charles was behind it.

Why on earth didn't I guess what was going on? I surely wouldn't have put anything like that past him.

Dr Georgiou seems to read that question in my mind. 'Part of the dynamic of gaslighting is that the victim feels so insecure in herself that it never occurs to her to think her partner might be responsible for any unexplained occurrences. He's trained her to believe that everything is her fault, so she naturally assumes the blame. Usually she's somewhat insecure to begin with, perhaps prone to people-pleasing, averse to conflict, not quite sure of her own identity or her place in the world. A typical "nice girl," in point of fact.'

I'm a little appalled to recognize myself in that description. My pre-Charles self, at least. Although I'd forced myself to stand up to my father and sometimes to Charles himself, there was a big part of me that always thought it would be so much easier simply to go along. Because – ultimately – I didn't matter. The whole reason I'd fallen in love with Charles in the first place was that he made me feel – for those brief months of our courtship – that I *did* matter. But when he peeled back the façade and revealed the beast within, it was easy to accept on a subconscious level that my importance – to him and in the world at large – had been nothing more than an illusion, a happy dream.

But now I have Emma, and my importance to her is real and forever. I cling to that. For her sake, I have to become the strong woman I've been pretending to be ever since that positive pregnancy test a year and a half ago. Become that woman not only on the surface but all the way down.

Dr Georgiou gazes at me a moment longer, then says, 'This session has given you a lot to think about. We'll wrap it up for now. But I do recommend we meet again, because you still need to process the trauma of your husband's death.'

I blink and come out of my reverie. 'Yes. I'd definitely like to meet again.'

We make an appointment for next week at her office. I feel like I've taken the first step toward making Strong Abby a reality.

*Friday morning. March 2, 2018*

*Peter*

Friday morning. The captain calls me in to remind me this is Abby's last day of grace.

'We don't even have the full autopsy report yet. Or the labs. How can you expect me to make an arrest when I don't have all the evidence?'

'I checked with the ME. You'll have all that by this afternoon.'

'And you'll give me all of, what, a couple of hours to make sense of it, determine not only the manner of death but the person responsible, and make an arrest. Sir, I have to say that seems a little harsh.'

He leans forward over the desk, his famous glare boring into me. 'I'm getting heat on this from higher up, Rocher. That young man had connections. His people want this solved yesterday. If we can't give them a solution, we have to at least give them an arrest. Now put your personal feelings aside and get on with it.'

I suck it up. What else can I do? 'Yes, sir.'

I have to take Abby back to her house this morning. Maybe she'll remember, or I'll find something there that will shed some light. If not physical evidence, at least some kind of hunch, some inkling. At this point, the only instinct I have is that Abby is innocent. And that is manifestly not enough.

I pick Abby up at the hospital at eleven a.m., discharge time. She looks fresh and pretty in a dark green sweater and jeans. Ellen must have brought these with her nightclothes earlier in the week; the clothes she came in with are in the evidence locker. I doubt Abby will want to see them again.

'Ready to go?'

'Absolutely.' She smiles. 'I've had enough of hospitals to last me a good long while.'

We drive to the house in silence. When I shoot a glance her way, I see her gazing out the window with the look of someone seeing a place for the first time. I guess she is sort of living in a whole new world now.

We pull up in front of the house. I open the car door for her, go up the walk, remove the crime scene tape, and unlock the front door. Abby hangs back. Her peaked face is almost gray and her eyes wide, as if she's watching a horror movie.

'I'm not sure I can do this,' she says in a small voice.

'I'll tell you what. How about if we go in through the garage? That way you won't be walking straight in on . . . the scene. And that's what you did that day anyway, right?'

She nods, swallowing. Officially, this visit is for the purpose of packing up the things she needs to take to her sister's house, but I'm hoping for revelations about the night of the murder, and Abby knows it.

I open the garage, where their two cars still sit side by side. Forensics did a quick search and fingerprinting on them but didn't take them in for the full treatment, as they didn't appear to be connected with the case. I unlock the door to the mudroom, which leads into the kitchen. From there Abby can get to her bedroom without going through the living room, although that room is visible from the hallway.

She starts to walk through the kitchen, then falters. Her head jerks like a bird's and she freezes. 'Did you hear that?' she says in a harsh whisper.

'What?' All I've heard is the wind in the trees outside.

'He's calling me. Oh, God . . . No. I won't answer. I won't go to him. Emma's asleep, and I have to put her down. I won't have him spewing his filth at her.'

Abby's arms go up as if she's holding her child to her shoulder. Her eyes are glazed. This is exactly what I hoped for – she's reliving the moment. I wish to God I didn't have to make her do it.

She walks through into the hall and then the nursery, and bends over the crib. Then she straightens, looking around in confusion. Her eyes light on me, and slowly they clear.

'Peter. But . . . I was back there. That night. Just for a second, I was back.'

She wavers like she's about to faint, so I help her into the rocking chair. 'You said he was calling you. So Charles was still alive when you got home?'

'I guess so . . . I guess he must have been. I heard him calling – but he sounded strange, kind of faint and slurred. I thought he was drunk. I didn't want to go to him and risk waking Emma.'

'What happened then? After you put the baby down?'

She looks up at me. 'I don't know. It faded out after that, and I was back here. Now.'

'OK.' At least we have something to go on. If Crenshaw sounded strange, it's possible he had already been injured and was in the process of bleeding to death right then. But what could have happened to his attacker? Had he still been in the house? How did he get out – through the front door, presumably, if Abby didn't see him – without being spotted by Dunstable or the nosy neighbor?

Or – I have to acknowledge this possibility, much as I hate to – it's conceivable Crenshaw was alive and well, if maybe a little drunk, and it was in fact Abby who killed him.

'Are you feeling OK now?' I ask her.

She nods.

'You go ahead and pack up your stuff. I'm going to have a look around.' It's true forensics searched the place thoroughly, but sometimes they miss the big picture in their focus on the details. I'm trained to look at both.

I go back to the living room. Except for the blood on the rug and a thin layer of dust that's accumulated over the last few days, the room is immaculate. Kind of unnaturally so for a home with a baby. From what little I know of Abby, she doesn't strike me as OCD; I think it must have been Crenshaw who insisted on this level of order. The kitchen, too, shows not a crumb on the counter, not a dish out of place. I remember the report said they found one used glass on the counter with a trace of whisky and a greater amount of water, as if it had been rinsed out.

I need to get inside Crenshaw's head. A picture is forming from what other people say about him – externally controlled in public, even charming when he wished, but a mass of seething passions and neuroses underneath. A man like that would need an outlet somewhere – besides bullying his wife. Some private space for the chaos within him to bubble over. A journal or something, maybe. Forensics found nothing here of that nature, and I found nothing in his office or on his computer. He'd hide it in some spot where he could be alone – his study, maybe, or his car.

Forensics went over his study pretty thoroughly. I'll take my chances on the car.

The red Porsche Cayman is sparkling clean inside and out, except for the fingerprint powder forensics left behind. Crenshaw's pride and joy, no doubt, and the face he showed to the world – even more so than this house, which he shared with his wife and baby. I slip on some gloves and check all the pockets and compartments – sunglasses, auto manual, registration, and insurance card in the glove compartment; one used Starbucks cup in the driver's cupholder. I check for loose panels on the doors – nothing.

Then the trunk. A kit containing jack, jumper cords, and so forth. A cotton bag with some old fur inside. A holly-patterned gift box holding several T-shirts, labeled *To Pavel*. Right, the brother-in-law. Not suspicious in themselves, but odd. What was Charles doing with an old fur? And why would a Christmas gift still have been in his car in February? I put those aside to show Abby.

Up with the floor panel that conceals the spare tire. Nothing obvious here. But wait – is that the corner of something black showing between the spokes of the mag wheel? I shine my flash on it – yes, definitely something. I lift the tire. Underneath the center of the wheel is a small black leather-bound notebook.

I take a handkerchief and carefully lift it out, then ease open the cover. Inscribed in a small, crabbed hand on the endpaper are the words, *Private property of Charles Adam Crenshaw, Junior. Do not read. If found, call 831-555-4300.* His cell phone number.

Sorry, pal, but you're dead and I'm the police. I turn over the first page and see a list of dates. They go back to July two years ago – about the time the Crenshaws would have returned from their honeymoon.

After each date is a notation, most of which have to do with Abby but some with his parents or colleagues. The first page reads:

*7/14. A wore the black bustier and was very nice to me. Must get flowers.*

*7/16. A pleaded another of her fake headaches. She will be punished.*

*7/21. Dinner with M and D. D humiliated me as usual. Someday he'll realize I'm twice the man he is. M and A both failed to defend me, though they looked uncomfortable.*

*They're weak, like all women. And I thought A would be different.*

*7/24. Stole a juicy case from under Colin's nose without him even realizing it. That'll serve him right for not going out with us the other night.*

*7/25. Came home to A gone and dirty dishes in the sink. Unacceptable. A must learn that I make the rules.*

I flip a few pages to verify that the list goes on. Feeling sick, I pocket the notebook, pick up the fur and gift, and go inside to see if Abby's ready to go. I'll read the whole thing later when I'm on my own. With a barf bag at my side.

I've been thinking I needed to get inside Crenshaw's head. But I don't think I was quite ready for what I'll find there.

# THIRTY-THREE

*Friday, February 23, 2018*

I wore the earrings to Charles's office Christmas party on the twenty-sixth and to Colin's New Year's Eve party, where Charles spent the whole night flirting with Monica Hopkins. She looked so uncomfortable, I felt sorry for her. Then Charles went back to work, my life went back to normal (meaning no dressy nights out), and after Valentine's Day passed with no special observance on Charles's side, I decided it was time to sell the earrings.

But they were not in my jewelry box.

I searched the dresser top, the drawers, the floor. I pulled the dresser out and looked behind it. I examined the dress I'd last worn the earrings with, in case they'd gotten snagged on it, although I distinctly remembered taking both earrings out and restoring them to their box. I even searched my car.

No earrings.

A burglary in which only a pair of diamond earrings was stolen was certainly more credible than one in which the sole loot was a dozen eggs. But it would have to be an extremely clever burglar to leave no other sign of his presence – no broken window, forced door, or tripped alarm, no mess in our pristinely clean house. I was sure Consuelo was trustworthy – more than once, she'd handed me cash she'd found in random places around the house.

I could hardly ask Charles if he'd seen the earrings without having some excuse for having looked for them in the first place. But that night he announced we were going out to dinner with a client the following night and I should 'fix myself up.'

I waited until I was dressed and doing my hair at my dressing table to pretend to look for the earrings. I opened my jewelry box and gave what I hoped was a convincing gasp.

'My diamond earrings!' I turned to Charles in mock dismay. 'They're gone!'

'Don't be silly,' he said. 'They can't be gone. You've misplaced them.'

'But I distinctly remember putting them back in the box after New Year's Eve.'

He raised one eyebrow at me. 'Let me look.'

He repeated my actions from the day before but of course found nothing. He stood and faced me, almost nose to nose. I shrank back.

'You've lost them.' His voice grew louder, menacing. 'Those earrings cost me a month's salary, and you've lost them.' He paced in a circle, throwing his hands in the air. 'Why do I bother giving you anything?'

Something about his performance rang false, but that made no sense. Surely he must be genuinely angry.

'I swear to you, Charles, I put them back in the box. I can't imagine what's happened to them.'

He rounded on me. 'You sold them. You sold them to pay for Emma's surgery.'

'No!' I hoped my wounded outrage rang true. 'I didn't, Charles, I swear I didn't. I haven't seen or touched them since New Year's Eve.'

He ceased his raging abruptly and glanced at his watch. 'We're going to be late. Are you ready? You'll have to go without.'

With shaking fingers I put on my second-best earrings, which I liked better anyway, and slid into my coat. Could I have had another blackout without even realizing it? And if so, what had I done with the earrings? Had I in fact taken them and sold them? I couldn't check the balance in the surgery account now. It would have to wait till I could be alone.

After ordering at the restaurant, I excused myself and went to the restroom. From the stall I logged on to the online account on my phone.

The balance was the same as before – $35,045. If I had sold the earrings, I hadn't deposited the money.

I scoured my wallet, then the rest of my purse. No wad of cash, no check, no receipt. Not the slightest evidence the earrings had ever left the house.

I must be going mad.

I was distracted all through dinner with worrying about the earrings. I noticed peripherally that the client, Nathan Prendergast, was a youngish, attractive man, and I was vaguely aware that his eyes kept drifting in my direction and he addressed a disproportionate amount of his conversation to me. I strove to walk the fine line of being nice to him – that was the point of dinner with a client, after all – without encouraging his attentions, and to the best of my belief, I succeeded.

When we parted outside the restaurant, Nathan pressed my hand with some remark about having enjoyed the evening – the company even more than the excellent food. It felt good to be admired again. Since Emma's birth I'd felt like a frumpy milk machine rather than an attractive woman, despite Charles's unrelenting attentions; his rampant libido was clearly much more about him than about me. It's possible that as we walked through the darkness to the car, I permitted myself a tiny smile.

Charles was silent through the drive home, for which I was grateful, but I could sense a building fury radiating off him in waves. When we arrived, he went straight to the living room and poured himself another drink. He'd already been drinking all evening; it was a miracle we'd made it home safely, but he wouldn't hear of me driving his precious Porsche. He paced about the living room, whisky in hand, while I paid and dismissed the sitter, who had her own car, and checked to make sure Emma was sleeping soundly. Then he pounced.

He came right up to me and hissed into my face through gritted teeth. 'You slut! You whore! You couldn't keep your eyes off him, could you? I bet you were playing footsie under the table all through dinner. Hell, I wouldn't be surprised if you gave him a hand job right there in the restaurant.'

I was too stunned to answer. His accusation was absurd even on the logistical level – Nathan had been sitting across the table from Charles and me – not to mention in every other way.

I gathered my wits and took a step back. 'Charles, you're imagining things. It was Nathan who couldn't take his eyes off me. I did nothing to encourage him.'

Charles closed the space between us. His bloodshot eyes glared into mine. 'You played into his hands the whole time – smiling and simpering and batting your eyelashes. God, you make me sick.' He grabbed me by the shoulders and gave me a shake.

I'd never found Charles as physically terrifying as I did in that moment. He rarely drank this much, and I'd never seen him lose control so completely. What had I done to set him off? Had I stepped over that fine line without realizing it?

I knew from experience that further defending myself would simply make him angrier. So would trying to leave the house – he could easily stop me, and then there'd be hell to pay. I could think of only one thing that might calm him down. It wouldn't be pleasant, but it would be better than landing in the hospital with broken ribs – or worse. And it would ensure his anger wouldn't spill over on to Emma.

I put on my sweetest voice and lifted a hand to stroke his cheek. 'Charles, darling' – I never called him *darling* – 'you know you're the only man for me. Who could ever compare with my dashing, handsome husband? Let me show you how much I want you.' Swallowing my revulsion, I kissed him deeply and let my other hand wander toward his crotch.

His hands tightened on my shoulders till I nearly cried out. His jaw muscles clenched under my hand, then gradually loosened as my other hand found its target. Then he rammed his tongue down my throat, pushed me down on the sofa, pulled up my dress and ripped off my underclothes.

He'd never been so rough with me as he was that night – not even the night Pavel brought me the desk. I struggled to no avail, tried to push him off me, but he was too strong for me at any time, and at this moment he seemed to have the unnatural power of a berserker. I cried out in pain more than once, begged him to stop, but he took my struggles and cries for pleasure and stepped up his brutality, bruising every tender orifice in my body. It seemed like hours – the longest hours of my life – before he finally shuddered and grunted his release, then collapsed on top of me.

I waited a suffocating ten minutes to be sure he wouldn't wake, then, with a colossal effort, pushed him over on to his side and extricated myself. I poured an unaccustomed whisky of my own – it burned my throat, but with a cleansing fire. Then I collected my shoes and my ruined underclothes and stumbled to the bathroom for a long, scalding shower.

But even the hottest water could never make me feel clean after that. I couldn't imagine ever being able to look my husband in the face again without vomiting. I dried off, wiped the smeared makeup from my shadowed and defeated eyes, dressed in jeans and a sweater, and threw a few things in a bag. I padded past the living room to the nursery – Charles was now snoring stertorously on the couch – grabbed the diaper bag and added some extra essentials, lifted my blessedly sleeping daughter from her crib, and tiptoed out of the house. Ellen wouldn't be thrilled to be awakened after midnight again, but with one look at my face, she would understand.

# THIRTY-FOUR

*Friday morning, March 2, 2018*

*Abby*

At the house – not *my* house; it never really was and will certainly never be again – Peter leaves me to pack up everything I want to take to Ellen's while he pokes around some more. He looks a little startled when he comes back to see that I've filled three big suitcases of clothing and personal belongings plus four large plastic storage boxes of books and Emma's paraphernalia. I can move fast when I'm motivated. And I am highly motivated never to have to return to this house.

'Good thing I can fold down the back seat,' he says. 'We should just about be able to fit all this in.'

'I'm sorry, I know it's a lot. But I don't want to have to come back here for a while.' I pause, and the compassion in his eyes almost undoes me. 'Preferably never.'

'Understood.' He hefts a couple of the boxes, and I follow him, rolling two suitcases. One more trip for the rest of the stuff. We pack the car, he locks the house up tight, and we drive away – for the last time, if I have anything to say about it. I hope the Crenshaws Senior will be able to find a buyer for this place. But it's no skin off my nose if they don't. I'm glad, in a way, that Charles left me nothing but the wedding gifts I never chose and a few dollars in a bank account. I don't have to feel beholden to him, even dead. I'll get someone to sell off the china and silver for me, and I'll take Jacqueline's insurance money – God bless her – and never look back.

Peter says casually, 'Oh, by the way, I found a couple of things in Charles's car that seemed a little odd – an old fur and a gift box labeled *To Pavel.* Those mean anything to you?'

I freeze. I'm back on that frightening day before Christmas when I thought I was going out of my mind. 'They mean I'm not going crazy after all. Those things disappeared months ago, and I could never figure out what happened to them. So Charles had them all along. Did you find a pair of diamond earrings, by any chance?'

'No. But I didn't look through the bag or the gift box thoroughly.'

'He probably returned them to the store. Sounds like he needed the money.'

Peter looks as though he's about to say something more, then decides not to.

'You found something else, didn't you?' I ask.

'I can't tell you. Well, I don't want to tell you. But I may have found something that will finally shed some light on this case.'

My heart stops, then jolts painfully. He must have found something that incriminates me. Why else would he not want to tell me? Am I a murderer after all?

How cruel an irony would it be if I finally got free of Charles only to spend the rest of my life in prison for killing him?

*Peter*

I drop Abby off at her sister's house and linger in the doorway a minute to watch the reunion between mother and child. So much love and joy in Abby's face. She clings to Emma so tight I think she'll never let go. I guess my mother felt that way about me once. I wonder if any other woman ever will.

I bring in all the stuff. Ellen looks a little overwhelmed but points me up a back stairway to a nice little guest suite above the garage. Big bedroom with a full bath and a kitchenette in one corner. I feel good about leaving Abby here.

Abby thanks me, not only with words but with her eyes. I know it's just an overflow of that all-consuming mother love, but it cuts to the heart of me anyway. If she killed her husband, I'll quit the force.

I grab a burger from an In-N-Out drive-through and head back to Santa Cruz. Someday maybe we'll get an In-N-Out of our own. Plenty of taquerias, but if you want a decent burger, you have to sit down and pay ten to fifteen bucks for it. This is a treat, even if I do have to eat it one-handed while negotiating the curves and traffic on 17.

At the station, I log in the notebook I found in Crenshaw's car but keep it with me. Waiting on my desk is the full autopsy report, including toxicology. I grab on to it like a lifeline. The clock on this case is ticking so loudly I can hear nothing but its insistent pounding, which translates to *Ab-by, Ab-by* inside my head.

The report starts with a list of substances found in the blood, tissue, and stomach contents, including quite a bit of alcohol and a large quantity of opiates. I skim through, eager for the bottom line: cause and manner of death.

And there it is: inconclusive. *The quantity of opiates combined with alcohol could have proved fatal given sufficient time. The copious bleeding from the head wound indicates that the trauma was inflicted while the victim was still alive and that death did not occur immediately afterward. However, it is impossible to determine with certainty whether death occurred because of the head trauma, the opiate poisoning, or a combination of the two.*

And he can't be sure whether the drugs were administered by the victim himself or by someone else. The closest he can get is:

*Traces in the digestive tract, in addition to the absence of puncture wounds on the body, show the drugs were administered by mouth. The absence of any drug containers at the scene suggests, but does not prove, administration by a third party.*

It sure as hell does suggest a third party. I think this through. No empty pill bottles found at the immediate scene. Nothing in the garbage. Pills you can flush down the toilet, but not the bottle. Crenshaw would have had to dump the pills into some innocuous container – a plastic sandwich bag, for instance, or even his pocket – and then dispose of the bottle in a public trash can some distance away before returning to his house to take the pills. But why? Why cover your own tracks if you're committing suicide?

No note. No previous indication of suicidal intentions. Suicide by overdose of pills usually represents a cry for help rather than a genuine desire to die; it's too easy for something to go wrong. And a cry for help is usually accompanied by a note or at least some previous hint of the victim's intentions. And besides, suicide doesn't account for the head wound.

On the other hand, feeding someone a bunch of pills is a clumsy and uncertain method of murder. It's not easy to force pills down a conscious person's throat, nor to make an unconscious person swallow. It's conceivable someone could have knocked Crenshaw out, then stuck the pills in his mouth and poured whisky or water down his throat to wash them down. But if that were the case, surely he would have died of the head wound before he had time to digest the pills, and the cause of death would be clear. Also, the killer would have ended up covered in blood.

I look back at the autopsy report. No bruising around the mouth to suggest forced ingestion. No liquid splashed around the outside of the face. If this was murder, we're dealing with a killer who is either stupid or crazy – and also incredibly lucky. And I mean *incredibly* literally.

Once again, I'm faced with a death that couldn't have happened.

I refill my coffee and pace the office, looking for a different angle on this whole thing. What if the pills and the head wound have nothing to do with each other? What if it was both attempted suicide and attempted murder? Crenshaw took the pills himself, then after he was unconscious, someone came along and bashed his head in for him. But why? Why not simply let the pills take their course? Did the killer want to make absolutely sure that he would die? Or was it an excess of blind, unreasoning rage that simply wanted to lash out – the conscience being appeased by the fact that Crenshaw was already dying?

Pushing aside the thought that I know of only one person who might have felt such rage against Crenshaw, I call the ME to verify some assumptions.

'Forbes? Rocher here. Listen, I want to run a couple of things by you about this Crenshaw report.'

'Bash away.' He chuckles. Pathologists are easily amused by their own jokes.

'Any chance he would still have been conscious before the head wound?'

'Hard to say. I can guess how long before death he ingested the pills, but it's harder to pinpoint when the head wound occurred. I guess it's possible he was still conscious, though I wouldn't say likely.'

So a killer might not have known he'd taken a fatal dose of something, especially given the absence of any pill bottles. He or she might have simply thought Crenshaw was drunk – in which case the attack would make sense.

'On the opposite end of the possibilities, any chance the head wound could have come first?'

'Now that I would say is extremely unlikely. He wouldn't have been conscious after that wound. Plus the pills were fully digested, which means he must have taken them at least half an hour before death. I don't think he could have survived that long after the head trauma.' That tallies with Dunstable's account – Crenshaw was conscious and walking around thirty-five minutes before Abby made the 911 call.

I drum my fingers on the desk. 'What's your gut on this, Forbes?'

He gives a little laugh. 'You mean the part I can't put in the report? Hell, I don't know. It doesn't seem to make sense, no matter how you look at it. Only thing I can think of, he took the pills on purpose – or unknowingly, say, dissolved in a drink, though we found no trace of that – then hit his head on something accidentally while he was groggy. The wound could be consistent with the corner of a piece of furniture, for instance.'

Like that glass coffee table. I had that thought early on and then dismissed it because there was no bruising to suggest he'd been punched or shoved. But if he simply fell . . .

Then Abby couldn't be responsible. She wasn't home long enough to give him a doctored drink and wait for it to take effect. This looked a heck of a lot like attempted suicide and misadventure. The rush of relief I felt at that surprised even me.

'Thanks, Forbes. You're a lifesaver.'

'Glad to be of help,' he says drily. He thinks I'm being facetious, but I'm not.

If Crenshaw was planning a suicide attempt – and it had to be planned, since he had to get hold of the pills and then dispose of any container so carefully – surely he would have written something about it in his little black book. He might not have the decency to leave a note for his wife and family to say why he was doing it, but a mind like that would surely have recorded the planning and the motivation somewhere.

Crenshaw's notebook is going to be tough reading. I'd like to take it home and wash it down with a couple of beers, but I don't dare take evidence out of the station once it's logged in. I'll have to read it here. I grab some coffee and take the notebook into an empty interview room so I won't be disturbed. The clock is still ticking, but I have a few hours to go.

*Friday afternoon*

*Abby*

I spend the whole day playing with Emma, nursing Emma, holding Emma while she sleeps. I can't get enough of her after these days apart, and she can't get enough of me. If it turns out I did kill Charles – if they send me to jail – both Emma and I will die before the first month is out. I'm absolutely certain of that.

I tell Ellen about what I remembered. For once, I'm glad of Emma's deafness, because I don't want her to hear this, nor do I want to let her go long enough to talk to Ellen alone.

'That's all you remember?' she says. 'Him calling to you?'

'Him calling and me deliberately ignoring him. Yeah, that's it.'

She scrunches her brow. 'So he was alive when you got home. That still doesn't mean you killed him.'

'What else could it mean? That he'd already been attacked and I deliberately let him bleed to death? That's so comforting, El.'

Brisk headshake. 'Somebody else could have been in the house right then. Somebody could have come in afterwards. Either of those would have scared you enough to make you lose your memory. Or . . . you said he sounded strange?'

'Yeah. Like maybe he'd had too much to drink. Though that would have been odd for Charles, so early in the evening.'

'But if he was drunk, maybe he just slipped and hit his head on something. Maybe nobody killed him at all.'

I look up at her, dumbfounded. Why didn't I think of that? For that matter, why didn't Peter?

Probably because I lost my memory. With no eyewitnesses at all, the police might have worked out that it was an accident. But that tantalizing open door of a possible eyewitness with no memory let all sorts of speculations sneak in. Darn my messed-up brain, anyhow.

# THIRTY-FIVE

*Saturday, February 24, 2018*

My moonlight flit landed me at Ellen's around one in the morning. She let me in, took one look at me, and put me to bed in her guest suite without asking a single question. I guess the gist of the evening must have been written on my face.

I slept until Emma woke me, whimpering for her breakfast. I nursed her and we both drifted off again. Finally, around eight, she made it clear that sleepy time was over. I changed her diaper and took her down to the kitchen.

Ellen was cleaning up from breakfast, but she offered to make more eggs and bacon for me. 'Just coffee,' I said. 'Please.' My stomach, as well as the rest of my being, was still in revolt against what I'd been through.

Emma was straining toward Nicky and Katya, who were playing in the family room that opened off the kitchen. I set her down beside them, gave my niece and nephew a hug of greeting, and returned to the kitchen island to take the fresh coffee Ellen handed me. No cup had ever tasted so good. I needed the warmth as much as the caffeine – I felt icy to my core.

Ellen let me take a few sips in silence, but that was all her sisterly concern could endure. 'Can you talk about it?'

I shook my head. 'The last part of the evening – the part that drove me out of the house – was like a porn movie. You don't want to know.'

She reached across the island to cover my hand as it clutched the hot mug. 'Oh, Abby. You poor thing. Did something particular bring it on?'

I took a long breath and sighed it out. 'We went out to dinner with a client. The client was obviously attracted to me, and Charles got jealous. For no good reason, I need hardly say.'

Ellen gazed at me, clearly using all her self-discipline to keep her mouth shut.

I looked up at her finally. 'You don't need to say it. I know. I'm not going back. Except to get the rest of my stuff. Or maybe I'll send someone else to get it for me.'

'I'm sure Pavel would be happy to go.'

'I was thinking more like the police.'

Her eyes widened. 'You mean you're ready to bring charges? Good for you!'

I grimaced. 'I'd like to, but I'm not sure it would work. I kind of . . . I was afraid he was going to kill me. So I . . . sort of . . . deflected his attention.'

Ellen frowned as my meaning sank in. 'But you didn't consent to everything he did to you?'

I shuddered. 'God, no. I tried to stop him, but he was too strong for me.'

She drummed her fingers on the table. 'I guess you've showered and changed and everything.'

'Yeah. I had to get his smell off me.'

'But you'd still have . . . bruises and stuff, wouldn't you?'

I shifted my weight on the stool and winced. 'Yeah.'

'So if you went to the hospital now, you could probably prove rape.'

I thought of the ripped underclothes buried at the bottom of the bag I'd brought. 'Maybe.'

Then I thought about standing up in court opposite Charles. He'd insist it was consensual rough sex, and it would be his word against mine. It wasn't as if he'd threatened me with a knife or anything. I must have bruises on my shoulders where he'd grabbed me, but would that be enough?

Plus they'd make me go through it all again. Describe in front of a whole court exactly what he did to me. There was no way I could do that.

I buried my face in my hands. 'I don't know, El. I don't think I can go through with it. Besides, I don't need him to go to prison. I just need him out of my life.'

She pulled my hands from my face and skewered me with a look. 'And you think he'll go quietly? He's an abuser, Abby. Abusers don't let their victims walk away.'

My stomach went cold. Of course she was right.

'All right. Take me to the hospital. I'm not promising anything, but at least that way I'll have evidence to use against him if I need it.'

It was Saturday and Pavel was home, so we left him with the kids. There was no way I'd be able to get through this without Ellen at my side.

When I told the admitting nurse why I was there, she was all motherly concern. But when they took me back to examine me and I told the other nurse I'd showered and changed since the incident, she tutted. 'That's going to make it much more difficult to prove rape.'

'I know. I wasn't thinking. I needed to get . . . clean.'

She nodded. 'I know the feeling. We might still be able to get some DNA, though. Unless he used a condom.'

I stared. 'DNA? Why? There's no question of identification. It was my husband.'

Now it was her eyes that went wide. 'I see. That does put a different complexion on things.'

I could see in her eyes that *a different complexion* was code for *snowball's chance in hell of conviction*. I pulled the ripped pantyhose and panties out of my bag. 'Would these help?'

She took them in her gloved hands and looked them over. 'That's a step in the right direction.' She put the garments in an evidence bag. 'Let's get you examined.' She called the doctor in.

The doctor spoke reassuringly and was as gentle as she could possibly be. Nevertheless, that exam was only slightly less traumatic than the rape itself. By the end I was a quivering puddle of tears. I sat up, grabbed the nearest receptacle, and vomited my guts out.

If it hadn't been for Emma, I wouldn't have cared if Charles found me and killed me. Nothing could be worse than what I was going through now.

They gave me a few minutes in a waiting room with Ellen to try to pull myself together. Then a female police officer came in.

'Mrs Crenshaw? I'm Officer Jones. Can you tell me what happened?'

A violent shudder ran all through me. 'Do I have to go through it all again?'

A spasm of compassion crossed her face. 'You don't need to go into detail right now. I just need the gist of it.'

Ellen rubbed my back as I collected myself. 'Last night, my husband and I went out to dinner with one of his clients. Charles is prone to unreasonable jealousy. When we got home, he accused me of flirting with the client. He was angrier than I've ever seen him. He shook me, and I thought he was going to hit me. So I . . . I initiated sex to distract him, reassure him. But he got super rough with me. Did things I would never consent to if I had the choice.' I gestured to the doctor's report the officer held in her hand. 'It's all there.'

She perused the report for a minute. 'I see.' She looked back up at me. 'Do you want to press charges?'

I glanced at Ellen for support. 'I . . . I'm not sure. I was hoping I could sort of use this incident for insurance. In case he tries to come after me – I've left him – or if I need it in the divorce case to be sure I get custody of my daughter.'

Officer Jones gazed at me, her black eyes intent. 'We can keep this information on file for six months. If he does come after you and you want to take out a restraining order against him, this should help. You could try using it in divorce court, but I have to tell you a clever lawyer will make mincemeat of you if you don't press charges now.'

What was still solid of my insides turned to jelly. 'But won't they make mincemeat of me if I do press charges?'

She grimaced. 'Realistically, yes. Since you initiated the encounter, it could be pretty difficult to convince a jury of lack of consent. But if you act now, at least it won't seem like you're dragging in everything you can lay your hands on for a divorce case.'

I screwed my eyes shut and attempted to screw up my courage as well. But the mere thought of rehearsing this whole experience in front of a courtroom full of strangers, with Charles's lawyer hell-bent on making me look foolish, vengeful, or worse – no, I couldn't do it.

This incident was about me, not Emma. Emma was all I cared about – I wanted nothing else from Charles or that marriage. If it came to a custody fight, surely Charles's neglect of Emma, his unwillingness to help fund her surgery or participate in her care in any way, would be sufficient evidence of his unfitness as a parent. I would have to take my chances. And pray.

It was well past lunchtime when we got back to Ellen's. She fixed me a sandwich to eat while I nursed Emma, who was ultra-fussy by this time, being both hungry and overdue for her nap. I'd had my phone turned off since I left home the previous evening. But once Emma was asleep in my arms, I turned it back on.

I had about fifty texts and voicemails from Charles.

My first impulse was to delete them all without reading or listening to them. But then I thought if they contained any threats, I would need to hang on to them as evidence.

The voice messages began around seven in the morning with a sort of half-hearted apology: *Hey, babe, guess I got a little carried away last night. You taking Emma over the hill to the doctor or something? I'll make it up to you tonight.*

When I didn't respond, he got more serious: *Don't freeze me out, Abby. I'm trying to apologize here.* Then after a couple of hours, any hint of remorse gave way to anger: *What the hell, woman? Where are you? Answer me! You can't treat me like this!*

No acknowledgment that I might have some good reason for not answering. No concern for my or Emma's safety.

The anger intensified over a series of messages, then suddenly turned to pleading: *You wouldn't leave me, would you, babe? You know I need you. Come home. Please.*

After that, there was silence for about an hour. Half an hour before I began reading, he'd sent this text: *If you've left me, I'll kill myself.*

I was so tempted to answer *I've left you* and leave it at that. It would make everything so much easier if he died.

But I didn't really believe he would kill himself. He was far too fond of himself for that. Yet I couldn't dismiss the threat, either. Charles had been telling me for so long that I was to blame for everything that was wrong in our marriage. Consciously I rejected that, but some of it had sunk in. If he did kill himself, it would be my fault.

I temporized with a text, as brief as I could make it: *I need some space. I'll be in touch in a few days.* Then I deleted all the day's messages – possibly not the most strategic move, but I never wanted to see them again – and turned off my phone.

That night, I dreamed that Charles was dead. To be precise, I dreamed his death in half a dozen different ways: he hanged himself, shot himself, slit his wrists in the bathtub, drove his car off a cliff, drowned himself in the ocean, took an overdose of something. But in every case, I was the one who found him – always on the point of death, improbable as that might be – and watched the light go out of his eyes.

I tossed and turned all night, floating near the surface of consciousness after each discovery, finally waking, drenched with sweat, in the early hours of the morning. My mind was awash in horror and obscure guilt, because with each new death I had the feeling I could have prevented it, could have saved him, could have at least called an ambulance, but chose not to. And yet underneath all that was a steady current of satisfaction and intense relief. Which, of course, ratcheted up the guilt even more.

Shivering now in the winter dawn, I turned up the heat, wrapped myself in my cushy bathrobe, and made a cup of cocoa, praying Emma would stay asleep until I could still my shaking hands and calm my pounding heart. I forced myself to look at the dreams objectively: what did they actually mean? Not that Charles was truly dead, or would in fact kill himself; I'd never had a prescient dream and wasn't sure I believed in them.

Two things were clear. On some level, I wanted Charles dead. But I would never be able to live with myself if he committed suicide on my account. At some point, I would have to confront him in person and work out some solution that would keep us all alive. And preferably sane.

*Sunday morning, February 25, 2018*

Eventually the rest of the house awoke and got ready for church. Ellen was too busy feeding and dressing the kids to ask about the dark shadows under my eyes, and that was fine with me. Some things I couldn't discuss even with my sister.

She invited me to come to church with them, and I agreed. I hoped the service would bring me some measure of calm and clarity. Also, I couldn't be sure Charles wouldn't come looking for me – he could easily guess where I was staying – and I was not about to risk facing him on my own.

The service did steady my nerves, though it didn't bring me any miraculous insight into how I could move forward. But during the coffee hour, while the children played under Pavel's supervision, Ellen finally had the mental space to notice how exhausted and haunted I must have looked.

'How are you doing?' she asked in a low voice as we sipped our coffee and nibbled our *piroshki* in a quiet corner of the fellowship hall.

I shook my head. 'Not great. I didn't sleep very well. Yesterday – I never told you, but when we got back from the hospital, I had a slew of messages from Charles. They wound up with him saying if I'd left him, he would kill himself.'

Ellen's eyes went wide with horror. 'Oh, Abby.' She looked around the hall and spotted the priest, who had just come in after divesting and doing whatever other mysterious things an Orthodox priest does after finishing a liturgy. 'This is out of my depth. I think you should talk to Father Gregory.'

My heart skipped a beat. My past experience with church authority figures had not been good – the ones I'd met had all been too much like my father. But Father Gregory had a twinkle in his eye that suggested a sense of humor, and a kind smile peeked out from between his thick mustache and his waist-long beard. 'OK. But you stay with me.'

She nodded and squeezed my hand, then went to talk to Father

Gregory. After a subdued but intense few sentences, she led him back to our table.

'I've told him a little about your situation,' she said to me. 'Now you tell him what Charles texted you yesterday.'

I swallowed. 'You told him about – Friday night?'

Father Gregory reached out to touch my hand. 'I know your husband is abusive and you've left him. That's enough for now.'

His mere fingertips seemed to send a promise of comfort all through me. But I still couldn't look him in the eye. 'He sent me about fifty messages yesterday, going from apologetic to angry to desperate. The last one was *If you've left me, I'll kill myself.*'

He nodded thoughtfully. 'Did you respond?'

'I texted him that I needed some space and would be in touch in a few days.'

'Good answer.' He looked into my eyes until I was drawn to meet his gaze. 'Two things I want you to keep in mind, Abby. One, this is almost certainly an empty threat. Abusers will use any means to control their victims – guilt is one of the most powerful. And two – I can't emphasize this enough – whatever he chooses to do is *not your fault.*'

I blinked at him, startled but hopeful. 'Not my fault?'

His smile engulfed me in warmth. 'I give you not only my word but the word of God. You are responsible for your own actions – never for anyone else's.'

A blessed relief washed through me, along with something that might someday become peace. *Not my fault. Not my fault.* I repeated it in my head like a mantra.

Later that afternoon, when Emma was napping, I took a deep breath and turned on my phone. To my astonishment, there was only one message from Charles.

*I'll agree to a trial separation if that's what you want. Come home Monday at five and we'll talk like civilized adults.*

I could hardly believe my luck. Maybe Father Gregory had said a prayer for me. If so, his prayers were powerful indeed.

Something in me suspected a trap – the time was oddly specific, for one thing – but I couldn't pass up this opportunity for a peaceful resolution. I texted back: *I'll be there.*

# THIRTY-SIX

*Friday afternoon, March 2, 2018*

*Peter*

I skim through the early parts of Crenshaw's journal. It's pretty much all of a piece, although the vitriol and sheer irrationality escalate with time. He hardly mentions his daughter except to record his bitterness and disappointment, first over her being female, then over her being deaf. When he has to refer to the baby in connection with Abby, it's always as *her kid.*

My bile rises on behalf of both Abby and Emma, but I swallow it and force myself to keep reading.

A significant shift occurs in late October of last year. One entry reads:

> *Came home early and got a glance at A's laptop. The bitch is going behind my back – raising money, looking for work and housing. If she thinks she can get away from me she's got another think coming.*

And the following day:

> *Got up for a drink of water in the night and found A in front of the TV. Spoke to her and she didn't answer. Went right up to her and waved my hand in front of her face. Her eyes were open, glassy looking, but she didn't react. Freaked me out for a minute, then I figured she must be sleepwalking or something. Sleep-watching, I guess, LOL. This could present interesting possibilities. Will have to monitor the situation.*

Then a week or so later:

*This morning A was weird again, like the other night when I found her in front of the TV. She got up and made coffee but didn't seem to realize I was there. Drank her coffee and went back to bed, even though her kid was starting to whine. So I decided to play a little trick on her. Took all the eggs out of the carton and put it back empty. Threw the eggs away on the way to work. That should spook her. She's got to see she can't get along without me.*

This goes on in the same vein. In December he mentions *playing a trick* on Abby that involved leaving Emma awake and unsupervised in her nursery while Abby slept. If that bastard weren't already dead, I'd get him for criminal neglect. He's like a mischievous child, only fifty times more dangerous – he's hyper-focused on keeping Abby off balance so she'll be afraid to leave, and he doesn't care how much havoc he causes in the process.

Close to Christmas, he writes:

*Got A some impressive earrings for Christmas. On Dad's store credit, of course. She'll see how much I need her. And if she tries to return them to fund her kid's surgery, she'll get a nasty surprise – no money back!*

Then a month later:

*A still has the earrings. Been checking every so often. Surprised she hasn't tried to cash them in. Dad found out about the charge, though – went ballistic. Have to take them back. But I can use this to pull another little disappearing act. Bonus – I get to blame her for what I'm going to do!*

And then comes an entry that turns my stomach:

*Friday, February 23*
*Took A out to dinner with Prendergast. That asshole couldn't keep his eyes off her all night. A just as bad. Naturally she denied it. But I showed her who's boss. Fucked her up, down, and sideways, left her limp as a ragdoll. She won't pull a trick like that again.*

I have to duck to the restroom. Bye-bye, burger. I splash water on my face, pull myself together, and go back to the notebook. I have to keep reminding myself this guy is dead, because I badly want to wring his neck.

The next morning, he writes:

*Saturday, February 24*
  *A gone, with the kid. Texted, left voicemails. She won't pick up. Probably crawled off to her bitch sister's for a good cry. No worries. She'll be back. She knows she's too crazy to get by on her own.*

This was written on the Saturday before he died. I need a fresh cup of coffee so I can focus. Only a couple of pages to go.

The captain ambushes me at the coffee machine. He makes a show of looking at his watch. I know very well what time it is – three twenty-five on Friday afternoon.

'What are you doing in the station, Rocher? Why aren't you out arresting someone for the Crenshaw murder?'

'Sir, did you read the autopsy report? From that, it isn't clear we're even looking at murder. Crenshaw left a journal, and I've read up to the weekend before he died. He's going to tell me what happened – I can feel it in my bones.'

I don't realize what I've said until the captain's eyes go wide, then he peers at me like I have purple spots or something. 'Am I dreaming, or did I actually hear you say a *dead man* is going to tell you how he died?'

I pull at my tie. 'I didn't mean that exactly, sir, of course. But I do have a strong feeling he's written something that will lead me to the breakthrough I need. If I could only have a few more hours, sir. I need to finish reading this journal and then drive to San Jose to interview Abby Crenshaw again. I might need to take her back to the house to try one last time to jog her memory.' I look into his eyes – a thing I usually avoid – willing him to accede to my request. 'Please, sir. I promise I'll have a result before the evening is out.'

The captain comes right up to me so his bushy eyebrows almost brush my forehead. He's got a couple inches and quite a few pounds on me, so to have him loom over me like this makes me sweat.

'You go get that Crenshaw woman and take her to the house. If she remembers somebody else being responsible, fine. But if she doesn't, you better have a damn good reason not to arrest her. And I mean other than the word of a dead man.' He looms, if possible, even closer, and his stale cigarette breath makes me suppress a cough. 'Do I make myself clear?'

I step back and adjust my tie. 'Yes, sir. Perfectly clear.'

I escape back to the interview room, gulp most of my cooling coffee (it's too acidic for me to want to taste it anyhow), and resume my reading.

*Saturday, February 24*
*Finally an answer from A to all my messages. Or what passes for an answer. She 'needs some space.' I'll give her space. Outer space. I'll send her up in a rocket so high she'll never come down.*

*She needs to know I mean business. I need a plan that will shock her into her senses. Or out of them for good – that would suit me just as well.*

*Sunday, February 25*
*Plan in place for tomorrow evening. I've thought of everything. Called Jeff and got him to prescribe me some pain pills – told him I'd pulled my shoulder playing racquetball and didn't want to wait through the line at the ER. He swallowed it. Swallowed, LOL. Always knew it would come in handy to have a doctor in my pocket.*

*Texted A to come home Monday at 5. Said we'd 'talk like civilized adults.' That'll get her. She always wants to resolve things reasonably. As if a woman was capable of being reasonable. Anyway, she'll be here as planned, no matter what. She won't miss this chance.*

*Looked up online how many pills to take and when. I'll time it just right so I'll be out cold when she gets here, but I won't take enough to really do the job. She'll call an ambulance and rush me to the hospital, and when I wake up, she'll be all weepy and sorry, begging me never to do that again. She'll be putty in my hands after that.*

*I won't leave a note, though. Won't leave any evidence at*

*all. So if something goes wrong – which it won't – it'll look like it's all her fault. And it will be, of course. So I win either way.*

I knew it! That bastard did commit suicide. At least, he tried to fake it and something went wrong.

But given the pathologist's uncertainty about cause of death, I can't leave it here. I've got to account for that head wound one way or another. I've got to be able to prove – not least to myself – that Abby is innocent of any possible charge.

I call Abby to let her know I'm coming. Hopefully she can leave the baby with her sister for a couple hours. If she does remember more, Abby could end up being almost as distressed as she was by the actual event, and I don't want the baby exposed to that. I wish I didn't have to do this to Abby. But it'll be better for her in the long run not to be left wondering what happened.

I pick her up at the Stepanoviches' house. Abby's brother-in-law is home early, and the whole crew are playing on the floor in the family room – grownups laughing, kids squealing with delight. I hate to interrupt this. It's a perfect picture of a life I hope to have someday. Not that I could ever afford a house like this one on a cop's salary, but the house is only the stage – the play's the thing.

That thought brings the rest of the quotation in its wake – *wherein I'll catch the conscience of the king.* Come to think of it, I'm asking Abby to do something like what Hamlet had in mind for Claudius – except she's both actor and audience. And it's her memory I want to catch, not her conscience; as far as I can tell, her conscience is in good working order.

I stand in the doorway, waiting for a good moment, till Ellen whispers to Abby that I'm here. Abby looks up from where she's sitting on the floor and smiles at me. A nice, ordinary, welcoming smile, as if I were picking her up for a date instead of for a reenactment of the most traumatic event of her life.

Well, maybe someday. When all this is over. When she's had time to heal. She'll be skittish for a while, like the fox in *The Little Prince.* She may never warm up to me at all – what have I got to offer a woman like her? Not much in a material sense, but I can offer patience. Gentleness. Respect. She didn't see much of those things with Crenshaw.

She stands up to get her coat, and I shake myself back into present reality. I've got to hang on to some shred of objectivity for at least the next few hours. Then, God willing, both our parts in this sick drama will be over and real life can begin.

I told her on the phone what I had in mind, so there's no reason for much conversation as we drive. For my part, I need to concentrate on navigating the pouring rain and the Friday rush-hour traffic. I imagine her thoughts are dwelling on things even less pleasant than those.

We get to the house about five thirty, close enough to the time she arrived there on Monday for the light to be about the same. The captain impounded her car this afternoon – one more last-ditch effort to come up with evidence against her – so I pull the car into her space in the garage. I glance over at Abby. She's staring straight ahead, unblinking. Hard to tell in the gloom, but I think she may be going into a kind of trance, the way she did when we came here before. Good. That's exactly what I need.

She climbs out of the car, opens the back door, and makes as if to get a sleeping Emma out of her car seat. Just as she did this morning, she carries the imaginary baby in through the mudroom to the kitchen, where she stops for a moment as if listening to something. Then she gives her head a shake and hurries on through in the direction of the nursery. I follow as quietly and unobtrusively as I can, recording video of her movements on my phone. I should have had a witness for this – ideally a psychologist, or at least another cop – but we're understaffed at the moment, so video will have to do.

Abby lays her invisible burden gently in the crib and keeps her hand still for a minute, as if resting on the baby's belly. Then she slowly withdraws her hand, waits to be sure the baby doesn't wake, and tiptoes out of the room.

She closes the nursery door quietly behind her and stands there a minute as though gathering her strength. She gets that listening look again. 'Coming, Charles,' she calls. Muttering to herself – I can't catch the words – she moves through the hall into the living room. She comes into sight of the couch and the coffee table and stops.

'Charles, what's wrong?' Then her eyes go wide with horror. She screams and rushes forward to the spot where the body was found. She makes as if to touch it, then starts backward, hands to her mouth. She stands there shaking for a few seconds, then a change comes over her – she's not getting closer to reality but seemingly retreating farther from it.

Moving like an automaton, she walks at a measured pace into the kitchen and pulls a roll of paper towels off its holder. From the sink ledge, she makes as if to pick something up – a large sponge, maybe. The forensics report mentioned finding one that held traces of blood. She wets the imaginary sponge and takes it with the paper towels back into the living room. She pulls the coffee table out a little farther from the couch. Avoiding the invisible body and the pool of blood that would have been spreading around it, she slowly and deliberately wipes the invisible blood from the corner of the glass coffee table and from the leather cushions of the couch, using first the paper towels and then the damp sponge. She contemplates the rug, apparently deciding there's nothing she can do about that.

She throws the used paper towels into the cold fireplace – there must have been a fire going at the time of the death, though I don't remember it – and takes the sponge back to the kitchen, where she rinses it thoroughly and leaves it on the edge of the sink. She puts the roll of paper towels back on the holder. I don't suppose the forensic guys thought to test the ashes of the fire.

Still moving robotically, Abby returns to the living room. There she seems to wake up – though still not into the current moment – and starts back in horror again at seeing the body. She gives a gasp that is halfway to a scream, rushes forward, crouches outside the bloodstained area, and lays her fingers against where Crenshaw's neck would be, presumably checking for a pulse. Then she stands, backs up, and pulls out her phone.

I check the time on my watch. Five forty-five. This whole show has taken fifteen minutes – exactly the time that elapsed from when Dunstable saw Abby arrive home Monday night until she placed the call to 911.

I end the video and sag against the wall. Abby Crenshaw is innocent of any involvement in her husband's death.

Before she can place another 911 call, I go up to her and gently take the phone from her hand. 'Abby,' I say, looking into her face. 'Abby, wake up. It's over.'

She blinks, looking first at her phone as it leaves her hand, then up at me. A look of recognition comes into her eyes. Her face drains of color as if she's about to faint, so I put out my arms to catch her. She falls into them and sobs against my chest.

'Oh, Peter,' she gasps out between sobs, 'I didn't do it. I didn't kill Charles after all.'

# THIRTY-SEVEN

*Friday afternoon, March 2, 2018*

*Abby*

I come out of my nightmare in Peter's arms. It feels like exactly where I'm meant to be. And I know that nightmare was not a dream but the truth.

Finally, I know. I am not crazy. And I did not kill Charles. I may have wanted to kill him – at least wanted him dead – but his death is not on my conscience.

The relief of that realization feels in my body almost like the aftermath of finding him dead. I'm completely drained. I can't begin to think about the implications at this moment.

Peter leads me to the loveseat – not that couch of horrors, thank God – and sits down beside me, keeping one arm around my shoulders. After a minute, he asks gently, 'Can you tell me what you heard, what you saw? What you did was obvious, but I couldn't always tell what you were reacting to.'

I take a big breath, try to pull myself together. 'When I came in, he was calling to me. His voice sounded slurred – I thought he was drunk. I was tempted to turn right around and go back to Ellen's, but I was starting a migraine and didn't think I was safe to drive. I put Emma down and went into the living room.'

My throat is dry. I ask Peter for a glass of water, and he fetches it from the kitchen. While I drink, he asks, 'I did wonder about one thing. I know you were coming from Ellen's house and expecting a confrontation. I'm kind of surprised you would bring Emma with you.'

'I had no choice. Ellen had to take her kids somewhere she couldn't bring Emma along, and Pavel couldn't get home in time. I was counting on Emma falling asleep in the car, which she did.'

'I see. Go on. You went into the living room?'

I nod. 'Charles was standing there in front of the couch – between the couch and the coffee table. He looked awful, swaying on his feet, but scared. He wouldn't be scared if he was drunk. He took a step toward me, then his eyes turned up in his head and he fell. His head hit the corner of the table. There was so much blood . . .'

I stop, unable to go on. Peter gently rubs my back. 'It's OK, Abby. I saw what happened from there.' I take a drink of water, and he clears his throat. 'Abby . . . Charles wasn't drunk. He'd taken an overdose of pain pills. He wrote about it in a notebook I found in his car. He planned to take just enough so he'd pass out and scare you into believing he'd genuinely tried to commit suicide. But he also planned on you rushing him to the hospital in time for him to recover. The fall was an accident. He never meant to die.'

I stare at Peter, overwhelmed by all of this. I can't sort through the seething mass of thoughts and emotions. I'm relieved Charles is dead, beyond relieved and grateful that I'm innocent, furious at him for planning to trap me that way, appalled at how it all went wrong. But underneath all that, there's still something I don't understand.

'Even now, after going through what we just did, there's a blank spot in my memory. I remember seeing him lying there bleeding, and I remember calling nine-one-one, but I feel like I'm missing something in between.' I look up at Peter as a new horror dawns. 'Was he still alive after he fell? Did I stand there and let him die?'

He looks at me with such compassion that I almost melt into the floor. 'It looked to me as if you probably went into your usual kind of blackout right after he fell. You changed at that point, started acting sort of automatically, irrationally. You tried to clean up some of the blood. Then you went back to where the body was, and you seemed to come out of it. You reacted all over again, checked his pulse, then pulled out your phone to call nine-one-one.'

I try to digest all this. 'So while he was . . . dying . . . I was in a migraine blackout? I was cleaning up blood while he bled to death?' Now there's something to haunt me for the rest of my days.

He shakes his head. 'According to the pathologist, he died either from the head wound or from the pills, or a combination of the two. He didn't bleed to death. Even if you'd called an ambulance right away, there's virtually no chance they'd have been able to save him. It was only a few minutes – they could hardly have even gotten here in the time.'

I nod, struggling to accept that I'm genuinely not in any way to blame. 'One thing I still don't get, though. If the actual blackout lasted only those few minutes, why couldn't I remember anything from the time I got home?'

Peter frowns in concentration. 'I'm no doctor, but my guess is there were two different things going on in your head. The time in the middle, when you were cleaning up the blood, was one of your migraine blackouts, the kind you've never had memory of and probably never will. In this case, it's just as well.' He grimaces, and I shudder in agreement. 'For the rest of it, you were probably fully conscious at the time it happened. But the trauma of discovering the body caused a temporary loss of memory of the larger event. That's not uncommon, even in people who are not prone to blackouts of any other kind.'

I close my eyes and let out a long breath. My head flops back against the cushions. I've never been so utterly exhausted in my life.

'Can we get out of here, please?' I say in a small voice, which is all I can muster.

'Absolutely.' Peter stands and helps me to my feet. He keeps an arm around me as we walk to his car. It feels good to have his arm around me. Safe. Cared for. Like I never felt with Charles.

He helps me into the car and says, 'I need to check in with my boss before we leave.' He's taking out his phone as I drift off – to a land blessedly free of any kind of dreams.

*Friday evening*

*Peter*

I call the captain. I'd love to see his face when I tell him, but I need to get Abby home.

He picks up with 'Have you arrested her?'

Despite his peremptory tone and the red face that no doubt accompanies it, I'm smiling. 'Sir, I'm happy to report there's no need to arrest anyone. Abby remembered everything, and her memory coincides perfectly with the plan Crenshaw recorded in his journal. He set up a fake suicide attempt, but it went wrong – he fell and hit his head. The only criminal here is Crenshaw himself.'

A moment of highly satisfactory silence, then a barely hissed, 'Oh, shit. How the hell is Crenshaw Senior going to take that?'

I can't muster any compassion for the father, but I can spare a pang for Jacqueline having to deal with him when he finds out. As for her, I think she'll consider it the least of the possible evils.

'I'll get you my full written report in the morning, sir. My recommendation to the coroner will be attempted suicide leading to death by misadventure.'

He mumbles something and hangs up. I wouldn't take his job on a plate.

I drive Abby back to her sister's. She dozes along the way – no surprise there; she must be exhausted after that ordeal. Thank God she has Ellen and Pavel in her life. So many abused women have no support at all. I can leave Abby there with a clear conscience and no fear for her safety. She couldn't have a better environment in which to heal.

But I drive away with a sinking heart nevertheless. Apart from the inquest, which will probably happen early next week, I'll have no excuse to see Abby again.

By the time I reach the summit of Highway 17, I've come to a decision. I may have no further excuse to see Abby as a policeman. But once the inquest is over, I'll have every reason to see her – as a man.

*Abby*

When we arrive at Ellen's, I wake up long enough to stumble into the house and up to my room. Ellen helps me to bed, and I sleep the first truly peaceful sleep I've had in a year and a half – no Charles to worry about, living or dead; no interruptions from Emma, who's being cared for by Ellen on the other side of the house; no hospital staff bustling in to perform their mysterious rites every couple of hours throughout the night.

I wake around noon on Saturday, unbelievably refreshed. My breasts are bursting, so I go straight downstairs to feed my little girl. Ellen's been placating her with stored breast milk and Cheerios, so she's not starving, but she's ecstatic to see me, nevertheless. 'It's all right, sweetheart,' I coo to her as she nurses. 'Everything's going to be all right from now on.'

Ellen gives me some space while I'm nursing, but once Emma is finished and down for a nap, she pulls me into the kitchen to ply me with food and questions.

'Detective Rocher gave me the gist of what happened when he dropped you off. Can you tell me any more?' She hands me a mug of steaming coffee like a bribe.

I clutch the mug with both hands but shake my head. 'I don't want to go through it all again. Not now. Maybe later. Or you could just come to the inquest – I'll have to tell it all then.'

She makes a face but doesn't protest. 'I understand. Of course you don't want to relive it. The important thing is that it's over, and you're innocent. You can start again.'

Yes. I can start again. The knowledge floods through me like a warm, energizing tide. I can become Strong Abby, Abby who is loved and needed by her family, Abby who can care for her daughter admirably, Abby who is not to blame for the failure of her marriage or for her husband's death. Or, for that matter, the failure of her parents' marriage or her mother's death. Abby who can become a force for good in the world. Abby the legal defender of the innocent and abused, now having a deeper knowledge of what it means to be both.

Abby who will shortly have plenty of money of her very own. 'Did I tell you about the life insurance?'

'No. Did Charles have insurance after all?'

'No, but Jacqueline did. She took out a two-million-dollar policy on his life, with half going to me and half into a trust for Emma. I won't have to worry about money for some time.'

Ellen gives me a hug, almost spilling the coffee. 'Oh, honey, that's fantastic!' She pulls back and looks me in the eye. 'But you know you're more than welcome to stay here as long as you want.

Even if money isn't an issue, you're still going to need support. You'll need some time to heal from all this.'

I give her a smile that's teary with gratitude – for this offer, and for being my big sister who's always there for me. 'Thanks, sis. I think I'll take you up on that.'

I can schedule Emma's surgery now – she'll be ten months old, and thus eligible, in a couple of weeks. And after that, she'll need to be talked to every waking hour, ideally by a variety of voices – male and female, child and adult. Living here with Ellen, Pavel, and the kids will be perfect for her until the therapy period is finished. After that – who knows?

I realize with a thrill that my future is completely open. Emma is the only immutable factor, and I wouldn't change her for the world. But now I can choose when – even whether – to begin my law career. I can stay in this area or relocate wherever I like. I can create a home that expresses *my* taste and caters to Emma's and my needs. I can reinvent myself as anything I choose to be. I can even dream of maybe someday – when other decisions are made and when all of this is a dim and distant memory – learning to love again. To love genuinely, with my whole being, a man who will truly love me back.

And with that thought, a face swims into my mind.

Peter's face.

It isn't a movie-star-handsome face. I won't trust handsome ever again. But it's a nice face, a kind face, a caring and strong and reliable face.

A face I could happily look at for the rest of my life.